MURDER: DOUBLE OR NOTHING

THE SOUTHERN CALIFORNIA MYSTERY SERIES

by Lida Sideris

MURDER AND OTHER UNNATURAL DISASTERS (#1)
MURDER GONE MISSING (#2)
MURDER: DOUBLE OR NOTHING (#3)

MURDER: DOUBLE OR NOTHING

A Southern California Mystery

by Lida Sideris

LEVEL
BEST BOOKS

Murder: Double or Nothing
A Southern California Mystery

First Edition | July 2019

Level Best Books
www.levelbestbooks.com

This is a work of fiction. Any references to historical events, real people, or real locales are used fictitiously. Other names, characters, places, and incidents are the product of the author's imagination, and any resemblance to actual events or locales or persons, living or dead, is entirely coincidental.

Trade Paperback ISBN: 978-1-947915-16-9
Also Available in e-book

Cover and Interior design: Shawn Reilly Simmons

Printed in the United States of America

To MomV, the ultimate cheerleader

CHAPTER 1

Dead Serious

H e pedaled the bicycle hard and fast down the narrow, deserted alley, stealing glances behind him. It was a late, warm Friday afternoon somewhere on the eastside of Los Angeles where police protection was scarce and hoodlums plentiful. Two- and three-story buildings huddled together on both sides of the rider. Graffiti stained the walls.

Hunched over the handlebars, the cyclist whizzed past a dented metal dumpster, unsettling newspapers and milk cartons pressed against a doorway. The collar of a gingham dress shirt stuck up beneath his red pullover and a backpack flopped behind him. Chuck Taylors clinched his nerdiness, as did the argyle socks. He looked fresh out of a computer lab, on his way to the library. There was nothing unusual about him, if you didn't count the bulging eyes, gritted teeth and heavy panting. His expression belonged on a trapped animal.

A black sedan barreled around the corner, tires grinding and coughing up pieces of asphalt. Leaning his torso out of the passenger window, a muscular guy in a white T-shirt clutched a revolver. He aimed at the cyclist, fired three times and missed.

The rider angled around a corner and skidded to a stop. Dropping the bicycle on its side, he stumbled over the upturned wheel moments before the car crushed the bike beneath its fat

tires, spitting out a tangle of metal and chrome. The car parked, and two thugs spilled out. They
raced after the cyclist, guns drawn. The nerd careened toward the side of a brick building and jumped up, arms outstretched above his head. The silver cuff around his wrist glinted as he grabbed the bottom rung of a fire escape ladder, legs flailing wildly. The ladder creaked and swayed. He'd barely started the climb when the hoodlums fired. And missed again.

"Oh, brother," I whispered.

The nerd scrambled onto a landing and dove through an open window.

"Cut," a gruff voice rang out.

"No one's going to believe this," I muttered.

"Do you mind?"

I stood apart from the assorted movie crew and on-lookers, but one lanky guy hovered behind my shoulder, his arms crossed against his chest. His sunbaked face turned a shade of red that complemented the brick building behind me. Short, coarse hair was cut close to his head. His chin hosted a well-groomed goatee showing no signs of gray despite the strands in his plucked and arched brows. The guy lowered his shades along the bridge of his nose to get a better look at me.

"Do you have *any* idea what 'quiet on the set' means?" His words tumbled out through clenched teeth.

"I spoke *after* you yelled, 'cut'. And I was talking to my-self." It didn't add to my credibility, but it was the truth.

"You were mumbling the whole time."

"Well, I couldn't help it. The scene wasn't realistic," I told him.

"We're not shooting a documentary here," he said. "It's a movie, for Christ's sake. An edge-of-your-seat whodunit."

"But there'll be people like me watching who'll know. You just can't squeeze out bullets like a squirt gun." I was new to my lawyer gig at the movie studio, but not so new to PI work and guns. Thanks to my father. "It's hard to miss at such close range."

2

"How would you know?" He glared my way. "Did I hire you? Do you even work here?" He gave me a slow once over and squinted at the badge on my chest.

My tailored, sea green sheath dress and three-inch pumps had to give me some status. Even my usual tangle of hair had cooperated into a French twist. That was a first. I was a female force to be recognized.

"Carrie what?" His squint still pinned to my badge.

"Corrie. Corrie Locke. I work on the business side of the studio."

"Is that so?" His lips turned inward. "Well, mind your own business. You should not be judging the fake shooting ability of my actors. This wasn't even the final take." He lifted his manicured chin and his voice. "I want her removed from the set." His finger pointed to my head.

"Is this a comedy?" I asked. "Because that scene might work if it is."

"It's dead serious. As in police drama serious. Viewers are going to flock to this film. Know why? Because it's going to be a highly watchable murder mystery."

"Maybe the cyclist could be wounded. Even a surface wound would do."

He looked around and yelled, "Why is she still here?"

I was now working on the main lot of Ameripictures Studios in Culver City, a town steeped in Southern California movie-making history. I'd been relocated nearly a month ago from a production arm in Newport Beach. A trouble free month, I might add. Unlike the stint in Newport, I'd avoided private investigation work completely on the main lot. My trouble free streak was going strong. Until now.

A tall guy in a loose shirt and baggy shorts hustled in my direction. Another guy with longish hair and blue-tinted aviators eyed me from the corner. I turned on my heel and was about to vacate the fictional city street when a long scream froze me in place. All eyes aimed for the brick building. White shades covered every window, except one. The fire escape had led the nerd to the only open window. A woman with inky black hair now poked her head out of it. "Help, help!" she said. "He's been stabbed."

* * *

There was a mad scramble on the street below the window. People dashed in different directions, knocking aside anyone still rooted in place. I muscled my way through the throng and rounded the corner to the building's entrance. One security guard rushed inside, while another stepped out, posting himself by the front door. All the structures on this street were facades, except this one. Behind the bricks sat small offices, including an accounting office where I'd been headed before I got distracted by the bicycle scene. The temperamental guy who'd tried to kick me off the set stomped ahead of me, elbowing his way to the entry. The guard opened the double doors wide enough for the guy to slip through.

I blazed a path to the same entrance and held up my badge, covering the bottom portion with my index finger. The grizzled guard stared down at me. He looked like a former line-backer. Former meaning a few decades ago.

"I'm from legal and business affairs," I told him. "I need to get a read on the situation."

"Legal?" he asked in a voice the size of a wrecking ball.

"I'm a lawyer. I represent the studio."

"A junior lawyer by the looks of you."

"Hardly. It's been a while since I passed the bar exam." Nearly seven whole months.

"You gotta wait 'til the cops arrive," he said.

If a crime had been committed, precious minutes were ticking by, and someone with crime scene experience needed to get in there. That would be me. "Not a good idea," I said. "Suppose somebody makes an inaccurate statement to the police? That could jeopardize this production. The chief will be angry."

I'd only laid eyes on the studio chief once. And that was on the front page of *Variety*. My finger remained steady on my badge while I spoke. The small print beneath it placed me in the children's film division. Kiddie flicks, as it was fondly known among insiders. Being an associate attorney at a film studio gave me a lot of credibility, to outsiders anyway, but it didn't seem to be making any waves with this guy.

"The people inside this building need to be prepped on what *not* to say to the cops," I told him. "They might blurt out confidential information. That would get you into big trouble. You can avoid that by letting me in. Move aside, please."

The guard locked eyes with mine. His stony glare made my skin itch. "Let the adults handle this. You sure you're not still in high school?"

"As sure as I know you're...obstructing justice." I clenched my teeth. I'd graduated high school nearly a decade ago.

"Someone senior needs to give you permission."

I pulled out my cell phone. "I'm calling my boss." I punched in a number and told him, "Vice President Marshall Cooperman won't be happy about this. But you're probably used to dealing with executive level temper tantrums." I started the call, expecting the guard to interrupt and say I could go through. He didn't. I placed the phone to my ear.

"Corrie Locke's office," my legal assistant Veera answered the call.

"Marshall, I'm on the back lot. There's an emergency situation."

"Is that code for I should stall Marshall 'cause you can't get back to the office right away?" Veera spoke quietly into the phone.

"You heard about it? Already?" I shot a look at the guard. His stiff brows didn't budge. "I tried, but this security guard..." I peered at his badge. "...Ward Vanderpat...won't cooperate."

"Security guard?" Veera raised her voice. "You want me to come down and handle him? You know I know how the security guard mind works. I'll shake some sense into him right away."

Veera Bankhead had worked as a security guard before she'd talked her way into becoming my legal assistant a few months ago. Nearly six feet tall and built to last, she could probably shake a whole lot of sense into him, as well as the entire studio security team.

"No—" I said.

"I'm on my way," she said.

"Don't—"

Veera disconnected.

Oh-oh. This was getting complicated. I shoved the phone into my purse and turned to the guard. "Now you did it. My boss is coming down in person to talk to you."

"So let him." He turned his back to me.

Why was no one taking me seriously today? All I'd wanted to do was help. And get a read on what happened before anyone tampered with a possible crime scene. I'd shadowed my PI dad enough times to know how it was done. Crime scene tampering was all too common.

I stepped back and dragged my feet away from the building. There really was no reason for me to get involved. I could almost hear the stack of contracts on my desk crying out for attention. Oh, wait. That was the wail of a siren. I whirled around. A squad car burst through a pair of iron gates, capturing the crowd's attention. I made a dash for the entry. Vanderpat dove for the door the same time I did, jumping in front of me and blocking my path. I stopped just shy of a collision. I had to hand it to him. He had an ample amount of agility for an older guy.

"Okay by me if you want to fly this mission without a compass." I turned and marched down the fake city street, headed for my office. For all I knew, the woman who'd screamed could have been mistaken. Maybe someone was playing a joke. Could even be a publicity stunt.

I picked up my pace, then paused by the end of the fictional street, eyeing the studio alley running behind the brick building. Was there another entry besides the one the guard blocked?

I'd only taken a few steps when a runner barreled around the corner, racing past like a rabbit with a coyote on its bushy tail. His skin was the color of molasses; his face soaked with sweat. He wore a red sweater over a gingham shirt, and had the same bulging-eyed expression as the nerd on the bike. The only thing missing was the backpack. His hands pumped up and down displaying a silver cuff around one wrist. My mouth dropped open. It was him. The guy on the bike on the movie set. The one who'd been stabbed.

CHAPTER 2

The Doppelganger

I dashed after the nerd, keeping him in my line of sight, until he ripped around a corner at the back end of the studio lot. By the time I rounded the same corner, he'd vanished.

"What the..." The runner looked a whole lot like the rider in the last scene.

While I debated the next move, a police car pulled beside me, red lights flashing. A tall, buff officer stepped out and sidled up to me. He sported bushy brows, an overgrown crew cut and mirrored lenses.

"Did you see him?" I panted and looked around.

"I need to see your name and ID, Miss," he said. "Why were you running?"

"I was chasing someone." I pointed down the sidewalk. "He disappeared."

He peered at my badge. "Corrie Locke, children's motion picture division." He raised his brows. "You're employed here?"

His badge read Officer Samuel Ramirez.

"Only when I'm not running after suspects."

"Who were you after?"

"An actor in the movie being filmed on the back lot, by the brick building."

His brows shot up. "How did you know he was in the

film?"

"I know what he looks like. I watched the last scene. He rode a bicycle and climbed a fire escape into the building."

He stared over my head. "It wasn't him running."

"Yes, it was."

"No, it wasn't."

"What do you know that I don't?" I asked.

"The actor you describe was found in the building where the movie was being filmed."

"Found?"

"He's dead."

I sucked in my breath. A lump formed in the middle of my throat. So that's why the woman was screaming. "Are we talking about the same guy?"

"You're going to have to come with me, Miss."

"Where?"

"Back to the building—"

I'd slid into the passenger seat before he'd finished speaking. I closed the door and buckled up.

The officer opened my door. "I've never had a person of interest get into the patrol car so eagerly."

"I've been trying to get a read on the crime scene for the past ten minutes, and ...what did you call me?"

"In the back, please." He pulled open the rear door.

I stepped out and landed on the hard plastic seat in the back. It was cramped and as comfortable as sitting on a boulder in a telephone booth. The officer slipped behind the wheel. A steel mesh cage separated us.

"Do you mind telling me where you were at the time of the murder?" He flipped a U-turn and cruised back to the brick building.

"Where I was *when*?" I spit out the last word. "Yes, I do. Mind, that is. Besides, I already told you." I leaned forward and gave him a hard look. His gun-leather looked stiff. I could practically see the water droplets behind his ears. "You're new to the force, aren't you?"

"Well, I just...I'm not answering questions. I'm asking them. That's why you're in the car."

I folded my arms across my chest. "Consider this. No one runs away without a good reason. I wanted to know the reason. That's why I was chasing the guy."

"I didn't see you chasing anyone. I saw you running."

"After a possible suspect. Or a victim." This was getting more confusing by the moment. "I was outside of the building with about fifty other people."

"What?"

"At the time of the murder."

"Oh, right. I'll need to verify that." He parked the car near the brick building and pulled out a small notepad. The tip of his tongue slipped from side-to-side over his top lip while he scribbled. "Can you name at least one person who saw you there?"

"I talked to the director, I think. I don't know his name. And a security guard. Ward Vanderpat."

He nodded. "Let's go inside."

He opened my door. We stepped out of the car and into the narrow street. There was an entry at the back of the brick building, now guarded by another uniform. I pushed past him.

"Hey!" The cop at the door said.

"It's okay," Officer Ramirez told him. "I'm taking her in for questioning."

"Looks like she's taking you."

Officer Ramirez hotfooted after me. "Hold on, Miss."

I slowed so he could catch up.

"After you." He waved me forward and followed me up a back staircase darkened by time and foot traffic, and into a narrow hallway with beige walls and wood flooring that creaked with every step. The whole building groaned and shuddered. The structure was one of three relics still standing from the Golden Age of Hollywood. It even had its own mail chute; a brass box running from floor to ceiling with a glass front, used in the olden days to carry mail down to the basement mailroom. The corridors hosted colorful posters featuring films from the thirties and forties. Musty air invaded my nostrils.

Officer Ramirez hung a left, ushering me into a wide hallway with fresher air and the hum of quiet voices. He paused near an open door. Crime scene tape ran from the entry of the kill room to the main staircase.

"Miss, I suggest you stand away." He pointed down the hall. "It's grisly in there."

"Thank you. That's very thoughtful."

I retreated a few paces. He turned his back to me and headed for the room. He stopped by the entrance. I tiptoed forward, peeking over his shoulder.

The window facing the side of the building sat open; blinds rolled to the top. A small group milled about, mostly officers and security stepping around a sprawled body, laying face down, across a geometric rug. I craned my neck. My mouth dropped open. It was him. The guy running past me ten minutes ago. Same clothes, same hair, same everything, except for the bloody mess around him. Maybe he had a twin?

"Who've we got here?" A voice behind me barked.

I jumped and whirled around. A wiry guy with pale, droopy eyes fanned a heavy dose of fury my way. His suit, his shirt and sober striped tie all echoed a different shade of gray. He had detective written all over him.

Officer Ramirez stepped forward. "I found her running down the alley, Sir. I brought her in for questioning. Her name's Corrie Locke. She works in the kiddie cartoons department."

"That's children's motion picture division," I told him. Geez. If he couldn't get that simple fact straight, how did he handle the hard stuff?

"This is Detective Jeb Sorkel," Officer Ramirez made introductions. "Like snorkel but without the 'n'."

"You were running?" Detective Sorkel shook his head. "Not hard to guess why."

"I was after—" I started.

"Cowards run to escape the law. But they always get caught."

"I'd say it's about fifty-fifty," Officer Ramirez said.

Detective Sorkel focused his glare on him.

"Sorry, Sir." Officer Ramirez lowered his chin.

Detective Sorkel returned to me. "They're always caught on my watch."

"The guy I was chasing was a dead ringer for the body on the floor in there." I pointed my thumb to the room behind me. "No pun intended."

"Don't even think about playing games with me." Sorkel pushed his droopy gaze past me to the officer. "Ramirez, did you run a check on her?" His stare cascaded over me. "Get a mouth swab ready. A lot of druggies running loose around here."

"I'm not on drugs," I said, turning toward Ramirez. "No swabbing."

"I'll do a warrant check." The officer trotted down the hallway.

"Corrie!"

A full-bodied woman pounded up the staircase and burst into the scene. Veera rocked a burgundy pantsuit and heels that pushed her well over her usual six feet high mark. Her caramel colored hair sat in a neat knot at her crown; her cocoa hued complexion glowed. She marched up to the detective. "What's going on here?"

Sorkel leaned forward and spoke in a low voice. "Unless you're with the crime scene unit or have the cup of coffee I ordered, get out."

"She's with me." I stepped closer. "I'm a studio lawyer and this is Veera Bankhead, my assistant."

"That's right. Although I wouldn't mind joining the crime scene unit." Veera turned to me. "I looked all over for that security guard. He's disappeared off the face of this earth." She peered over my shoulder at the body. A shudder ran through her. Her hand shot to her mouth, covering it. She gulped and lowered her hand. "Holy Jiminy Cricket." She turned to me and clicked her tongue. "You didn't say we had another case to crack."

Veera had been a big help on my last two homicide investigations. She harbored a not-so-secret ambition to partner-up and open our own PI office.

"That's because we don't," I said.

"I want you crime scene crashers away from here. Play out your Nancy Drew fantasies somewhere else, ladies," Detective Sorkel said and turned to Veera. "You, get out." His glare burned in my direction. "You'll stay until after Ramirez returns with your background check. Come with me."

The stairs took another pounding and a large man joined us. It was Vanderpat.

The detective threw up his hands. "What the hell is going on? Friends and family day at the crime scene? Where's the studio security watching at the front?"

"That's me. Ward Vanderpat. I've been trying to keep everyone out. But this one managed to slip in." He pointed to Veera.

"I got special moves for times like these," Veera told him. She peered at his badge. "You're Vanderpat?"

"That's right."

"How do we know you're not responsible for that in there?" She pointed to the body.

"You must be out of your mind," Vanderpat responded.

"Well, it happened on your watch, so you got some responsibility," Veera said.

"Vanderpat, escort this person out of here." Detective Sorkel gestured toward Veera and stared hard at Vanderpat, "I *will* hold you personally responsible if anyone else gets inside this building."

"It won't happen again," Vanderpat said.

Veera looked at me. "Okay with you, boss?"

"See you back at the office," I said.

"Alright," she whispered to me, "I'll find out what this security guard knows." Vanderpat followed her out.

"Now," Detective Sorkel turned to me. "You. This way."

I paused long enough to scan the victim and the area around him. He lay, face down, in a pool of blood that seeped past the rug and onto the hardwood floor. His backpack occupied a corner chair near the window. A desk was pressed against the wall. A small lamp lay on its side between the body and an antique white, two-shelf bookcase. An assortment of soft drinks lined the top of the case. Books filled each shelf, but the ones on the lower shelf were splattered with blood.

"I'm not going to ask you again. Get moving before I have you locked up for disobeying the lead detective." Sorkel had stopped mid-hallway to glower at me.

I took a step. "Alright…" And stopped. Paramedics padded up the staircase and slid into the crime scene.

Sorkel darted past me, pausing long enough to tell me, "Down the hallway. Wait there until I'm done." He followed the medics inside.

I hovered near the doorway. I couldn't help myself. Even the most reformed individuals face challenges giving up their old ways, and I was hardly reformed. Truth is, I found crime scenes thrilling. And the two cases I'd recently solved only boosted that thrill, not to mention the confidence to step up when it came to the chance of cracking a new case wide open.

"If a piece of thread is overlooked," Dad used to say. "A criminal could escape detection. The solution to a crime is in the details."

I craved details. While Sorkel spoke to the latest arrivals, I inched closer. My gaze scanned the victim and locked on his sneakers. I caught my breath.

CHAPTER 3

Join the Club

"**W**hat?" Sorkel asked me.

"What do you mean *what*?" I stood off to the side of the entry. My thoughts were racing, and I'd learned that racing thoughts need to slow down before I make a statement, especially to the cops.

"You look like you saw a ghost," Sorkel said.

"I guess, the body...all that blood. It's finally getting to me, I'm having a delayed reaction." I held my hand over my heart.

"You should not have been in there," he said. "Get moving."

I flipped a U-ey. Sorkel herded me to the end of the hall and gestured inside an open door. I slipped into a compact room furnished with leftover pieces circa 1960 if the shiny wood surfaces, straight-line chairs and one-armed sofa meant anything. Weak sunlight trickled in through partially open slats of the blinds covering the only window. A fan whirred on the ceiling. There he was again, the director with the goatee and short-cropped hair. He slumped a shoulder against a wall. His head jerked up when I strolled in, eyes narrowing. Two women sat on either end of the sofa. One jumped up and approached Sorkel.

"Did you catch who did it?" Her badge read Debbylynn Diamond, costume department. She wore black from her elbow-length hair and satin top to her culottes and glittery ankle boots. Her head was the one I'd seen sticking out the window, calling for help.

Sorkel curled his lips. "How's that supposed to happen when the woman who found the body was channeling Helen Keller?"

Debbylynn stomped a boot and squeezed out some tears. "I was stunned and upset. I can't get over it."

"You found him?" I asked her.

She nodded and gulped. "So much...blood." She swallowed a sob.

"Was he dead when you found him?" I asked.

"I'm not sure. I was afraid to touch him. But I finally shook him. He didn't move." She broke into tears.

"You took his pulse?" I asked.

"I ask the questions," Sorkel told me and turned to Debbylynn. "Did you check for a pulse?"

She sank onto the sofa. "No. I yelled for help."

I perched on the edge of a lacquered desk and pointed to the guy with the goatee. "I was with him when she screamed."

The detective turned to the guy. "Can you verify that, Kruger?"

The man rolled his eyes. "It's Kramer. Burton Kramer. I'm the director of *Bullets Flying*." He pivoted in my direction. "I never saw her before in my life."

"This must have been a big shock to your system," I told him. "Or you might have a few wires loose in your brain. Either way, it was less than thirty minutes ago," I said. "We argued over your questionable shooting scene."

"What are you? An arms expert?" Burton snickered.

This was what I got for offering constructive criticism. "I was with him when the victim climbed in the window," I told Sorkel. "I had to let him know the shooting was unrealistic."

Burton lifted his chin and turned his face away. "I can't believe you're still harping on that."

"I left to go back to my office when this guy ran past me, and I chased after him." I planted my hands on my hips.

"Do you do that often?" Sorkel asked. "Chase pretend people?"

"Let me see." I tapped my chin with a fingernail and looked at the ceiling before meeting Sorkel's gaze again. "No. I only chase real people running away from real crime scenes."

Burton flipped back to me and stepped closer. "Did the chief sic you on me? Or was it the head of production? Wait, you're an undercover cop. I shoulda figured that. That's how you know about guns."

"I will gladly verify she is not one of us." Detective Sorkel aimed his radar at Burton. "Why would you need to worry about undercover cops?"

"The studio wants to shut me down."

"Is that what they told you?" Sorkel asked.

"Course not," Burton replied.

"Then how do you know?" Sorkel circled Kramer.

"They've got spies everywhere watching me," Burton said. "I shoulda shot independent."

"And why exactly would they want to stop you?" Sorkel wanted to know.

"I'm over budget." Burton shrugged. "So who isn't? Who do they think I am? Clint Eastwood?"

Sorkel pointed to me. "So she *was* with you when it happened."

Burton shrugged. "That's right. Why should I do her any favors? She criticized my scene."

"I was trying to be helpful," I added.

"Did Shaw Kota seem upset lately?" Sorkel asked Burton.

"Who's Kota?" I asked.

"What did I say about questions?" Sorkel said. He flicked a thumb behind him. "He's the guy without a pulse back there." He turned to Burton. "Was he upset?"

"Understatement," Burton replied. "It's Shaw's fault I ran over budget. When we started filming, he was on time, knew his lines. Then all of a sudden he won't leave his trailer, stumbles over simple dialogue, and takes breaks, all of the time. The guy couldn't even read the cue cards."

"That's because you created tension on the set," Debbylynn said. "All those retakes." She flipped back her hair.

"No, Burton's right," the other woman said, sniffling. Her badge ID'd her as Rhoda Way, catering department. "Shaw had to be dragged out of his dressing room today."

"When did this lack of cooperation start?" Sorkel asked.

"A couple days ago," Burton said.

"I need to go now." Rhoda stood and ran her fingers through her beachy blonde bob. She pulled down her short, poofy skirt. "All I did was walk in to replenish the snacks and drinks. I saw Deb standing over him. I don't know what she was doing."

"What does that mean?" Debbylynn asked.

"For all I know, you stuffed a pillow over his head," Rhoda said. "And stabbed him. Then screamed so everyone would believe it was someone else. That's makes sense to me."

"That's not true." Debbylynn jumped to her feet.

Sorkel wedged himself between them and focused on Debbylynn. "How well did you know the victim?"

"We saw each other during costume changes," Debbylynn replied.

"You saw each other more than that," Rhoda said.

"You got eyes on me all the time?" Debbylynn said. "Give it a break."

"What do you know?" Sorkel asked Rhoda.

"They've been an item from the start," Rhoda said. "I saw him sneaking into her closet in the wee hours of the morning."

"What closet?" I asked.

"That's what we call her costume closet," Rhoda said. "It's also her office."

"Since when is that a crime?" Debbylynn asked. "Yes, we dated, but everyone knows we broke up a few days ago."

"That break-up must've been tough if you were dating a

while," I said, tiptoeing around questions.

Debbylynn turned her lips inward. "It was. We dated for over a month."

"Did you notice any changes in Shaw Kota?" Sorkel asked her.

She crossed her arms over her chest. "He seemed fidgety lately. Hardly said a word."

"And when he did talk, he was absent minded," Rhoda added. A loud sob blew out of her mouth, but her expression remained unchanged. "What's everyone staring at?" She looked around the room. "I had a little Botox last night. It'll settle down. I feel really sad right now."

Sorkel turned to me. "Why were you discussing the shooting scene with Burton Kramer? What do you know about guns?"

"My father was a private investigator. He taught me about guns." And a little bit more.

Sorkel pulled his pistol out from the inside of his jacket and held it up.

"Colt government model," I said. "Looks like a customized 380."

Sorkel put the gun back in the holster and nodded. "Okay, at least you know something. Which is more than I can say for anyone else in here."

"Maybe it was his stand-in I saw running." I turned to Burton. "Shaw had one, right?"

"All major talent have one," Burton replied. "Wish I had one right now."

"What's a stand-in?" Sorkel asked.

"A close replica that takes the actor's place during rehearsals and lighting set-ups," Burton said. "They help us directors figure out camera angles for the shoot."

"Does this stand-in look like Shaw?" Sorkel asked.

"Nearly identical," Burton said.

"Where is he?" I asked.

"I ask the questions," Sorkel reminded me. He turned to

Burton. "Where's the stand-in?"

"How should I know? I've been stuck here since Shaw was whacked." He looked around the room. "I mean since the unfortunate incident." He turned to Sorkel. "Listen, Shaw Kota was a fine, A-list actor," Burton said. "He was poised to be India's next superstar. I plucked him up out of obscurity and brought him here. I'm going to miss him, that's for sure." He pulled out his cell phone. "I need to call my assistant so we can find a replacement fast. The show's gotta go on or we'll be outta jobs real soon."

The detective snatched the cell phone away. "You'll get this back when we're done."

Officer Ramirez charged into the room. He nodded toward me. "She checks out, Sir. Her record's clean." He leaned in and whispered loudly in the detective's ear. "Except that—"

"That charge was dismissed," I said. "No intent to commit a burglary. I was just carrying around some common household tools in my trunk."

Officer Ramirez blinked my way. "I was going to say you helped solve the Ty Calvin murder investigation. Your dad was that famous investigator."

"You mean Monty Locke?" Sorkel asked.

"Really?" Burton stood and peered closely at me. "Ty Calvin? The NBA superstar? I've been trying to get courtside seats for years." He turned to the detective. "You know, she and I did talk guns." He leaned closer to me and said, "I'll take your suggestions under consideration."

Sorkel turned to Debbylynn. "Why did you go into the room?"

"It was time for a costume change," she replied.

"Did you notice anything unusual about what he was wearing?" I asked.

"Yes, I did," Debbylynn said. "When I gave him his wardrobe this morning, THERE WAS NO BLOOD ON IT." Her sobs turned into hiccups.

I made a mental note to circle back to her later. The

break-up could be motive.

The detective threw up his hands and turned to Ramirez. "Find me Shaw's stand-in and get everyone out of here. Except you." His gaze landed on me a moment before turning back to the group. "Make sure none of you leaves town. If you don't respond immediately when I call, I'm coming after you."

"Hard to do if I don't have my phone," Burton said.

"Here," Sorkel handed the phone to Burton. "Out."

Burton pulled out his business card and pushed it into my hand. "We'll need to consult about the shooting scenes."

I took the card and everyone, but Sorkel, filed out after Ramirez. The detective shoved his hands in his pants pockets and stared my way. "I want details."

"I told you everything."

"I've heard about the cases you solved with your father. You've been exposed to police and investigative work before, so you have some idea of what to look for. I'm not saying you saw anyone, but even if the man you say you were running after was the identical twin of the dead guy, something had to be different between the two of them."

Something had been different. That's the realization that had hit me when I stood in the doorway viewing Shaw's body. I'd pictured the guy running away. Just before he turned the corner, I'd zeroed in on his sneakers. "They wore different socks."

"Who did?"

"The star, Shaw, wore black argyle socks. I noticed them when he pedaled the bike during filming. The victim..." I nodded toward the hallway "...his socks are black. No design."

"You sure about that?"

"Check with wardrobe."

"I might do that. Of course, he could've changed socks, if there'd been any time." Sorkel stroked his chin. "These pop-up actors have weird quirks. Anything else?"

"I wasn't close enough to see much. Except..."

"A tattoo? A ring? How about a scar?"

"When he ran by, he smelled..."

"Like cologne? Aftershave? Can you give me a brand?"

"Bubble gum. That's what it was. I smelled bubble gum when he ran by."

Sorkel exhaled. "I see." Sorkel took a turn around the room. "What else did you smell? Candy canes or lollipops?" He turned and mumbled, "Sweet lady justice."

"Now you're making me hungry."

"Ramirez!"

The officer came running.

"Get her out of here."

"Wait," I said. "You should smell the victim. His clothes or something in that room might smell like bubblegum, if the two were close together."

Ramirez' stare shifted to Detective Sorkel. "Sir?"

He narrowed his gaze and spoke through closed lips. "Give it a quick sniff."

Ramirez bounded down the hallway.

"You'd better not be wasting my time," Sorkel said.

Another uniform stepped into the room. "Sir, we found something."

CHAPTER 4

Go Away Murder

I was hot on the trail of Detective Sorkel's rubber soles, down the stairs and out of the brick building. I kept twenty paces back, while he and Officer Ramirez wound their way through the back lot to a boxy structure behind the studio commissary. Ramirez had stopped long enough to tell me he didn't smell bubble gum on the deceased, but his allergies were bothering him, so his sense of smell was weak. He also asked me the way to soundstage ten. I gave him directions and followed, pushing aside thoughts of the contract pile-up on my desk.

Stage ten was one of thirty stages on the lot. And it was where the interior shots of the *Bullets Flying* movie were being filmed. Sorkel entered through a backdoor. Officer Ramirez turned and stood guard. I showed up moments later.

"I can't let you in," he said. "Entry is for law enforcement only."

"I'm practically law enforcement, you know that." I stared up at him.

"We'll both get into trouble."

"I don't want to get you into trouble. But why does the detective need to see the makeup artist?"

The corners of his brown eyes crinkled and he grinned. "You're good. But you're also smart enough to know I can't tell you who he's talking to in there."

This guy oozed enough sincerity to fill Lake Superior.

"So, it's not the makeup artist," I said.

He clamped his lips together.

Stage ten housed dressing rooms, offices, as well as the makeup and costume departments. Which meant the killer could be anyone affiliated with the production. Or not. I tapped a finger against my lips. What did they find?

"Was the knife found?" I asked.

The officer's lips parted and his eyes rounded. "I can't really...say." He turned his head away from me.

Can't or didn't know? He looked pretty clueless to me.

"They found blood that could be a match, right?"

"They did?"

So he was clueless. "I'll leave you to your work."

I hustled past the commissary and aimed for my office. My quiet, humdrum office. It was still warm for a late Friday afternoon. The sun put in a solid day's work, and was going strong. I felt the heat and switched direction. So many questions swirled around in my head. I strolled past the brick building.

The crowd had thinned, but Vanderpat still lurked around the entry. The door was open and his hulky frame was half-inside, attention fixed upstairs. As I closed in, his stern gaze locked on mine. I decided to try small talk, just to show I had no hard feelings.

"Where were you at the time of the murder?" A perfectly reasonable question.

He puffed out his chest. "Why don't you let the grown-ups handle the important matters? Go back to your desk like a good little girl and forget this ever happened."

My temperature rose. I debated stomping on his foot with my heel. My gaze dropped to his shoes. The black leather looked smash resistant. We locked stares again. "I was wrong about you. I believed this could be handled more efficiently in-house than by law enforcement. But with guys like you working security, that would be impossible, wouldn't it? Does this happen when you're fresh out of chew or are you always this ornery?"

"If you don't leave right now, I'm going to make things very difficult for you."

"Wait. You're saying you haven't been doing that already?"

He eyed my badge. "Kiddie flicks?"

"Children's motion picture division. Walt Disney. Ever hear of him? He had a whole movie studio just for that." I uprooted my feet and tramped away.

I'd nearly turned the corner toward my office when I heard a shout behind me.

"Hey, you!" A gravelly voice called out. "Gun lady."

I turned my head.

"Wait up." Burton Kramer jogged over.

"What are the cops doing in stage ten?" I asked, not one to give up easily.

"How should I know?"

"You're in charge, aren't you? You're shooting scenes in there."

"Yeah. So?" He put up his hands.

"They found something. Know anything about it?"

"Uh, right. Blood on a tissue in a wastebasket. It's being sent to some lab somewhere. I tried to tell 'em the key grip had a bloody nose at lunch. He gets them all the time." He licked his lips. "You got a lead on courtside tickets?"

Seriously? "I'm fresh out of leads."

"You're mad 'cause I didn't fess up right away about us conversing." He spread his hands apart. "I'll make it up to you."

Burton dropped back and I picked up speed. I didn't let up until I'd stepped into the two-storied lobby of the producers' building. This was where all the business and legal affairs offices were housed. Casting offices sat in one corner, but the rest of the place belonged to people like me. Or like I was trying to be. I skipped up a wide staircase to the second floor.

Minutes later, I tiptoed into our suite, the legal and business affairs department of the children's motion picture division. All was quiet except for the hum of computers and copy machines. Where was Veera? And more importantly, where was Marshall? Just thinking about my boss made my skin crawl.

I skated past my office and craned my neck to peek around the corner into his office. His chair was empty. His TV screen blank. I let out a breath, slackened my shoulders, and pivoted toward my office, whistling a jaunty tune. I'd get back to work like nothing happened. He'd never even know I was gone.

I stepped into my space and put on the brakes.

"Have a seat." Marshall sat behind my desk. His grainy brown stare didn't budge. He waved a thin hand toward a chair.

Marshall Cooperman, Vice President, Business and Legal Affairs, Children's Motion Picture Division, doled out assignments and migraines freely, especially to me. I sat.

"You've been gone a while." Marshall spoke like an octopus capturing his prey after squirting out a cloud of black ink. I could barely see through the cloud.

"I couldn't get to the accounting meeting," I said. "Crime scene tape got in the way."

"I heard about that." He linked his fingers. "Were you... involved?"

"No." His emphasis on involved referred to a murder at the Newport Beach division a few months ago. That time I'd become "involved" by doing a little sleuthing on the side. I stood, hoping he'd do the same. "I'll reschedule the meeting with the accountant for next week." I licked my fevered lips.

"Never mind about that. I'll take care of it."

"You will?" That was a first, and highly suspect. Marshall never stepped in to take over any of my tasks. Something was up.

He made a pyramid with his fingers and bounced the tips together. "There are going to be some changes."

I sank back down. My heart beat a little quicker. This was a man who only shared bad news. Good news I had to unearth for myself.

"Changes? As in my moving into a bigger office?" I asked. There was a larger office next door to mine with a much better view. Or was he going to sack me for neglecting my lawyerly duties?

"As in a new assignment for you. An assignment that'll be a little different."

"How little?" I asked.

"Lacy Halloway."

I stood again. Lacy was an old time actress who'd contracted to voice a hard-edged moth in an animated series called, *Big Little Flies*. Lacy never returned my calls, ignored me whenever she came into our suite, and would speak and make eye contact only with Marshall. Even her agent, her publicist, and her dog walker ignored me. "That assignment's not a good idea. She won't like it."

"Lacy specifically asked for you."

"By name? Because I don't think she knows it."

"Here." He held out a sticky note. "That's her personal cell phone number. She's waiting for your call."

I took the note. "Is this about a contract?"

"She didn't say." Marshall finally stood and glided for the door. "She wants you to work for her. In what capacity, I don't know. You'll have to update me, afterward."

I shook my head. "I'll call, but she'll end up talking to you."

"Look, give her your undivided attention." He tossed a glance over his shoulder and crossed the threshold. "She's an important client. Stroke her." Marshall ambled out.

He forgot to add, "Or else." He didn't need to. If I made Lacy the least bit unhappy, my head would roll, right out of the studio lot and into the nearest gutter. My heart thumped against my chest. I huffed and picked up the phone. I dialed the number.

"Don't pick up, don't pick up..." I whispered. I could handle murder suspects, illegal weapons, and crime scenes, but when it came to communicating with top brass and big studio stars, well, let's just say it was like spooning honey out of a bee-hive.

A low raspy voice answered, "Why are you calling me?"

"This is Corrie Locke, Miss Halloway. Marshall—"

"I'm in the commissary."

"You know who I am?"

The line went dead.

Did she or didn't she know who was calling her? This was going to be a colossal waste of time unless she took me ser-iously, and gave me a chance to show her I was every bit as good a lawyer as Marshall. Well, maybe not as good as Marshall. But as good as any new lawyer who was navigating her way around ne-gotiating and drafting talent contracts.

"There you are." Veera walked into my office. "I've been looking all over for you."

"I just got back." I grabbed a legal pad. "And now I'm going to a meeting."

"I'll make my update quick." Veera walked me out the suite. "That Vanderpat's tight-lipped as can be. I tried to shake him down. Told him how I used to work top level security for the Chinese mob before I entered the legal profession, but he wouldn't talk."

Veera had worked parking lot security for a company that made computer parts, women's hosiery, and reproductions of antique Ming vases – a wide array of goods, so naturally she sus-pected mafia ties. She'd left that job to be my assistant and to concentrate on her night law school classes.

"I concluded he's the kind of guard with no ambition, and he's no team player," she said. "He's been stuck in that security guard role for so long, he doesn't give it all he's got any more."

"That man's trying too hard to get me out of his way. There has to be a reason. But, I've got another problem right now."

"I'm here for you, C, you know that."

"I'm about to meet with Lacy Halloway."

Veera gave a slow nod and grinned. "Look at you. Making

me proud. Moving up the corporate ladder right before my very eyes. If it gets a little shaky at the bottom, you know I'll be holding the ladder steady."

"You will?"

"Lacy'll never go back to Marshall once she sees you got what it takes. You can make deals better than he can."

I was speechless. Could I handle Lacy? I pushed back my shoulders and lifted my chin. "Thank you, Veera." I swallowed the lump in my throat. "Maybe you're right. After all, we're just two women of vastly different generations who both work in the entertainment industry." Lacy had a solid four decades on me, but that didn't matter. "We must have something in common, right? I wonder if she likes Bogart movies. Maybe she's even met him. It shouldn't be hard to talk business with her." I rubbed my hands together. Why were my palms damp?

Ten minutes later, I entered the mostly empty, high-ceilinged commissary. It was five-thirty, and most of the studio had clocked out already. My footsteps echoed along the sleek, stone floors. The spacious dining area featured multi-tiered seating, the usual vintage movie posters and high-backed, cushioned booths. A server glided past, pausing long enough to guide me to a private dining room.

Lacy Halloway sat in the center of the space, behind a large round table. Her tangerine sweater complemented her coral colored hair and necklace. Big green eyes scrutinized me through spidery lashes. A plate of vegetable crudité sat untouched in front of her. She pointed to the seat across from her. I took it.

"You," she called out to a server standing just outside the door.

He scrambled over.

"One BLT on sourdough. Except without the bacon or tomato. This BLT's going to have basil, lettuce and turkey. White meat. Not the rolled up stuff. And skip the mayo. Slap on some pesto, then grill the whole shebang. Got that?"

"Of course." He bowed his head and turned to me.

"Iced tea, please."

He darted out of the line of fire. Lacy sat back in her chair and eyed me. A sliding glass door to my left opened to a small patio with white latticework crawling with leafy green vines. I gripped my knee to keep it from bouncing. The room temperature was comfortable, but it didn't matter much to my sweat glands. They'd shifted into overdrive. Fortunately, the cotton fabric of my sheath dress was thick enough to keep my sweating under wraps, for now. Meanwhile, it was all I could do to hold her stare.

"I abhor inexperience," she told me.

That about summed up my legal career. "Who doesn't?"

She pursed her lips. "Do you dance?"

Her career had started out in Hollywood musicals. "Before dinner?"

Her thin reddish brows dropped. Her lips tightened. If I waved a red handkerchief, she'd charge at me.

"Well, let's say I can move my...limbs in a way that loosely resembles the concept of dance. I'm sure there's a sub-Saharan tribe that would appreciate it." I chuckled. Why was I talking so much? "Do you like Bogart movies?"

She grabbed a French roll and tore off a piece with her teeth. The server arrived with her entrée and my iced tea. Lacy didn't blink. He quickly made his exit and stood outside the doorway.

I lowered my chin. "Is this about your latest deal? Because I can help you with it." My voice crept up a notch, and I grabbed my glass of ice tea.

"Not even close." She leaned in close to me. "It's about a homicide."

CHAPTER 5

The Bait Dangler

"**A** homicide?" The glass of iced tea was halfway to my lips when my hand froze. My stomach hit the floor. Two homicides in one day were two too many.

Lacy snapped her fingers at the server. "Decaf latte with raw sugar." She turned to me. "I'm craving sugar and coffee, but I can't handle caffeine anymore. Messes with my equilibrium."

"What homicide?" I lowered the glass to the table.

"There's a film in production starring my godson." She stared past me. "He was...killed today." Her voice dropped.

"Shaw Kota was your godson?" I said. "I'm so sorry."

The server raced in and placed the latte next to Lacy. He zoomed out and took his place near the doorway.

"I can't rely on the police to find out what happened."

I knew what was coming next. Just because I'd worked a few cases with Dad, the whole world thought I'd inherited his sleuthing skills. It's true, I'd picked up a few pointers. I'd also kept his collection of illegal weaponry and knew my way around them. But if I failed Lacy, my studio days would be over.

Lacy leaned toward me. "You're going to find out who's responsible."

"Maybe you haven't noticed yet, but I'm an attorney in the legal and business affairs department of this studio. Not a private investigator or with law enforcement or—"

"Don't patronize me. I know all about you. I know all about your investigation of the Newport Beach division. The cops were no help. Your...discovery...forced a cleansing in the kiddie flicks department. That's how you ended up here."

"Marshall told you?" My boss scooped up gossip like a ditch digger scooped dirt on a construction site.

"I have my sources. I also know you found a killer for a murder no one even knew about."

I blew out a sigh. I took that case because of my best friend, Michael. He'd happened upon a crime scene and left a little something incriminating behind. I kept him off police radar until we found the killer. How could I turn down helping my closest pal?

"And now, you're going to find out who killed Shaw Kota." Lacy glowered at me full steam. My hair was beginning to curl.

"My job at the studio is to negotiate and draft contracts."

She squinted an eye and moved her head from side to side. "You don't really want to choke down any more contracts, do you? They're so hard to digest."

Was it that obvious? I pictured the stack of paperwork on my desk. My motivation dragged around my ankles like a pair of sweatpants without an elastic waistband.

"A happy Lacy Halloway means a happy children's motion picture division, which means a happy movie studio." She linked her fingers. "We're all interconnected."

I stood. "I need to get back to my office." Meaning, I needed time to think this over.

"The script was perfect for Shaw." Lacy's voice cracked. "And you're perfect for solving this case."

I kept on standing, but one of my knees was buckling. "You may be able to control everyone else that crosses your path, but you can't control me."

"Control?" She sat back. "Is that what you think I'm doing? Honey, I'm just trying to help you live up to your potential. From what I've read, you're good at solving hard-to-crack crimes. And I'm guessing you're good at…" she leaned in close. "…breaking the friggin' law without all hell breaking loose. Just like your daddy. You played a big part in his investigations. Even a starring role now and then. This lawyer gig you pretend to be so hot on dulls in comparison. What I want to know is why you even bother?"

"It has a little something to do with my penchant for staying alive."

"Overrated. You can't really be alive if you don't take risks now and then."

"Driving the 405 freeway is enough of a risk for me."

"Oh, spare me. Taking risks isn't just a necessary part of life, it helps us find out what we're made of. What are you made of? Silk? Or steel?"

I felt like I'd been waiting my whole life for that question. I'm a fan of silk, but I'm a bigger fan of people of steel, like Superman and Wonder Woman. Still, I wasn't going to be rushed into anything. I had a steady paycheck to consider. "I suggest you hire a real PI instead of a rookie."

"I asked for you, in particular." She bit into her sandwich.

"Why?"

"Maybe it's because I'm dedicated to bringing out the best in people," Lacy spoke with her mouth full, spitting up crumbs. "I'm done here." She swallowed the last bit and rose, pushing back her chair with the backs of her knees. "Let's blow this gelato joint." She checked the diamond-studded watch around her wrist. "We'll meet again at nine o'clock."

"Tomorrow morning?"

"Tonight." She dug around inside her handbag and pulled out a card. She tossed it on the table. "That's my home address. We'll discuss the details." She turned on her ballet flats and left just as the server stumbled in.

"Is everything alright?" he asked.

Lacy floated by him without a word.

"Put it on her tab," I said and hurried after Lacy. "Wait."

She pushed through the entry doors.

I followed her. "I can't make it tonight."

"Why the hell not?" She turned to face me.

"I...I have a date."

Lacy picked up her pace again. "So bring him...or her along."

"That won't work," I said. My date was too important to cancel or postpone.

"I promise I'll liven things up for you both."

"You don't understand—"

"No, *you* don't understand," she said. "You just don't get it."

Two popular TV actors strolled past and said hello to Lacy. She ignored them and quietly said, "That boy meant everything to me." Lacy jumped from hard to soft in no time at all, like a cheap mattress. All the jumping around was confusing my backbone.

"First, I need some questions answered," I said.

"Fire away."

"Where were you around three this afternoon?" I asked her.

"On soundstage two, working on a song for that cartoon I'm voicing." She blew out a long blast of air through her teeth. "Security walked in to tell me about...Shaw."

"You need to understand I'm not a private investigator. I helped my father on some cases, and took a few on afterward, but that was beginner's luck. You'd be better off with a professional."

She huffed. "Don't tell me what I'd be better off with. Meet with me tonight and, if you want out afterward, I'll back off, and you can go back to your exhilarating contracts."

"I—"

She put up a hand decked out in turquoise rings. "We're done." She shook her head. "I've been around the block a couple of thousand times, my daughter hasn't spoken to me in years, and I'm yesterday's news to the toddlers running Hollywood today. I don't have time to waste." She moved closer. "You know what? If you show up tonight, fine. And if you don't, c'est la vie."

"Wow, that was an abrupt turnaround. Thanks for understanding." I'd make that date tonight, after all.

"There is one small item I forgot to mention," Lacy said.

I stopped in my tracks. She really was a control freak. She was dangling bait and I was hungry. "Why am I not surprised?"

Lacy held out the back of a hand in front of her face, lifted her chin and admired her pearly pink fingernails.

"Don't tell me," I said. "I have to show up tonight to find out, right?"

"No." She wagged a finger at me and stopped. "But that's a good idea. I'll save it for later."

"I need to know now."

Lacy stared at me a beat. "It's about your father."

CHAPTER 6

Change in Plans

Lacy zipped her lips after that bit about Dad, claiming exhaustion and promising more later, and we parted ways. I pulled out my phone to call Michael. As I walked to my car, he called me. He could read my mind even when we weren't together. I was on his radar that way.

"Can't wait 'til tonight," he said. "It's going to be the icing on top of a great, no a spectacular, week. School's out for the summer and well, you know, I'm grateful for the way things played out. Being bumped up to associate dean, it's been—"

"Michael, about tonight..."

"That's why I'm calling. I'm on my way. I left early."

Michael worked at a private tech college in downtown LA. "You did?"

"I didn't want to be late. Not that I'm ever late. We're going to have the best time. I'll make us dinner and all you need to do is sit back and enjoy. You won't have to lift a finger, my lady. Or would you rather go out to eat? We've got reservations at..."

While Michael talked up our plans tonight, the back of my neck started to prickle. I paused to look over my shoulder. A couple of women crossed a wide strip of lawn to get to the nearest parking structure, but someone was tailing me, about thirty paces back. Dark hair, parted in the center, brushed the tops of his shoulders; his eyes were hidden behind blue-tinted aviator glasses. He wore a shapeless brown jacket and loose-fitting jeans splattered with white paint. He gripped a brown fedora hat in one hand.

"Michael, I can't make it tonight." I slowed my steps and turned a corner.

"What? We've been planning this for a while. Isn't our date tonight?"

During our last murder investigation I'd surprised us both by declaring my love for him. I was fairly sure he was about to make his own declaration, but we were interrupted with news about my dad being spotted in one of his old haunts, which put me in a tailspin. My father had died over a year ago. My mom and I had scattered his ashes over the deep blue Pacific, but it turned out her means of identifying Dad's body was a bit sketchy. With Michael's help, I'd been searching for clues about a living dad for weeks, but came up empty-handed. That's when Michael asked me on our first date. Did he care about me like I did for him, or was it a sympathy date?

"Can I call you back in twenty minutes? I need to take care of business first." I peered over my shoulder. The guy had turned the same corner and stopped to fiddle with his cell phone.

"Uh, sure. You want to reschedule? Because if you do…"

"I want to—"

"Call me back when you're ready and we'll talk."

Michael's voice had dropped a notch, leaving behind only a trace of his former enthusiasm.

"Okay." I disconnected. I was a scaredy cat, plain and simple. To switch gears from friendship to romance could divide us in two, if things turned sour. My dating track record didn't exactly give me an edge.

I shoved dating thoughts aside and glanced behind me again. The guy had picked up his pace. He was closer now. I paused and pulled out my phone, feigning a call until he rounded a corner and left my line of vision. I faced forward and continued to toss glances over my shoulder while I padded along.

I waited at the entry and took one last look. This constant being-on-the-watch for tails and shady characters was Dad's fault. My way of viewing the world had become skewed toward the bad and the ugly.

I wound my way upstairs, pushing through the homeward bound foot traffic. When I reached our suite, I caught Veera blazing a trail up and down the hallway outside my office.

"You got back quicker than I thought," she said. "Is she throwing over Marshall for you? She'd better, if she's smart."

"Not exactly," I said.

Veera landed in the middle of the small leather sofa in my office, and I gave her a play-by-play of my meeting with Lacy.

"She's a trip, isn't she?" Veera said when I finished.

"Down the rapids of the Colorado river. I've got a hunch there's something she's not telling me."

"You mean besides that tidbit about your dad?"

"Yep. How would you feel if you'd learned your godson had been killed?"

"I'd be a mess. Crazed out of my mind with grief."

I nodded. "Same here. She seemed pretty casual about it." I grabbed a stress ball shaped like a lemon off my desk and gave it a squeeze. "Of course, she didn't seem like the teary-eyed type."

"Hmm." Veera stroked her chin. "Some people don't get all emotional in front of others. She could explode in private. You don't want to be there when that happens."

"Yet, she's an actress who loves attention."

"Maybe that's just a front," Veera said.

"When did Marshall leave?" I asked.

"Right after you did. Something about playing ball."

So he knew my talk with Lacy didn't concern him, or he would have stuck around to make sure I handled our star client appropriately.

"You going to meet her tonight?" Veera said. "Isn't this

your date night?"

"It is, or it was."

"Don't you go putting up with anybody's BS. I don't care if she is our biggest client. She could be taking you for a ride through the Mojave desert without any A/C."

Veera had a knack for cutting to the core of things. "No one's taking me for a ride."

"Okay." Veera rose to her feet. "Then let's get the rules straight before you meet with her."

"What rules?"

Veera held up her index finger. "The Rules of Proper Private Investigation. Learned during my on-the-job training."

"Since when are we proper?"

"Rule number one." Veera walked a small circle around my office. "Don't agree to investigate anything until after you collect the facts."

"Solid."

"Rule number two." She reached into a pocket and pulled out a sucker. She removed the wrapper. "Investigate to determine if the facts are what the client said they are."

"Veera, you are on a roll. Any more?"

"Number three. No law breaking." She sucked on the pop.

"Oh boy."

"Then there's rule number three, subsection A, which says if you should break a law accidentally or on account of an emergency situation, run like hell."

"That's the only way to run," I agreed.

"This could mean a promotion for us both, if we do the job right. You know she'd use you and not Marshall for all her contracts."

"Nothing like a little pressure to get the job done."

"Meanwhile, I'm going to ask around some more." Veera pulled out peach gloss and made her lips shine. "Starting with the commissary. I'm gonna see how often our victim dined there, and ask around about that Vanderpat."

"Good move."

"I'll have some of the delicious cornbread while I'm asking."

Minutes later, Veera left to tackle the commissary, and I finished up a contract, meaning I reviewed one paragraph before hitting the road. It was Friday afternoon, after all. I made it to my parking space without any sign of the guy in the fedora.

I sank behind the wheel of my age-old BMW and dialed Michael's number. He'd been the one I always went to about problems and failed relationships. Who would I go to if we parted ways? My mother?

"That'll be the day," I mumbled.

Michael answered on the first ring.

"We can do this," he said. "We can make anything work if we want to. If you want to. I know I do. Do we have a date tonight?"

"No, I mean, yes. Well, maybe. You're not going to believe what happened." I spilled the beans about the murder and Lacy, and about going to her home tonight. "I said no to her the whole time, until she dangled that bit about Dad."

"I totally get it. We should go."

"We should? Why?" I pulled onto Pico Boulevard.

"Because we thrive on danger. At least you do. I'll provide all the sunlight, water and nutrients to keep you thriving."

"I like that. Even if I'm not a ficus tree."

"Besides," Michael was saying. "Sometimes, things are put on our path for a reason."

"Like a banana peel?" I wasn't keen on slipping and falling. "You really don't mind about tonight?"

"Mind? How could I? Maybe she's got the one clue about your dad we've missed. That would be incredible, right? Besides, I'll make us dinner when we get back."

This was why I loved the guy. "See you soon."

Twenty minutes later, I pulled onto the 10 freeway. I motored toward home and got off on Lincoln where the cars were jammed together tighter than a string of pearls. Usually, I'd be huffing and puffing my impatience, but tonight, I was sedate.

I turned onto Longfellow and cruised down the hill to my driveway. I was about to pull in, when I slammed on the brakes. A black Town Car with limousine-tinted windows blocked the entry. I landed on the horn. The sedan didn't budge, but the right rear door popped open.

CHAPTER 7

Visions

I lived a few blocks away from the golden sands of Hermosa Beach in a cozy little bootleg unit over the garage in the front of a duplex. What could be better than that? Well, for starters, the landlady was gone most of the time, flying the friendly skies. Miss Trudy became a flight attendant not long after Orville and Wilbur invented the first flying machine. The travel bug hadn't just bitten her, it had roosted on her shoulder and built a sturdy nest. The very best part? She was a friend of Mom's so she cut me some slack on the rent. The only downside was she stuck to rules like pink on cotton candy. No loud music between ten pm and eight am, no obscenities within earshot (I only swore when driving LA freeways), and no dogs allowed. I could live with the first two rules, but I was glad Miss Trudy wasn't around to see what had scrambled out of the Town Car. A fawn colored pug with a curly tail and small floppy ears trotted over to a patch of grass by the driveway. I parked on the street behind the car and sidestepped to the open door.

"That's Basil." Lacy's raspy voice croaked from the car's interior.

I peered inside. "What are you doing here?" I didn't need to ask how she found my address. Marshall never said no to any of Lacy's demands.

She shuffled out of the sedan, raised her arms and arched her back in a long stretch. "I moved up our meeting time."

"And the meeting place, and didn't bother telling me."

She turned to stare at my duplex. "I like spontaneity. And I wanted to get to know you better, on your own turf." She waved the driver away. "Park and wait," she told him and slammed her door. She picked up Basil.

Moments later, the sedan disappeared, and I'd pulled into my garage. I skipped up the short staircase to my unit, with Lacy climbing at a leisurely pace behind me. I unlocked the front door and motioned for her to enter. She stepped into my living room, one of three rooms in a place small enough to fold up and carry in a knapsack. My furnishings were only the bare necessities: a futon, a lamp, a coffee table and a dartboard to decorate my wall. A table and two chairs sat in a tiny space in my kitchenette. A bed and a dresser livened up my bedroom, and a small bathroom was squeezed between the bedroom and hall closet.

Basil grunted, tongue hanging out.

"That needs to go." Lacy pointed to a yellow throw pillow on the futon.

"I like the splash of color."

"Yellow reminds Basil of fire hydrants."

I grabbed the pillow and tossed it into my bedroom. "Should I order pizza?"

"No. I brought food for us." Lacy sank down on the futon, Basil on her lap. She reached into her handbag and pulled out two Snickers bars. She handed me one.

"Great, thanks. Just what I wanted for dinner," I said. "Care for some M&Ms for dessert?"

"Don't be impertinent."

"And my father?"

"He was never impertinent," Lacy said.

"You said you had information on him."

She squirmed and Basil jumped off her lap with a snort. He scurried along, nose to the wood floor and disappeared into my kitchenette. "Do you have any tequila?"

"No," I said.

She bit off a piece of the Snickers bar and chewed while her bright green eyes scanned the room. "I called Monty a few years ago."

"And?"

"We talked about my visions."

"What kind of visions?" My father had his share of kooky clients, so I wasn't surprised. Except you'd think she would have mentioned her acquaintance with Dad earlier, like during any one of the dozen times she'd passed by my office on her way to see Marshall.

"I didn't know you were his daughter until I read your profile in last week's studio newsletter."

So not only did she have visions, she wasn't too shabby at mind reading either.

"I don't control my visions," Lacy said. "They pop into my head."

"Were you a client of my fathers?"

She stood and gravitated toward the dartboard. "This looks more beat-up than usual. What kind of darts do you use?"

"The kind that make a big impact." My dartboard served as a practice area for throwing my shuriken, otherwise known as a Japanese throwing star, my favorite weapon of distraction. Since shuriken were illegal in California, they sat in a locked box in the closet, with the other illegals inherited from my father.

Lacy's gaze traveled up the wall to a small black camera aiming at the front door. She pointed to it and stared my way.

"It's a Crib cam, home security. Makes my mom feel more comfy about my living alone." Mom knew all about my weaponry. You'd think that would help her sleep better at night. "No one can break in without my knowing."

Lacy gave me a squinty eye. "I had a vision showing you capturing the killer. That's why I came to you."

"And did the vision tell you who the killer was?"

She took another bite. "My visions don't contain minutiae. Are you always so skeptical? Monty was more open-minded."

"I'm not my father," I folded my arms across my chest. "Did he ever use any of your visions?"

"I led him to the case of that missing banker in Marina Del Rey." She chomped the last of her Snickers bar and brushed invisible candy crumbs off her hands.

A banker had been kidnapped a few years ago, without a trace. Dad found him holed up in a shed belonging to the kidnapper. Dad said he'd gotten a tip that a customer was holding him ransom. Had Lacy provided the tip?

"You led him to the shed?"

"After a few wrong turns, but yes, I did."

"Why not go straight to the cops?" I asked.

"Think I didn't try them first? They wouldn't believe me." She shrugged a shoulder. "Something about my past tips not playing out. They can be hit or miss. It's the way they unfurl out of my head."

"How many past tips did you give the cops?"

She shook her head. "Too many. But that was back when I was getting into my stride. By the time I got to your dad, I knew what I was seeing."

"Did you have any other visions about Shaw?"

"I'm surprised I got any. It doesn't work with people I'm close to." She reclaimed her spot on the futon.

I walked over to the blinds on my front window and tilted a couple of slats with my fingers. I peeked through. The sun had gone to sleep when I wasn't looking, leaving behind a shiny-faced moon. Most of the street parking was taken for the evening, but Lacy's sedan was parked up the street. I turned back to her. Most kooks got in the way more than they helped. This kook looked like a pressure cooker about to blow her top.

She patted the futon. "Sit." Basil leapt onto her lap. "I'll tell you about your father."

I slowly walked over and sat at the opposite end, bracing myself for a ridiculous vision.

Lacy dug a hand into her purse and pulled out an envelope. She pulled out a photo and held it up to me. "Recognize anyone?"

It was a picture of Lacy and my father from about five years ago, if Dad's shorter hair meant anything. He'd let it grow longer before he—

"We became close."

"That can't be," I said.

I peered at the photo. He stood by Lacy's side, tall, broad-shouldered, longish snowy white hair swept back from his angular face, dark eyes alert behind wire rimmed glasses. His mouth hinted at a grin, but a deep groove lingered between his brows resembling a slight frown. That's how Dad looked when he was in deep concentration. His hands rested at his sides, but Lacy's arm reached up and around his shoulders.

I rose and slid toward the front door. "My father was not the type of person to get close to anyone. How could he possibly be close to you?"

"He's going to help you solve this."

"Dad? You mean in his astral form?"

She shook her head. "No, in his human form."

"You do know he died a year ago?" His last cup of coffee was laced with ricin. His killer was never found.

She nodded.

"Which means he's physically not around to help," I said.

She scooted to the edge of the futon. "I can only tell you what the spirits show me. But there's more."

"Of course, there is."

"Shaw wasn't exactly my godson."

CHAPTER 8

Walking Things Over

Lacy stayed another ten minutes. Enough time to finish the Snickers bar she'd gifted me, and explain she'd met Shaw only six months ago in Kolkata. She'd made the trek to "clarify" her visions, but got sidetracked by a food fest that added eight pounds to her slender frame. That's where Shaw entered the picture. They'd bonded over chickpea patties and sweet pancakes. The only background she'd had on Shaw included his having played parts in two Bollywood films, and his dream of coming to America as an actor. He'd also lost his parents in a freak rickshaw accident where they'd been hit by a truck. That was enough for her to anoint him as her protégé after they'd dipped their toes in the Ganges River.

"If we dipped anything more than our toes, we'd probably get typhoid. The Ganges is filthy," she'd said. "I would have brought him to Hollywood right away, except he had no passport."

He'd eventually taken care of that technicality, and she'd sent money to bring him over.

"So you see, Shaw is...like a godson, even though there'd been no formal anointing," Lacy said. "I'm also an ordained minister, by the way."

I told her I'd need the weekend to think things through.

But I'd already made up my mind. That's what I told Michael when he arrived minutes after Lacy's departure.

"She's a fruitcake," I said. "And you know I'm a lover of everything cake, except fruitcake."

"I'm along for the ride, either way," Michael said. "Even if our ride has no steering wheel. If you want to nose around, I'll throw my nose in the ring right beside yours."

"That's so sweet." I stood on my toes and kissed him.

I slipped into a T-shirt and jeans, and we left my place for a stroll along the stretch of greenbelt running between Ardmore and Valley. The softly padded wood chip trail wandered between the two roads, hosting ice plants galore and an assortment of native shrubs, trees and flowers. It was cool and quiet this time of night, except for the whirr of passing car engines and the occasional jet overhead. I shared a few more details with Michael about the day's happenings. We talked uninterrupted and got some exercise in. Who could ask for more? Me, for one. I was hungry. Lasagna and garlic bread served hot from the oven would have been appreciated. My stomach grumbled.

I threw Michael a sidelong glance. He wore a jacket with his jeans tonight, his usual Chuck Taylors, and the beginnings of a beard. He was attractive without being handsome, unassuming without being dull, and humble and ambitious at the same time. He set my heart aflutter with his pure goodness. The big question was, what did he see in me? The girl with the wild hair, and an unwavering penchant for high-end clothes borrowed from Mom's closets no matter how many locks and hiding places she'd installed. PI work had made me a thief, a weapons expert and a consummate bender of truths. How would he react if I took him in my arms and kissed him passionately? How would I feel? He turned his head to me and smiled.

"Michael, you look—"

"Corrie, you look..."

We'd spoken at the same time. We stopped to stare at each other.

"Yes?" I prompted.

"Hungry. When was the last time you ate anything?"

"Are you kidding me? Who cares about eating at a time like this?" I marched ahead.

"Is this not a good time to eat?" Michael caught up to me.

"No, I mean, oh, never mind." He could be so clueless sometimes.

"Maybe we should go through the facts of the murder scene again. And try and make sense of it."

My mind was on romance, while his was on murder. Our wires were totally crossed. I gritted my teeth to keep me from spitting out my next words. "You are so exasperating sometimes." He'd asked me on a date, but behaved as usual.

"Really?" He stopped in his tracks. "Is this because—"

"Yes, it is." I slapped a frond hanging off a stocky palm tree. Neither one of us knew what I was talking about.

"If you don't want to help Lacy Halloway, I get that. But I also know you can't turn away anyone who needs your help, even if it is an eccentric old movie star who's not been nice to you in the past." He put an arm around me and continued our walk at a brisker pace. "This is not about you getting fired or about your lawyer job. It's about your special talent. A little unusual, but special. Being out there solving these incredibly challenging cases before the cops barely know what's going on. How many people can do that?"

"I've never seen you so charged up before."

"My point is you're going to help Lacy. And I'm going to help you, help her. She needs us. She wants to be your friend. Why look, she even brought a Snickers bar to share with you. That's like breaking bread."

"That's not exactly true," I said.

"It's a gesture of friendship."

"She's not like regular people. Besides, she ended up eating both candy bars herself."

"Here's what we do."

I was so appreciative that he always jumped right in, without any prodding by me.

"We ask questions. If nothing turns up in a few days, we walk away. No one can say we didn't try, right?" He stopped and faced me again. He shoved his hands in the pockets of his trousers and beamed, lighting up our portion of the greenbelt.

I placed my hand on his shoulder. "Just a few weeks ago, you thought you'd be arrested. You don't want to get that close to a sketchy situation again, do you?"

"That was the old me. It's better to be hot or cold, not tepid, and that's the tepid way of handling things. I've been tepid for too long."

I kicked a pebble on my path. "The whole thing did nearly happen right in front of me. That's like the universe ordering me to get involved." Besides, I couldn't resist a thrill ride. I was a true adrenaline junkie.

We locked eyes. "It feels right."

He leaned in, his hands lightly touching my cheeks. I lifted my chin, and it happened. The warmth of his lips on mine, softly at first, and then, more passionately. My heart fluttered while the world around us stopped moving.

Michael opened his eyes the same time I did.

"Wow-wee. What have we been waiting for?" he said.

"That's what I want to know."

"Let's go back to your place. I'll make us that great dinner, if that's what you want. Or..." He grabbed my hand, chasing away the cold. We walked hand-in-hand, up the greenbelt toward my street. He turned to stare at me. "Gee, you look nice tonight."

"So do you. Think we could—"

We'd barely stepped onto the road when a rumbling engine roar drowned out my next words. A Dodge Charger barreled around the corner and onto Ardmore, cutting off an SUV that screeched to a stop. The driver of the Dodge punched the accelerator, turned on its high beams, and aimed straight for us.

CHAPTER 9

Full Speed Ahead

Bright lights blinded me as I grabbed Michael's arm and yanked him back as hard as I could. The Dodge lunged toward us, the deep rumbling engine swallowing up all other sounds. We landed on a dirt mound next to the greenbelt.

"Did you see that maniac?" Michael asked, out of breath. "You okay, Corrie?"

I lay on my side, right arm lodged beneath me. I lifted my head. "I think so. I'm not missing any body parts. You?"

"I'm all here." Michael lay a foot away.

He was struggling to sit up. The woman driving the SUV jumped out and joined us.

"Oh, my God! That was crazy. I called 9-1-1," the woman said. "You both alright?"

We slowly rose to our feet.

"I think so," Michael said.

I hunched over, palms resting against the tops of my thighs. A long scratch bled along my forearm. My legs trembled and my insides were all shook up. The Dodge was black with shiny rims and tinted windows. The place for the license plate sat empty. I'd leapt back when I saw the car, but a beam from the streetlight had streamed through the driver's side when the car rocketed by.

"A fedora," I said.

"What?" Michael asked.

Two runners joined our group. "We saw what happened," one of them said. "Are you okay?"

"We're fine, thanks." Michael wiped the leaves and pebbles off my clothes and swished them off his jacket.

"She was insane," the SUV driver told the runners. "She cut me off."

"She?" I said. "You saw the person behind the wheel?"

"It was the kind of female motorist that gives the rest of us a bad rap," the SUV driver said.

"How do you know it was a she?" I asked.

"Her shoulder-length hair, but the hat was unisex."

"What kind of hat?" Michael wanted to know.

"Old school," the lady said. "I think they're making a come-back."

"Like the kind Bogart wore in his movies?" I asked.

"Who?" she asked.

"She means a fedora," a runner said. He pulled up a picture on his smartphone and showed the SUV driver. "Did it look like this?"

"Yeah, that's it," the SUV driver said.

Two cops stopped by minutes later. One took statements, while the other waited in the squad car. The officer in the car stepped out.

"The Dodge you described was located a mile away," he said. "In an alley east of El Oeste. We've cordoned off the area."

"What about the driver?" I asked.

"We're looking for her," he replied.

"We'll be in touch," the other cop said.

Michael and I hobbled across Ardmore toward my duplex.

"It wasn't a her," I said.

"What wasn't?" Michael asked when we made it across safely.

"The driver that tried to run us down was a man." I told him about the guy on the studio lot and how I'd caught sight of the Dodge driver.

"Why didn't you tell the police?" Michael wanted to know. "They'll look for the wrong person."

"It's too complicated to explain. I'll let Sorkel know."

"Wow, this went from a low dose of danger to very high in no time at all," Michael said. "We're going to need a bodyguard."

"That would be Veera," I said.

"I was thinking James. Two bodyguards would be even better," Michael added.

"James?" He was Michael's other best chum, and a guy with whom I'd shared a shaky past until recently when we'd called a truce. Our past disagreements--and kisses--didn't mean a thing anymore. Of course, Michael didn't need to know about any of that.

"We can use an assistant district attorney's help," Michael said. "And he's an ace with weapons, where I'm terrible."

"That's not exactly true," I said. Michael did have an aversion to weaponry, but he managed to work the two-inch blade I'd gifted him like a pro.

"We need back-up. Trying to run you down, and me in the process, is a classic gangster move," Michael said. "You think he's the guy you saw running off? Maybe he wore a wig to throw off the scent."

"Could be. He has to be connected with Shaw's murder."

"How do we prove that?" Michael said.

"Not sure yet. Oh no." My gaze landed on my driveway.

"What's wrong?"

"We have company."

CHAPTER 10

Where Spirits Lie

"You're a hesitator," Lacy said, eying Michael. She stood in my driveway cradling Basil in her arms. The pug's tongue hung out; his head bobbed up and down while he panted, googly eyes all over us.

"Who me? No," Michael said. "I don't hesitate. Not really. Well, maybe once in a while. But I take action, too. In fact, I was just about to make dinner for us. We've had a rough night. I'm Michael Parris, by the way." He looked at me, then back at Lacy. "Wait." His eyes rounded. "I'm standing next to a movie giant. Your films...they're phenomenal."

Lacy stroked Basil. Her lips turned up at the ends in a hint of a grin before settling back into the usual straight line. "Merci."

"Why did you return?" I asked her.

She narrowed her gaze. "Hello to you, too. I realized we hadn't settled anything." She tilted her head toward the black sedan. The engine was still running. The driver sat behind the wheel. "Let's go for a ride."

"Where?" I asked.

"My beach house."

"We can talk here." I couldn't imagine a good reason to go to her to place.

"You need to see where Shaw lived. Get a feel for what happened. That only works if you see things up close." She set Basil down, and he trotted to a hydrangea bush.

"Actually, she can get a pretty good feel even from a distance," Michael said. "In fact, she doesn't even need to be there to know what's going on."

"Stay out of this," Lacy told him. "I liked you better as a hesitator."

I crossed my arms over my chest. "First, I've got a few questions." I told her about the longhaired guy at the studio that had followed me, and about the near miss by the Dodge. "What do you know that I don't?"

Lacy clamped her lips together, regarding me with a sidelong stare. "Shaw had his own life."

"He lived with you," I said. "Did he have many visitors?"

"Never," Lacy said, her eyes shifted to Basil trotting over to her.

"Where did he go when he wasn't acting?" Michael asked.

"He hung out with people he'd met on the set, or..." Lacy paused a few beats.

"Yes?" I asked.

She shrugged. "Made friends with new people. I have no idea. Maybe this incident with the Dodge had nothing to do with Shaw."

"That would be quite a coincidence," I said.

Her gaze dropped to my arm. "You're leaking."

I'd declined paramedics, so the cops had bandaged my arm, but blood seeped out from beneath, dripping onto the pavement.

"Wow, let me take care of that," Michael said. He led me up my staircase and into my unit. We stepped into the bathroom, where Michael properly patched me up.

"Sorry, Corrie, this didn't turn out to be the date night I had in mind."

"If I can get rid of Lacy," I said. "We can still have our date."

Lacy cleared her throat. We turned our heads. She stood

just outside the bathroom doorway. "After tonight, if you still say no, I'll respect your wishes," she said. "But no respect from me until then."

Her ballet flats were rooted to the wood floor. She was like a permanent piece of lint. There was no getting rid of her.

"I don't need to see your house," I said.

She threw back her head. "Ha! You're not going to. You'll be confined to one room. Shaw's." Her eyes shot to Michael. "You're off the hook tonight, but you'll still owe her a dinner. Food'll be ready at my place when we arrive."

"What are we having?" Michael asked.

Lacy took a step closer to him. "White cheddar lobster mac n' cheese."

Michael and I swapped glances. Moments later, he rode shotgun, and I'd slipped into the back of the Town Car with Lacy and Basil.

PI work was a powerful stimulant, I confess. Especially when the case fell into my lap, curled up and started to purr. I couldn't help but stroke it. Lacy was right. My legal job was drab in comparison. Safer, but drab. It was like holding the reins of a fast moving stagecoach filled with unknown treasure versus driving the oxcart in a wagon crammed with clanging pots and pans. I stole a look at Lacy. There were no signs she'd lost someone dear to her today. Was it all bottled up? Or maybe she truly didn't care. She caught me watching her.

"You're wrong," she said.

"You're not only a psychic, but a mind-reader, too?" That was becoming more and more apparent.

She turned her face toward the window. "I've become an expert at hiding my feelings. What's going on inside of my head is nobody's business."

I turned away and pictured dinner. I could almost taste the mac n' cheese. Hot, buttery garlic bread would make the dinner complete.

"Sylvia makes great garlic bread."

My head snapped toward Lacy.

"What? She does," Lacy said. "Syl's my housekeeper."

The Town Car whisked us along at a steady pace down Coast Highway to Malibu. It was stop-and-go until the road sloped and ran beside the beach. That was when the driver, who hadn't uttered a word the whole time, wound up the sedan and accelerated between cars.

"Whoa, ho ho!" Michael said. "You're really getting into this, aren't you, man."

"Ping used to valet-park cars at Playboy Mansion parties. He knows what he's doing," Lacy explained.

Meanwhile, my feet were firmly planted on the floor. I gripped the door handle. Ping continued to unspool the car down the highway, but Lacy paid no mind. Michael talked up video games and Greek food, which he tended to do when he was nervous.

"I don't want to alarm anyone, but I might just display the meager contents of my stomach," I said.

Michael leaned sideways and regarded Lacy. "You should take her throwing up seriously."

Lacy shot me a look. "Slow down, Ping."

Ping eased off the accelerator and glided to the slow lane.

"Here." Lacy reached into the side pocket of her seat and pulled out a small packet of saltine crackers.

I took them from her. Basil stuck his chin on my knee. I offered him a cracker, which he instantly gobbled. I ate the other one myself. "Delicious."

Lacy sat back and rolled her eyes over me. "It wouldn't hurt for you to eat once in a while."

"Oh, there's nothing wrong with her appetite," Michael said, sounding a lot like my mother. "She just forgets to eat sometimes."

"How is that possible?" Lacy wanted to know.

"That's what happens when you work in a film studio with a stack of contracts on your desk and a homicide to distract you," I said.

"Does that happen often?" Lacy asked.

"About once a month," I replied.

* * *

Twenty minutes later, we'd pulled into a gravel driveway of a modest home wedged between two beachfront mansions. The houses peered out over the glimmering evening sea, snatches of which could be seen in the slits between structures, thanks to a moon the size of a dessert plate. From the highway, a thick cluster of trees and shrubs enveloped Lacy's home. Her Town Car rustled up the drive and parked in front of a two-car garage. On one side of the garage, a privacy gate sat partly ajar. I opened my door and Basil jumped outside. The sweet scent of jasmine mingled with the velvety seaside air. Michael hopped onto the gravel and Ping opened Lacy's door.

She stepped out and marched through the gate, with Basil trotting behind her. Ping stood watch by the car. Lacy pushed open a tall wooden door and a motion sensor light flipped on. We tailed her into a narrow courtyard, sweeping past a tall, copper water fountain shaped like a tree; it played a rain shower symphony. Irregular shaped, flat stones led us to the front of the house, all glass and posts and beams.

"This must be a pretty safe neighborhood," Michael said.

"This is Malibu, for God's sakes, not Brandon, South Dakota. We've got crime going up the ying-yang. Which is why the gate should have been locked. Same with the courtyard door." Lacy cupped a hand to her mouth and screeched, "Sylvia! What the hell is going on?"

CHAPTER 11

The Whiteness

T he front door to the house stood ajar.

"Syl?" Lacy paused before the threshold, and pushed it open wider. She shouted. "Are you home?" She lowered her voice. "You'd better be."

"We'll find her," I said. "She's probably inside somewhere and left the door open for you."

Heavy footsteps padded along the outside of the house. Two men in black appeared in the courtyard, along with a guy with droopy eyes in a dark gray suit. Revolver in hand, Detective Sorkel put on the brakes when his gaze landed on me. "Why are you here?"

"Who were you expecting?" I asked.

"Who the hell are you?" Lacy zeroed in on Sorkel.

"This is a courtesy call, Miss Halloway." Sorkel reached a hand inside his coat and flashed his badge. "Detective Sorkel, LAPD."

"What is a courtesy call?" Lacy asked.

"They're investigating you," I said.

"Not without my lawyer, they're not." Lacy lifted her chin and stuck out her bottom lip.

"We understand that...the victim, Shaw Kota, in today's unfortunate homicide at the studio, had been living here with you for the past three months," Sorkel told her.

"Shouldn't you be looking for the killer instead of questioning Miss Halloway?" Michael asked. "Can't you see how distraught she is?"

Lacy lifted a brow and glanced at Michael. "He's right."

"I'd like to take a look at the vict...Mr. Kota's room," Sorkel said.

"Wait," Michael said and turned to me. "Can they just come in like that?"

Barely seven months had gone by since I'd passed the bar exam. I'd been a terrible law abider ever since. My legal knowledge was newly hatched and wobbly. I wasn't sure what was and wasn't allowable. "No, they can't." I planted my hands on my hips. "Come back with a search warrant, Detective." I played my wild card. The only type of card I carried.

Sorkel lifted his brows, puckered his thin lips and gave a slow nod. "You're going to want to cooperate—"

"Not now." Lacy put her fingers to her temples and massaged them. "It's been a terrible day. I need to clarify my thoughts." She marched into her house, and slammed the door.

"Who are you?" Sorkel aimed his glare at Michael.

Michael dug his hand in his coat pocket and pulled out his driver's license. "Michael Parris. Associate Dean, Computer Science Department at LA Tech College."

"I don't know what you're doing here or if you're involved —" Sorkel started.

"I'm involved with her." Michael pointed to me. "I mean, I'm not involved with this murder. At all."

I didn't need to place my hand on Michael's chest to feel his pounding heart. Homicide investigations and suspects had rattled his nerves a lot lately.

Sorkel glanced at the driver's license. "Were you at Ameripictures late this afternoon?"

"Uh, no. I was in the LA Tech faculty lounge at four, meeting the new college president. We finished up in about an hour and a half. We had a very productive meeting."

Sorkel handed Michael's license back to him and turned to me. "You understand the consequences of not cooperating, don't you?"

"You have no solid leads," I told Sorkel.

"Tell..." he cocked his head toward the house. "...Miss Halloway we'll be back in the morning. If she wants to find Shaw's killer, she needs to work *with* us." Sorkel took a few steps, then returned. "Unless, of course, she's the killer. Hard to know without taking a closer look." He lowered his head and his tone. "We can't confirm her whereabouts at the time of Shaw's death." He and the cops stormed off the same way they came in.

"Do you think she did it?" Michael asked after they left.

"Lacy says she was on a soundstage when it happened," I said.

"But was she?"

"We'll have to find out." I knocked on Lacy's door.

"Come in!" Lacy screeched.

We entered a high-ceilinged living area, all done up in white and polished metal, surgical office style. The place was unfussy; the fanciest piece was a baby grand piano, also in white. Even the artwork was white with touches of metal. The floor offered up dark wood, as did the floating staircase with its metal handrails. The only flash of color came from Lacy's hair and sweater. She stood at the foot of the stairs.

"Why was the front door open?" Michael asked.

"Where's Sylvia?" I looked around.

"Those are my questions," Lacy replied and turned up her glare. "Why don't you add that to your list of things to figure out?"

"Any sign of a struggle upstairs or someone breaking in?" I asked.

"Nothing," Lacy said.

"Should I go back and get the cops?" Michael asked.

"Not yet," Lacy said. "That's what you two are here for. To do their job quietly. And quickly."

"When was the last time you spoke to Sylvia?" I asked

Lacy.

"When I sat in your driveway, waiting for you to show up."

"So less than an hour ago." I strolled over to a large covered pot on the kitchen stove. I lifted the lid. Cooked macaroni noodles sat in cool water. "She started the dinner, but didn't finish." I replaced the lid. "You try calling her?"

"Of course, I did," Lacy replied. "No answer. Quit with the dumb questions and move on to the smart ones."

"Speaking of smart, is that her phone over there?" Michael walked over to a side table sitting by a hallway. A smart phone with a flowery cover perched on the edge.

"Let me see that." Lacy marched over and grabbed the phone. She held it at arm's length. She peered at the screen.

The house was quiet. I could barely hear the cars buzzing along Coast Highway once the front door was closed. The only sounds were Basil's labored breathing and a clock ticking in another room. Michael moved around the spacious kitchen.

"Her daughter texted her thirty minutes ago," Lacy said. "Syl didn't reply. That's not like her."

"No signs of a struggle," Michael said.

"What was her relationship like with Shaw?" I asked.

Lacy trudged over to a small sofa. "Sylvia gets along with everybody. She's been with me nine years. That's a record."

With Lacy's temperament, that was no surprise.

"Did she know about what happened today?" Michael asked.

Lacy nodded and held her head in her hands. She closed her eyes. "I'm having...a vision."

"How does that work exactly?" I asked.

"You know," Michael whispered to me. "It's like a flash or words across a screen."

"How would you know?" I whispered back.

"It's a well known fact—"

"Shhhh!" Lacy said, eyes closed. A few moments passed and she said, "It's gone."

"Just like that?" I said. "Do you remember any of it?"

Lacy nodded. "The vision was showing me that Syl's still here. But not in a good way."

"You mean she's..." Michael started.

Lacy put up a hand, turned, and climbed to the top of the stairs. She disappeared around a corner.

"No one knows what she means," I said. "Including her."

"But what if she's the real deal?" Michael asked. "Maybe her visions are fact. Or close to fact."

Michael was the most logical guy I knew and now here he was, a believer in the fake occult. "This is a woman who wrote a whole book about being captured by aliens and living on their planet for six years before returning to earth. That's tabloid stuff." I poked around the living area.

"Why would she fake a story like that?" He poked around with me.

"Her career was on the fritz." I opened the drawers of a bureau sitting near the hallway. "She went on a lecture tour afterward. And got the attention needed to revive her sagging acting career. It helped her break into voicing children's flicks."

The drawers were filled with knick-knacks and cloth napkins. I stepped into the kitchen and strolled around a long table, past a brick fireplace painted white. A short hallway appeared at the end. I followed it to a door leading to a bathroom. I tapped on another door across from the first one. When no one answered, I peeked inside a small bedroom with the same lack of color as the rest of the place. It housed a bed, a desk and a chair. A sweater was draped over the chair. A small flat screen TV hung on a wall.

Michael followed me in. "Do you see what I see?"

I did a visual inspection and stopped at the small satchel sitting on the ground by the bed. "No woman leaves the house without her purse." I grabbed it and rummaged around inside. "A wallet, set of keys, lipstick and half a bagel. Nothing unusual. Except..." I looked inside the wallet and pulled out a wad of cash.

"Whoa," Michael said.

I did a quick count. "There's about eight hundred dollars here."

"What kind of housekeeper carries around that much money?"

"Today's Friday. Maybe it was payday." I opened up a dresser drawer filled with undergarments, folded neatly. There was also a pile of lottery tickets.

"Okay, I'll buy that, for now." Michael stroked his stubbly chin. "I hear white can be soothing. But I'm not feeling soothed. I'm feeling insane asylum."

"That's because we've been hanging around Lacy."

"Maybe there is no Sylvia," Michael said in a spooky voice with a spooky laugh.

"Really? You're in a joking mood?"

"Corrie!" Lacy shouted.

I hurried out with Michael close behind, back to the living room. Lacy waited at the top of the stairs.

"What do you two think you're doing?" Lacy asked.

"Searching for clues about Sylvia..." I started.

"My godson is dead, my longtime housekeeper has vanished, and you're touring my home?"

"Like I said, we were searching for clues..." As you demanded. She really was a fruitcake.

"The all white look is really peaceful," Michael said.

"Did you find anything?" she asked.

"Was today payday for your staff?" Michael asked.

"Yes, so what?" Lacy said.

"Just curious if you paid in cash or check..." Michael said.

"We didn't find anything yet," I said at the same time, trying to drown Michael out. I didn't want her to know I'd rummaged around Sylvia's purse. "How about you?"

"You bet I did. Get up here," Lacy said and fixed her eyes on Michael. "And I always pay in cash."

We joined Lacy on the landing at the top of the staircase.

"In the guest room." Lacy pointed to a closed door at the

end of the hallway. "I heard a noise."

Michael and I tiptoed down the wide corridor. "When was the last time you had a guest stay here?" I asked.

"Two years ago, when I needed my therapist 24-7."

"What kind of noise did you hear?" Michael asked. He stood near another closed door. He cocked his ear and leaned closer to the door.

"Thumping," Lacy said.

"Kind of like my heartbeat right now," Michael said.

"That's Shaw's room," Lacy told him.

Michael straightened and stepped away.

"I don't hear anything. Maybe it's the plumbing," I said, looking around.

"Since when do pipes sound like a Saint Bernard's tail wagging against a wall?" Lacy said. "Listen." Lacy tilted her head, fingers pushing an earlobe forward.

The only sound came from a passing siren.

"I still don't hear any—" I started.

"What was that?" Michael asked. "Sounded like someone crying."

"More like moaning," Lacy said.

"You said it was a thumping," I reminded her.

"Yeah, well, now it's changed to moaning," Lacy said.

I picked up my feet. Leading the way, I stomped to the guest room door. This would be proof positive that Lacy was off her rocker. I pressed my ear against the cold wood. The room was quiet. I lifted my ear. "There's nothing—"

Then I heard it. A high-pitched moan. I turned the doorknob and entered a dark space. I reached out my hand and patted the wall for a light switch. A thumping sound interrupted me and I stepped back. I paused and lifted my chin. All was quiet. I gulped and took a giant step into the room. I flipped on the light switch. Like the rest of the place, the guest room was decorated in white. Built-in bookshelves displayed Lacy's awards, and photos with other stars and VIPs. Basil trotted inside and up to a closed door. He sniffed along the bottom.

"That's the closet," Lacy whispered.

I glided forward and reached for the knob. Michael breathed softly at my shoulder.

"Did you happen to bring a weapon?" he whispered.

I shook my head. It's not like I never left home without one. "You?"

"Yes," he whispered. "I have this." He whipped out the knife I'd gifted him a few months ago.

"Sweet." I stepped forward and grabbed the brass doorknob. I pulled it open and flicked up a switch.

"Wow," Michael spoke. "Add a kitchen and toilet, and you can rent this out as another bedroom."

He was right. The closet was huge and formed a long L-shape. The whining noise looped its way from around the corner of the space.

Basil barked three times.

"In there," Lacy said from behind us.

I gingerly stepped around the corner, and stopped. Michael did the same.

"For heaven's sake," Lacy said as she came around.

CHAPTER 12

Lost and Found

A large busted woman in a black and white zebra print dress lay on her side, arms behind her back, duct tape hiding her mouth, and a blindfold over her eyes. More duct tape strapped her ankles together.

"Syl?" Lacy pushed past us and stood above the woman. "You alright?"

The woman groaned and rapped her feet against the wall behind her.

"Michael, call the cops," I said. "Ask for Detective Sorkel."

"Right." Michael pulled out his phone and exited the closet. Basil ran after him.

I knelt next to Sylvia, pulled off her blindfold and yanked off the duct tape.

"Owwwww!" she yelled loudly enough to awaken any seagulls snoozing on the beach. "Who are you? A police woman?" she asked me, smacking her lips together.

"This is the detective I hired, Syl," Lacy told her.

"Private investigator, kind of. I'm also a lawyer," I said. "Corrie Locke."

"Oh, nice to meet you." Sylvia wiggled her mouth around. "I'd say I'm at your service, but I'm really not right now." Her voice was low-pitched and nasally.

"No worries." I helped her sit up. I removed the cord and extended a hand, which she took after flexing her fingers. I helped her to her feet.

"Thanks." Sylvia tossed back a lock of platinum hair that fell in a long curlicue onto her forehead. Her wrinkles placed her in the longtime AARP member category.

"Who did this to you?" I asked.

"You think I know? I heard the doorbell and ran to answer it, figuring it was Lacy."

"Don't you have a key?" I asked Lacy.

"Syl's always here," Lacy said. "I don't need one."

"You never go out to the market or the dentist?" I asked.

"Everyone delivers these days, and my teeth are fine." She looked at Lacy. "I was expecting you. Not some no-good, dirty, low-down nefarious criminal." She ran a hand over her temple and closed her eyes. "I checked the peephole and nobody was there. So I opened it and there he was. This scumbag in a mask —"

"How do you know it was a he?" I asked Sylvia.

She chewed on her knuckle. "He had a deep voice."

"What did he say to you?" I asked.

"He mostly grunted and pointed," Sylvia replied.

"What kind of mask was he wearing?" I wanted to know.

"You know, the kind they wear at ski resorts."

"What else can you tell us?" I said. "How tall was he?"

"I'm not sure." She straightened out her dress and plumped her hair.

"What color eyes?"

"It was all a blur," Sylvia replied.

"Talk to her, Syl," Lacy said. "Answer her questions."

"Who could notice anything in such a dire situation? I was scared out of my mind."

Sylvia was about my height, five feet seven or so, with big hair and big everything else.

"Was he taller or shorter than you?" I asked.

"Taller. I felt so helpless."

Michael ran in with Basil at his heels. "Detective Sorkel's on his way."

"Who are you?" Sylvia asked.

"He's with her," Lacy replied and turned to Michael. "Run your name by me again."

"Michael Parris." He reached a hand out to Sylvia. "I'm helping Corrie."

"Enchanted, I'm sure," Sylvia said, clasping Michael's hand.

I pictured Shaw's lookalike as he ran past me. He'd been about my height, when I wore three-inch heels. That would put him at five feet, ten inches. It could have been the lookalike that came to Lacy's home.

"Was he a few inches taller or more?" I asked Sylvia.

Her hand shot to the side of her head. "More, I think."

"Why did he put you in this room?" I asked Sylvia. "Did he know about it or did you lead him here?"

Sylvia pushed her way out of the closet. "I need some air."

We followed her as she toddled down the stairs, stopping midway to grab the handrail. "You know." Sylvia turned to look up at me. "He popped into each bedroom before shoving me in that closet." Her hand shot to her chest. "I'm just so glad he didn't molest me. The guy obviously had self-control." She pushed back a stray platinum strand and made her way to the kitchen.

"Sylvia," I said, catching up to her. "The police will be here in a few minutes. We need details."

"I can't think straight." Sylvia trotted to the refrigerator. "I'm all tensed up." She tugged the door open and reached in for a bottle of wine.

"You need to get to the bottom of this," Lacy appeared by my side. "And everything. That's what you're here for."

Like I didn't know. I squeezed my lips together a moment and nodded. "But...if I don't find any clues in one week, I'm out." That was my way of showing her who was in charge.

"If you don't find a clue in three days, I'll kick you out."

Lida Sideris

And that was her way.

Michael poked his head between us. "No kicking anyone, please." He turned to Lacy. "Corrie's training wheels have been off for a while now. She's at the stage where she's using raw talent to hunt down killers, so I'm sure we'll be good. Pretty sure, anyway."

He'd better be right. I turned toward Sylvia. "We need to determine how the break-in here is related to Shaw's...what happened at the studio." I moved closer to her. She was clanging pots and pans as she pulled them out of a cabinet. "Step by step, take me through the events after you talked to Lacy on the phone this afternoon."

She padded over to the pantry and opened the door. "First, I went in here and got this little porcelain canister where I keep the dry macaroni." She pulled it out to show me. "Isn't this cute?"

Noodles in all shapes floated on the outside of the white canister.

"It even says macaroni in Italian. See?" She held it up and burst into tears.

Michael ran over to her with a tissue.

"Thank you." She took it from him, sniffling.

"Syl," Lacy said. "We've got to pull ourselves together to catch the bastard who did this to Shaw, and who tied you up. Can you do that?"

Sylvia nodded, dabbed at her eyes and sniffled. "I'm alright. But it's hard to concentrate. Today has been tragic."

"Try to recall the home intrusion," I said.

"My mind's a jumble," Sylvia said. "I'm usually very detail oriented. See?" She held out her hands, palms down. "I did this nail art myself."

Her fingernails were painted a deep mauve, except for her index finger, which was painted white and displayed a cherry blossom design.

Michael and I peered at her polish. Wow, maybe she didn't ever leave the house.

70

"Hey, you're really talented," Michael said.

"Thank you," Sylvia said with a small smile.

"Did you see anything else when you opened the front door?" I asked Sylvia.

Sylvia took out a block of cheese and started grating. "You mean, besides the guy in the mask? He pushed his way in and shoved me to the side. He told me if I said a word, he'd shoot me."

"He had a gun?" Michael asked.

"He must have."

"You didn't see it?" I asked.

"I don't remember." Sylvia stuffed some cheese in her mouth.

"Did you recognize his voice?" I asked. "Any accent? Did Shaw have one?"

Lacy sat on a white counter stool. "Shaw learned nearly perfect English from watching *Gilligan's Island* and *I Dream of Jeannie* reruns." Lacy strolled over to a living room window and pushed it open.

"Two of my favorite shows," Michael said.

"My abductor didn't seem to have an accent either." Sylvia grated harder. "Of course, he didn't talk much. He told me to turn around and that's when he tied my hands. Then he dragged me up the stairs."

Michael and I exchanged glances. Sylvia was a plus-sized woman. She wouldn't be easy to drag a few feet, let alone up a whole staircase.

"That must have hurt plenty," Michael said.

"It wasn't so bad. He didn't tie my feet until he pushed me into the guest room closet," Sylvia explained and took some mushrooms out of the refrigerator. "He did yank my arm once and I stumbled. I'm lucky I didn't fall and break something."

"I can sauté those," Michael offered. "Do you have any shallots?"

"In there." Sylvia pointed to the refrigerator and handed him the mushrooms. "There's some truffle oil in the pantry."

Sylvia whispered to me. "This guy's a keeper."

"Did the intruder say anything else to you?" I asked.

"Not that I can remember. Let's see, I've got fontina, gruyere..."

"Parmesan?" Michael asked.

"Can you just stop for a minute?" I gave Michael a *cut it out now* look. He had the habit of sometimes being overly helpful at the wrong time.

"Sylvia, cooperate," Lacy said.

Sylvia wiped her hands on a towel. "Cooking takes my mind off this terrible day. The intruder didn't say another word. He just threw me into the guest room closet like I was a rag doll. He stuck duct tape over my mouth. I could hardly breathe. I think I passed out." She licked a finger.

"So he popped into all the rooms? I asked her. "Did it seem as if he knew where the guest room closet was in advance?"

"I don't think so."

"Was he wearing gloves?" I asked.

Sylvia nodded. "Black knit. Everything's coming back to me now."

"What color were his eyes?"

"The color of coffee grounds."

Lacy sucked in her breath.

Sylvia's eyes welled up again. "Why would anyone do that to Shaw?" She blew her nose.

There was a pounding at the front door.

"Oh no," Sylvia said, grabbing a frying pan. "He's back."

CHAPTER 13

Secrets and Lies

L acy stood and closed her eyes a moment. "It's the police."
She shuffled over and opened the door.

Who couldn't figure that one out?

Sorkel made his entrance along with a few men in black. They searched the house while Sorkel asked Sylvia questions. She answered the same as she did before, but she added one new item,

"It's coming back in bits and pieces. When I got to the top of the stairs, the guy asked where Lacy's room was. I didn't say a word. But I might have blinked in that direction." She turned to Lacy and said, "I couldn't help myself. Sorry."

"It was a life or death situation." Lacy reclaimed the stool at the kitchen counter.

"That's what it felt like." Sylvia fluffed her hair. "I'm still shaking." She took a bite out of a small baguette.

"Was anything taken from your room?" Sorkel asked Lacy.

"I don't keep valuables in the house, Detective," Lacy replied. "Except for a few trinkets, which he's welcome to." She stood. "That's enough for today." She walked to the front door and opened it, gesturing for Sorkel to leave.

"Miss Halloway, we still need to—"

Lacy ran a hand along her forehead and shut her eyes. "I feel an explosion coming."

"Like in a bomb?" Sorkel asked.

"Like in my temper." Lacy slapped her palm on the counter.

Sorkel's gaze shot around the room and he shook his head. "Crazy bunch of..." he mumbled. "Miss Halloway, I'll leave. After I take a look at Shaw's room. There could be something significant—"

"Not tonight," Lacy said.

"You could get arrested—"

"Well, what are you waiting for?" She put out her hands and dropped them when Sorkel didn't move. "Just as I thought. Call tomorrow, Detective. Keep in mind, the sun rises at nine-thirty around here."

Sorkel's lips squirmed to one side. His attention landed on me. "You. A word." He stormed out with the cops behind him.

I joined him in the courtyard. He waited by the fountain, alone.

"We both know it would be in her best interest to cooperate," he said. "And in yours. I don't need to tell you that you could be impeding an investigation by withholding information."

"Yet, you're telling me anyway."

"Anything else going on in there?" Sorkel tossed his head toward Lacy's house.

"Tell me about the stand-in," I said.

"That's not a smart way to play your cards." He bunched his lips. "You really expect me to exchange information with you?" He shook his head. "Son of a gun. You first."

I was hoping he would say that. I brought him up to speed on the guy in the fedora and how he tried to run us down.

"I'll check with Hermosa Beach PD. Of course, it could be a complete and utter waste of time if it's unrelated to the studio murder. You have no proof it was the same person. All the more so if a witness confirmed the driver of the Dodge was a female."

"All she saw was long hair and a fedora," I said.

"Point is, an eyewitness says the driver was a woman."

I didn't believe that for one minute.

"Calvin Singh is the stand-in," Sorkel said. "We've got an officer tracking him down."

"Debbylynn found the body," I said. "How do we know she's not the killer?"

"You think I didn't consider that?" Sorkel gazed out over my head. "She was seen in a restroom on the first floor right around the time Shaw was killed."

"She could've been cleaning the blood off her hands."

Sorkel held my gaze. "I considered that as well. But the timing doesn't fit. Unless, she had help."

"I'd like a closer look at the crime scene," I said. "And the body."

"You've gotta be kidding me. Experts are scouring that room and the surrounding area. What are you going to find that they won't?"

"You'll never know unless you let me take a look." I tried to stare him down.

"You want an assignment? Watch Lacy. Find out where she was at the time of death."

"Something important might be missed by the CSI team. I can help."

"Forget it."

I huffed and stomped to the front door, stepped in and shut it behind me. Sylvia and
Michael were whipping up a salad in the kitchen. Lacy sat on the sofa, swirling a glass of chardonnay. Her shoulders slumped and her mouth sagged. Her glittery eyes rose to meet mine.

"I need another look at the crime scene," I told her. "But Sorkel refuses. You can make
that a condition of cooperating with him."

Lacy sipped the wine. "Your father said you had a knack for recreating crimes by visiting the scene. Is that true?"

"Yes."

"Follow me."

She planted the glass on a side table, stood and headed for the staircase. She climbed upstairs with me nipping at her heels.

"We should get closer to the people involved with the movie. Someone might know something they're not saying. I have an idea," I told her.

"No. You have no idea."

"Yes, I do."

"No, you don't. And you won't, until you know what's really going on. I haven't told you everything."

Not again.

CHAPTER 14

The Sock Exchange

I trailed Lacy down a hallway hosting bookshelves brimming with photos of her posing with well-known politicians, celebrities and a religious figure or two. While I gawked at her hall of fame, she stepped through a tall door, disappearing into the master bedroom. I followed a moment later, and entered a room dripping with the same whiteness - from the carpet to the ceiling - all snowy hued and pristine.

"Shut the door and lock it," Lacy said.

I did as she asked, while she pulled a cord that drew together a heavy set of drapes. She slid to a door near the master bath. "Go in the closet."

"Who's in there?" I asked.

"Not a who. A what. An orange shoebox. Open it."

I pushed open a pair of doors leading into a walk-in closet, with it's own massage room and mini nail parlor. One side housed rows of shelves holding shoeboxes. An orange shoebox rested on the center shelf. I lifted the lid. A small, robin's egg blue jewelry box sat inside. I opened the box to find a sparkling diamond. "Holy Tiffany's."

Lacy rustled behind me. "It's a twelve carat, radiant cut diamond ring with a platinum band and four eighteen carat yellow gold prongs. It was a gift to me, from one of the members of the Rat Pack."

"Seriously? You mean like Frank and Dean and Sammy, or like George and Brad?"

"What do you think? Don't ask which one."

"It's Dean, isn't it?" I asked. "He always was my favorite."

"Look at the note." Lacy breathed over my shoulder.

The ring box rested on a folded piece of paper. I reached in and unfolded a typed message. I read it out loud,

"*RA. Sit-O.* What does it mean? Someone's initials and a place, maybe?"

"That's for you to figure out. I found the note in the shoe-box tonight."

"How do you know it wasn't there before?"

"There are no shoes in the shoebox because I'm wearing the flats." Lacy held up a foot. "Guess where the shoes were this morning? That note wasn't there when I put the shoes on."

"Are you sure?" I asked. Was she pulling a fast one?

"Of course I am." She held my gaze. "I'm not senile."

"I don't understand," I said. "Someone broke in and tied Sylvia up just to leave this note?"

"Don't regurgitate," Lacy said. "It's very unbecoming."

"Hold on," I said. "What were the odds you'd find this message any time soon?"

"Favorable, if you're familiar with my routine." She ambled out of the closet.

I followed. "Care to elaborate? The more I know, the more helpful I can be."

"I wear these shoes daily. I have for the past two months. No one knew about the ring, except Shaw. And me."

"Not Sylvia?" After all, Sylvia was always here. What made Lacy think she didn't snoop around now and then?

Lacy shook her head. "Syl's got a good thing going here. Prison doesn't have the same appeal."

My inclination was to ask why she'd confide in a young person she'd only just met, but I didn't bother. Nothing made sense with Lacy. Why she'd cast Shaw in a leading role, why she ignored me when I tried to help with her contracts and why she wanted me to investigate now when she could hire a seasoned professional.

"Why not keep something so valuable in the bank?" Like a normal person would. Who keeps an expensive ring in a shoebox?

"Every evening before retiring, I remove the ring and wear it to bed," Lacy said. "I sleep more soundly with the ring on my finger."

Okaaaay. Some people needed teddy bears or sleeping pills to help them sleep. Lacy needed expensive jewelry. "Shaw must have confided in someone about the ring and your routine."

"Someone who'd ignore the opportunity to steal a valuable piece of jewelry? Who does that?" Lacy's voice cracked and a tear dripped down her cheek.

I weighed the possibility of Lacy planting the note, but then, who tied up Sylvia? Were they in cahoots? "The note has a meaning," I said. "Whoever put it there wanted you to see it because they thought you'd figure it out. What if it's someone that knows who killed Shaw?"

"Couldn't they just tell me instead of pussyfooting around?" Lacy wiped her eyes with her hands.

"What if the note was found by the wrong person? Like the killer? It was for your eyes only. Maybe it's pointing to something else you're supposed to find."

Lacy went quiet.

"Is there something important Shaw might have hidden?" I asked.

Her eyes shot to mine. "If I knew the answer, I wouldn't need you."

"I'll keep this." I raised the note in one hand and pictured Shaw in that final scene. More than ten minutes had passed before I bumped into his double. "Did Shaw have a thing for socks?"

"He liked them with color and patterns."

My heartbeat quickened. "What about when he was in

character?"

"His character wore the same socks he did."

"Really?" The key could be hidden in the sock exchange.

"It fit. He was an extension of Shaw." She narrowed her gaze. "What do socks have to do with the case?"

If I truly believed Lacy was being straight with me, I would have told her. "I noticed them when he was on the bicycle in that last scene being filmed."

Lacy huffed and turned her back to me. "Think you could do better than that."

"Did you collect Shaw's personal effects?" I asked.

"What?" She spun around.

"You identified his body, right?" I asked.

"I went to the coroner's office," her voice softened. "They showed me photographs and I used those to...you know the rest."

"What about the silver cuff on his wrist?" I asked.

Her spidery lashes curled. "How do you know about that?"

"I saw it," I said. "During the final scene. Do you have it?"

Lacy shook her head. "I was told there were no personal effects."

My mind moved at high speed. It could be that the stand-in killed Shaw, took the cuff and was toying with Lacy. But why? And what about the black socks on the body? Shaw wore argyle socks in the scene I'd watched. The dead guy wore black ones. Could the stand-in be dead and Shaw alive? Shaw planted the note to let Lacy know. *RA* could stand for...

"Really alive?" I muttered.

"What?" Lacy asked.

I didn't want to get her hopes up. "Detective Sorkel says no one can vouch for your whereabouts when Shaw was killed," I told Lacy. "That's not what you said to me."

"Of course, it's not. Would you be here now if you knew I had no alibi?"

"Where were you?" I asked.

"I *was* at the voice rehearsal in soundstage two...most of the day. But I was feeling cranky and we needed a re-write so I told the director I was taking a ten. Which turned out to be a twenty plus."

"Where'd you go?"

"Where I always go. To the Otis T. Morton building, home to all us golden oldies."

"Did anyone see you in there?" I asked.

"The place is abandoned these days. Gus might've seen me, if he wasn't snoozing. He's been doing security in the Otis since the seventies." She sidled up to the curtain and lifted a portion. She gazed out into the darkness. "I have my own key to the building and to Otis' office. I like to sit behind his desk. The entire third floor was his. There's a private dining area and bar, with its own patio, a music hall and a projection room."

Otis T. Morton had been the original head of the studio about sixty years ago. Why would Lacy spend time in there? I edged around to where I could read her expression. She met my gaze head-on.

"I'm pretty sure," I said. "They've changed the locks at least once since his reign."

"I always get my own copy. It's in my contract. His white leather walls and circular white desk emit an aura of power and tranquility you can't find nowadays. I need that vibe." She raised her hands and dropped them as she eyed the room. "The white in my house wasn't the interior decorator's idea. It was mine...it's an homage to a movie giant." She lowered her head. "I wouldn't be an actress today, if it wasn't for Otis."

"Those leather walls and furnishings have been missing for decades, Lacy. Are you ever going to level with me?" Maybe I *would* be better off doing the attorney job.

She jerked her head up. "I don't need to see to feel the presence."

"What does that even mean?"

She drifted over to her bed and sank down on it. "Okay. You need to know the truth."

Finally. I sauntered to the bed and plopped down on the opposite side, facing her.

"I headed for Otis' office, but got sidetracked by a scream. I ignored it...until I was nearly trampled by a stampede. I grabbed a kid running by and asked what happened." Lacy dropped her voice. "That's when I learned about Shaw."

I inched a little closer. I studied her face and body language for traces of lies.

"I made my way to the back of the building where Shaw'd been filming." She sniffled and wiped her nose on her sleeve. "I didn't want anyone to see me in the state I was in."

I leaned back and pulled a tissue out of a box on her nightstand. I handed it to her. She snatched it and pressed it against her eyes. She blew her nose loudly.

"I was about to pull open the door..." She closed her eyes. "...when I had a vision."

"My father again?" Lacy's acting awards were well deserved.

She shook her head. "Shaw appeared, running down an alley. Before I could finish the vision, I heard stomping and the door flew open. This person blew past me, nearly knocking me down as he raced out the door, into the alley." She stopped and tightened her lips. "It was Shaw."

I sat up straight. She finally had my full attention. "Are you sure?"

She threaded her fingers together and closed her eyes. "I'm sure of a lot of things, but not this. I opened my mouth to call him, but I choked up."

I stood and paced the floor. Had I told Lacy about the lookalike running past me? I stopped.

"Did you tell anyone about this?" I asked.

"Not even Syl. She'd have me doing therapy, double-time."

"Did you go after the guy?"

"He was long gone by the time I could move. After that, I made my way back to the soundstage. Just before I got inside, I got the official call about Shaw."

"And?"

"And what? I went haywire. I couldn't think. Everyone calling and offering condolences. I wasn't sure if I'd seen him running past. My mind was spinning. That's when I had the vision of Monty, and called Marshall about you."

I rubbed my temple with my fingers. There was a missing piece here somewhere. I told Lacy about my running into Shaw's double after the murder. Or was it Shaw himself?

She didn't say a word.

"No comment?"

"I'm stumped," Lacy said.

"We both agree we saw a runner that resembled Shaw."

"I can't be sure." She dabbed at her eye. "After I left you at the commissary, I went to the coroner's office."

"To ID the body?"

Lacy nodded. "They showed me post-mortem photographs." She sniffled. "I saw enough to make a positive identification. So either I imagined the young man pushing past me or it was a very realistic vision."

"Mine was no vision." Maybe it was the stand-in running out. And he fooled both of us.

Lacy stood and went to the curtains, parting them to reveal a pair of French doors. She opened them and stepped out into the night, and onto a large deck. I followed, inhaling the mingled scents of seaweed and briny air.

She lifted teary eyes to mine. "If the day ever comes when I can't tell the difference between my visions and reality, I'll have to do something drastic, like suck up to everyone."

"Do you wear glasses?" I asked.

"To read."

"How close were you to the guy running?"

"Face-to-face."

"So he looked blurry?"

Lacy lifted a brow. "Like he was behind a screen."

"Did he smell like Shaw?"

"You think I sniffed him as he ran by?"

"The person racing past me smelled like bubble gum," I said. "Did Shaw chew bubble gum?"

"Yes," Lacy said. "So did Calvin and a bunch of people on the set. They also ate jelly beans, cheese puffs and chocolate chips. That proves nothing."

I had to agree with her. "A guy looks like Shaw, dresses like him, runs off and disappears right after Shaw is supposedly killed? That's what I saw. That was no vision. Do you have a photo of Calvin?"

Lacy pushed back a curtain and returned into her bedroom. I followed in time to see her disappear into her closet. She rummaged through her handbag and pulled out her cellphone. She scrolled with a thumb and held the phone to me.

"I took this two weeks ago."

It was a photo of Shaw Kota dressed in a blue T-shirt and black shorts. One arm was slung around the shoulders of a guy who stood a little shorter, was built a little slighter, but with the same clothes. His highlighted hair was more tousled than Shaw's tamer black tresses. The guy's eyes were more almond shaped; his lips a tad fuller. Only Shaw wore a silver cuff around his wrist.

"Meet Calvin Singh," Lacy said and crossed her arms over her chest. "Is that the guy you saw running?"

Dammit. "Maybe." It could've been either of them. Or someone else. Shaw could've changed socks before he died or before he ran. If he ran. If he's alive. My head hurt from thinking.

There was a rap at the door.

"Dinner's served," Michael spoke on the other side.

I got up and opened the door. Michael stood there, hazel eyes bright, his mouth curling up at each end.

"I need a drink." Lacy pushed past us. She disappeared down the hallway and padded down the staircase.

"Um, Corrie?" He leaned down and whispered. "I found this in Shaw's room." A cell phone sat on his palm.

CHAPTER 15

The Floating Clue

"It's Shaw's phone," Michael said.

"How do you know?" I asked.

He leaned in close. "You know how."

He wasn't up to admitting it out loud. I respected that. "It's what nerds do, Michael. No one would blame you for breaking into Shaw's phone. Find anything useful?"

"Follow me," he said.

The white motif in the rest of the house took a hike in Shaw's quarters. The unmade bed was a tangle of sheets and pillows; the floor littered with piles of T-shirts, sweatshirts, jeans, empty plastic bottles, and patterned socks.

I waded through the maze of heaps and discards. "Looks like we stumbled onto the set of *Sanford and Son*." Throw in a few used car batteries, an old refrigerator and a mangy dog, and it would be an indoor junkyard.

"I see carefully planned disorder," Michael said, stepping over a pile. "Reminds me of my room when I was a kid."

"Except Shaw's no kid and your room doesn't look like this anymore."

"True, but I still see a logic to this disorder. I bet Shaw could find whatever he needed. Just like I could." He pointed toward a closed door. "Take a look in there."

I trekked through the mess and pulled open the door to a respectable sized walk-in closet. Clothes were hung neatly or folded on shelves. Along one edge of the floor sat tidy groupings of magazines, alphabetized by title. *American Scientist, Popular Science* and *Scientific American.* Small, partitioned boxes separated items like cotton swabs, brushes, string and floss. One box even contained a few lemons and a small knife.

"So he was capable of being organized when he wanted." I stepped back into the bedroom. Stacks of paper and magazines masked the top of an antique desk. I pitched my chin toward the desk. "Did you check the drawers?"

"All the usual stuff, pens, sticky notes and tape," Michael whispered behind me. "Did you notice these?" He made his way to the magazines.

I followed him. "What kind of actor reads *Popular Science* and *Scientific American?*" The skin behind my neck began to prickle. I swiveled around. Lacy hovered in the doorway. "Is this the state of normal in here?" I asked. "Or did the cops do this?"

She shrugged a shoulder. "Shaw kept the bedroom door closed most of the time. But this is what it looked like whenever I came in."

"You never asked him to straighten it up?" Michael asked.

"I respected his privacy. Besides, he needed space to... never mind." Lacy shut her mouth and opened it moments later. "Come downstairs." She exited.

I shut the door after she left and plodded around the piles. "Every time that woman opens her mouth, she's leaving out important information, or leading us down the wrong path." I gingerly moved around. "Tell me about Shaw's phone."

One of the many advantages of having a nerd for a best friend was his sweet tech skills.

"Took me all of thirty seconds to get in without the passcode."

"Impressive." I thought about my own passcode. "What's the point of having one?"

"To keep amateurs out and slow professionals down. In

Shaw's case, it's an older model smartphone." Michael held it up. "Easier to crack. I went through his email and heard a few voice-mail messages."

"And?"

"There was a message in Hindi or something similar, but there were a couple in English. All from yesterday. One was from someone on the movie set, telling him to get serious about his role or he'd be canned."

"Sounds like Burton Kramer," I said. "The director."

"But the other voicemail...the caller mentioned gear and a plan."

"Maybe he spoke in code." I was never very good at code cracking. But I knew someone who was. "This is where your buddy James comes in."

Michael and James had been pals since kindergarten. James Zachary was stop, drop and drool gorgeous, with a virile masculinity empty-headed females found irresistible. But, I had to admit, he was also clever and tough as iron when needed. I'd spent my adult years either avoiding him or treating him like a sack of rotten potatoes when we did interact...until our truce. I could barely remember how our feud started, which meant there was no reason for continuing our mutual dislike. Plus, he'd done nothing but help me on my last two cases, dropping everything and risking his legal career. Why he was so willing to assist, I couldn't figure. My "friendship" with James was going strong, but it helped that we hadn't seen each other since becoming new pals. Michael was our middleman.

"I'll text him." Michael pulled out his phone. "But he might not respond right away. He's switching offices. Transferring to the Los Angeles DA's office."

James had been an assistant district attorney in Orange County the past few years.

"That's too close for comfort," I mumbled.

"What?"

"It's a comfort," I spoke up. "Having him around." I needed more time to get used to this friendship thing with James.

"He's been called a lot of things, but never a 'comfort'." Michael texted James.

I broke out into a sweat just thinking about James, but Michael didn't need to know that. "Can I hear the voicemail message about the gear?"

"Aye-aye, Captain." Michael thumbed through Shaw's smartphone and held it to his ear. He pushed a button on the phone, handed it to me and went back to his texting. I pressed the phone to my ear and listened. A man's deep, crackly voice started talking.

"This is Wetzel. Can't meet today. The plan will..." A few seconds passed as the voice cut out and came back again. "...Wednesday. We're interested...protection. We'll work...clothing..." The voicemail message ended.

"Something's going down on Wednesday," I said, handing the phone back to Michael.

"But we don't know what or where or who Wetzel is," Michael said.

I strolled the bedroom. "We've got a name and a day. What's the 'plan'?"

"Could be part of a code." Michael snapped his fingers. "Judging by the magazines, I'll bet Wetzel's a doctor or a scientist. I'll do an Internet search." He turned his attention to his phone.

I continued my trek around the room. "Shaw's a sloppy neatnik, has a definite nerdy side—"

"And a great video game and vintage Star Wars poster collection," Michael added, looking up from his phone.

"Sounds like the perfect movie role for him. A nerd playing a nerd. Nerds are known for stumbling onto stuff out of their league, and that's what Shaw might have done." I toured the room and stopped by the closet. I stepped over the piles. "Where did you find the phone? On the floor?"

"The only Doctor Wetzel is a dentist in Whittier." Michael stuffed his phone in his pocket and moved closer to me. "The phone wasn't in plain sight. I had to dig deep for it, Corrie."

"You've got your PI game on. What made you come in here, anyway?" Something I should have thought of doing.

"I circled back because I remembered Lacy pointing out Shaw's room."

"Good. Why wouldn't he have the phone on him?" I asked.

"Sylvia told me he had two phones. One for work and a cell he brought with him from India. This was his India phone."

"Why leave this one here?"

"That's what happens when you've got too much going on. You forget to carry both phones. I came upstairs and poked around," Michael said. "That's when I found it."

"The phone?"

"No." Michael padded toward a wall next to the closet. He paused beside a tall stack of clothes. "This floating shelf."

He pointed to a piece of dark stained wood stuck to a wall. Three inches thick and two feet wide, the wood served as a shelf, hosting a framed photo of Shaw with Lacy, and a small bronze statue of Buddha.

"The phone was on that shelf?" I asked.

"Not on it. In it. Probably why the police missed it." Michael placed a hand on each side. "See? There's a false bottom." He pulled the lower portion down to reveal a drawer that tilted out and forward. A Springfield .45 pistol with a short barrel sat in a corner pinning down a small red notebook. "And this is where the room doesn't remind me of my room anymore." Michael pointed to an empty spot next to the notebook. "The phone was right there."

I peered down at the pistol. "It's an older model." I picked up the notebook and scanned through. The third page had an address:

Pantheon Space and Airborne Systems 2300 East El Segundo

"Whoa." Michael looked over my shoulder. "Why an aerospace company? Was that his target? Maybe he was a terrorist. That would explain the gun."

"The pistol's not loaded. The chamber indicator's in

down position. What kind of terrorist keeps an unloaded pistol?"

"The kind that doesn't plan on using it. But..." Michael's head swung around the room. "Maybe he's got another weapon. Hidden, underneath piles and piles." He bent over and examined a stack of items. "Lacy's involved, isn't she?"

I wasn't ready to tell Michael about the note beneath the ring box and Lacy's encounter behind the brick building. I needed to sort through it myself first. "Why would she give us free range in here if she thought we'd find something to incriminate her? Look at this." On the first two pages of the red notebook were notes about his role in the movie and other scribbling about shredding molecules. He lost me at molecules.

"Maybe this whole thing's a set-up," Michael said. "Planned chaos to keep us from finding out what really happened."

I gazed around at the mess. "Too much effort."

"Syl told me she was here alone when Shaw was killed. No alibi."

"You interrogated her?" I asked.

"She never even knew it. I asked her questions while we sautéed mushrooms."

"Michael, you are on such a hot streak. If I stay out of your way, I think you can crack this case in no time."

"Really?" Michael looked up at me with a big grin that fell off just as quickly. "No, I can't. I mean, I'm no good at crime-solving without you."

"I'm staying with you on this. All we need is evidence." I thumbed through the rest of the notebook. "This is mostly empty. And the last entry was dated two weeks ago. Why stop?"

"We'll find out. I've got two months of summer break before I go back to LA Tech, but I was..."

"Yes?"

"Going to keep looking for your dad..." Michael said. "... that is, if you wanted me to."

"I'm done with that. Let's focus on finding Shaw's killer."

Michael nodded and stepped back into the closet. He popped out his head. "We should find out if Wetzel works at the aerospace company. At Pantheon." He vanished back into the closet.

I dropped the red notebook in my purse and bent down. I picked up a large paper bag next to a pile. "We'll check on that." I texted Veera and asked her to research a Wetzel at Pantheon. She had security guard connections everywhere. "For now, let's collect magazines and determine what could be of interest to Shaw. Look for a pattern." I handed the bag to Michael.

He stepped out again, beaming. "I can do that. I know I'm not the star of this show, but I like being bumped up to magazine investigator. I can handle that."

I pulled out my smartphone. I snapped photos and took a video of the room.

A scratching sounded at the door, punctuated by grunting.

"She's back," Michael said.

CHAPTER 16

Game On

I waded around the piles and mounds and opened the door. My eyes shot to the floor. A wrinkly face stared up, panting, dark googly eyes fixed on mine. Michael peered over my shoulder.

"Basil? What is it, boy?" he asked. "Got something on your mind?"

I opened the door wider and stepped off to the side. Basil didn't budge. He continued panting, the tip of his round, pink tongue sticking out, bulging eyes hopping from me to Michael. Basil licked his nose and looked off to the side of the hallway.

"Okay, we'll be right down," Michael said.

Basil gave a high-pitched bark and scampered away, tail curled upward.

"You're welcome." Michael turned back into the room.

"Since when do you talk dog?" I asked.

"I've always talked their language. You just never noticed."

"Right." Maybe nerds and dogs shared the same mental wavelength.

Michael filled up the paper bag with the magazines and strolled out of the room. "Are you coming?"

"Where?"

"Basil said our dinner's going to be cleared away if we don't come down now."

"Oh, of course. I'll go downstairs, not because I believe that's what he said, but because I'm hungry, and I'm done here."

Michael and I high-tailed it to the kitchen. Lacy and Sylvia faced each other, sitting across the table. Sylvia's plate sat empty, like the bottle of pinot noir resting between them. But Lacy's dinner looked untouched. Basil lay by her feet.

"I thought you'd never come down," Sylvia said. "I was about to put everything away."

"Sorry," Michael said. "Once we start talking, we kind of forget the time."

"Talking?" Sylvia rolled her eyes. "Is that what they're calling it these days?" She unwrapped a stick of gum and folded it into her mouth. She bit down and chewed. "What's in the bag?"

"Oh," Michael said. "I found these science magazines in Shaw's closet." He turned to Lacy. "Mind if we browse through them?"

"What for?" Lacy sipped the last bit of wine in her glass.

"We think they might have...I mean..." Michael started, and stopped with a glance at Sylvia.

"You can speak freely in front of Syl," Lacy said. "She knows everything."

"We need to recreate the events leading up to what happened," I said.

"With magazines?" Lacy threw daggers at me with her eyes. "You're not going to find any friggin' thing in those pages. Is this how you operate? Your father wouldn't waste time with magazines. He'd ask for a list of people that I suspected were involved, and then he'd go out and find the one responsible. That's what I expected you to do."

"Why would anyone on your list talk to us?" I asked her.

"Because I would tell them to, that's why. They work for me," Lacy shouted loud enough to be heard at the Getty Villa sitting atop a hill a few miles away. "I own them while they're on my job. Capiche?"

"Oh, that's a good idea, Lacy," Michael said. "Can you make us a list?"

Lacy blinked and looked up at him with a stony stare. She tapped her empty glass and Sylvia rose. She cleared the table.

"Did you know Monty Locke?" Lacy asked Michael.

"Yes, yes, I did. He was one of the smartest men I've ever met," Michael replied. "And when he was out on a job, there was no stopping him. He solved a string of high profile cases and guess who helped on a few of those?"

"Jessica Fletcher?" Lacy said, and Sylvia giggled hysterically. She filled up their wine glasses.

"Or maybe it was Lieutenant Columbo," Sylvia said and more laughter erupted.

Michael joined in their merriment, while Basil stood and took a few steps back, head cocked. He had one thing on his mind, the leftovers on Lacy's plate. And I had one thing on mine.

"Does the name Wetzel mean anything to you, Lacy?" I asked.

She was in the middle of lifting her glass to her lips and didn't acknowledge my question until after a long sip. "Why should it?"

"I thought it might be someone connected to Shaw," I said and turned to Michael. "Let's leave those magazines outside, so we don't forget to take them when we leave. Okay with you, Lacy?"

"Ridiculous," she repeated.

"Come on," I told him. Half of me wanted to race home, but the other wanted to get to the bottom of this. Right now, I floated near the foamy part at the top.

He followed me to the front door, and I opened it. Sweet jasmine continued to scent the cool night air. Waves crashed along the beach behind us. We stepped outside to the tune of rainfall mimicked by the tree fountain. I closed the door.

"Shaw's going to have to be replaced," I whispered in the courtyard.

"So soon?" Michael asked. "I mean, you think they'll continue filming?"

"If they find the right person to take on the role."

"Shouldn't they shut down production?" Michael asked.

"They're too far along." I cast a glance behind me and lowered my voice. "I know a replacement. The new star's going to be our eyes and ears on the set. He's going to go places we can't. And he'll help us find out what really happened."

"That could work, assuming you could get your guy hired."

"Leave that to me."

Michael's brows dropped. "But how are you going to convince the substitute to spy for us?"

"Because I know him well."

"You're always one step ahead. You know the guy?"

"The perfect person."

"The stand-in, right?" Michael asked.

"Nope."

"Then who?"

"You."

CHAPTER 17

A Spy Among Us

"**M**e?" Michael's eyes grew to the size of half dollars. "I can't act."

"High school. Who starred as Curly in the stage production of *Oklahoma!* And got a standing ovation? Don't forget the encore."

Michael's open mouth broke into a huge grin. "I'd forgotten about that. I really nailed *Oh, what a beautiful morning.*" His shoulders slumped. "But that was a different kind of role. I was a singing cowboy. Not an actor."

"You were a sensation, Michael," I said. "You've got talent. Besides, acting isn't even a real job."

"But all I know are computers and science."

"Well, how about playing an actor for a week to bring a killer to justice?"

"Can I think about it?"

"Ten seconds."

Michael nodded and slid onto a nearby bench, doing a fine impression of that thinking man sculpture by Rodin...except Michael was fully clothed, of course.

I tapped my foot. It was one thing convincing Michael into doing it, but what about Lacy? She'd do it if it moved the investigation along, but she was so grouchy. She might just say no, because she could.

Michael stood. "There are times when one has to put personal feelings and major insecurities aside, in the name of justice."

His hands shot to his hips and he placed one foot on top of a large rock. Now he was doing a fine impersonation of Superman.

"Oh Michael!" I jumped up and wrapped my arms around his neck.

The front door swung open. Lacy and Sylvia stood framed in the doorway. Michael and I broke apart.

"What did I tell you?" Sylvia said.

"Your father would never break into a make-out session in the middle of a homicide investigation." Lacy crossed her arms over her chest. "Believe me, I tried."

"For your information, we were not making out," I said. "We were formulating a plan of action."

"That's right," Michael agreed. "It's a good one, too. Pretty good, anyway."

"Plan of action? Must be more of the modern lingo for make-out session," Sylvia told Lacy. They stepped back into the house. Michael and I slipped in behind them and closed the door.

"Kids today have no attention span at all," Lacy was telling Sylvia.

"They get distracted so easily. First, it was the magazines, now it's the smooching..." Sylvia said.

"We have someone to step in and replace Shaw," I said.

Lacy cut a sharp gaze my way. "Shaw won't be replaced. Filming's done."

"Oh, Lacy, that's a shame," Sylvia said. "This was going to be your first big production credit. You needed that."

"Like I need a rat's nest in my hair," Lacy replied.

"There are barely any women directors out there over the age of seven..." Sylvia stopped herself. "...over the age of sixty."

"You need to finish the movie," I said. "And for a very important reason."

"There is no reason, anymore," Lacy said.

"So we can catch a killer," I said. "You'll have an inside man." I unveiled my idea of making Michael the star, temporarily, until we caught the killer.

"That's actually a good idea. Look at him. He'd be the perfect spy," Sylvia said, chewing and snapping her gum loudly, eyes rolling over Michael. "He's got a face that belongs on a Nobel Peace prize winner."

"Really?" Michael beamed. "That's good, right?"

"First of all, he's not even an actor," Lacy said.

"I played Curly in *Oklahoma*," Michael said.

"He sings, too?" Sylvia asked, shaking her head and smiling. "What a guy."

"Back in high school," Michael said. "But I haven't played any parts since then."

"Well, it's long overdue," I said. "He did a fantastic job." I turned to Michael. "And this time you get to play yourself. A nerd on the run."

"But I'm not on the run."

"Well, you were a month ago," I said, referring to a little problem he had at LA Tech.

Michael nodded. "That's true. Sort of."

"You can draw on real life," I said. "Besides, our main purpose isn't for you to switch careers to acting, but to find a criminal during your summer break."

"He'll never pull it off," Lacy said.

"Oh, yes he will," I said. "It's just for a little while, so we have an insider." I moved closer to Lacy. "What are you afraid of?"

Her head rolled in my direction. She blew a huff of air. "I don't know the meaning of that word." She scrutinized a painting of a polar bear on her wall.

"He's our best chance," I said.

Lacy took a turn around the table and aimed her squint on Michael. "He does have a little of that Tom Hanks 'aw shucks' thing going on."

"Jimmy Stewart, too," Sylvia chimed in.

Lacy threw up her hands. "I don't have a better plan. It's not like anyone's going to talk to me about what happened. I'm the boss."

"They'll be impressed that you found someone so competent, so quickly," I added. "But you're going to need to distance yourself from Michael. Tell them he was a recommendation from a reliable source."

"I'll say top brass wants him," Lacy said. "Who's going to argue with the studio chief?"

"Sweet! We're going to wrap this up and hand it to you on a silver platter." Michael said to Lacy.

"Fine," Lacy said to me and turned to Michael. "But you're going to have to be coached. By me."

"I'd welcome that," Michael said. "Thank you."

"Isn't he adorable?" Sylvia smiled.

"Come by tomorrow, noonish," Lacy told him. "We'll go over the script. If you're no good, you're out before you're in."

"But wait, don't you have to do some rewriting?" Michael asked. "How are you going to work my character in?"

Lacy squeezed her chin between her thumb and forefinger. "Make it one o'clock. I'll have a new script by then."

Michael's eyes nearly popped out. "You're a writer, too?"

"I can't do everything," Lacy said. "I'm going to call the screenwriter and tell her to do the rewrite."

"There was a gun in Shaw's bedroom," I said.

Silence infiltrated the house.

"What do you know about that?" I asked Lacy.

"I gave it to him," she replied quietly. "It was mine. I thought if he ever found himself in circumstances—"

"What kind of circumstances?" I asked.

"Did something happen?" Michael wanted to know.

Lacy strolled across the room. "Syl has one, too. Just-in-case weapons we'd hopefully never need to use. I'm a well known personality and there are a lot of questionable people around."

"Maybe if I'd been packing, things would've gone differently today," Sylvia said. "Mine's in a makeup bag under my bathroom sink."

"I'll go to the studio this weekend and nose around," I said. "I'll need to meet with Burton, Debbylynn and Rhoda. They were the first on the scene after the murder. Can you set that up?" I turned to Lacy.

She gave a nod and a moment later, her hands flew to her head. She shut her eyes.

"Are you having a vision?" Michael asked her.

"No, I am not," Lacy replied. "I'm hearing things."

"In your head?" Michael said.

"No, I heard it, too," I said. "Is Ping outside in your car?"

"I gave him the rest of the night off," Lacy replied.

"What did you hear?" Sylvia asked.

"A crackle. Maybe a crunch," Lacy said. "By the front door."

I walked over to the entryway, Basil trotting at my heels.

"Doesn't he bark if someone's at the front door?" Michael asked.

"Not if it's someone he knows," Lacy replied.

I paused by the entry and listened. A car horn blasted and engines whooshed by on the highway. I opened the door. Michael and Lacy peered over my shoulder.

"No one's here," I said.

"What's that?" Lacy asked.

A large manila envelope balanced atop the nearest stepping stone.

CHAPTER 18

The Message

L acy's name was scrawled on the envelope in big block letters.

"Oh, my God. That's his writing," Sylvia said. "Shaw never learned to write cursive English."

I grabbed the envelope, passed it to Lacy and raced to the front of the house. Michael dashed toward the back. I pushed the gate open and strode up to the highway. A police vehicle was parked across the street. The officer stood by the driver's side of a car, parked in front of the squad car. No one else was around. I returned to the living room where Michael waited with Lacy and Sylvia.

"There's a cop parked out front, giving someone a ticket, meaning he probably didn't see anything," I said and addressed Michael. "What about you?"

"Just a small group hanging out on blankets near the surf."

"That's Shaw's writing?" I asked Lacy. "Looks pretty generic to me."

"He wrote in mixed capital and lowercase letters, like this," Lacy said quietly, turning the envelope around in her hands.

"Aren't you going to open it?" Michael asked.

Lacy handed it to me. "You do it."

I took it. Another clue pointing to Shaw being more alive than dead.

"Maybe we should give this to the cop outside," Michael said. "He can take it back to a police lab and test for clues and DNA."

I nodded. "Good idea."

Lacy snatched the envelope. "One of the reasons I hired you was so you'd do your own investigation, off police radar," she told me. "If I'd wanted them to handle it, I wouldn't have come to you."

She handed me the envelope and I ripped it open. A piece of paper was folded inside:

Sorry, Lacy Jean. RA sit-O

Lacy and I locked gazes. Was it possible she'd planted this second note, too?

"That's what Shaw called you." Sylvia's hand flew to her mouth. She turned to me. "Shaw was the only one who called her by her first and middle names."

"What's the rest referring to?" Michael asked. "RA? Return address? Red alert? The answer could be in a magazine."

"Fat chance," Lacy said.

"Then what?" I asked her. Her face looked pinched and slightly pink. The note upstairs had been typed. This one was handwritten. I folded the paper and slipped it back inside the envelope. "I need another example of Shaw's handwriting," I told Lacy.

Lacy threw me a killer look and disappeared upstairs. She returned in minutes, gripping a piece of paper in her hand.

"Here." She handed it to me. "These are items he wanted to add to Syl's shopping list last weekend. I forgot to give it to her."

"Red lentils, dried mangos, hot dogs, strawberry jam." I read and looked up at Lacy. "Eclectic list, isn't it? The writing looks like a match." I added the note to the envelope and headed for the front door. "Come on, Michael."

"Where are you going?" Lacy asked.

"I'm giving this to the cop across the street," I said.

"I thought you understood." Lacy planted a scowl on her lips. "No police."

"Look," I said, as Michael joined me at the door. "This is something the police can do. A handwriting analysis is simple enough. It'll keep them busy while we investigate."

Lacy tilted back her head and gave a slow nod. "I like it."

"Talk tomorrow." I left with Michael at my heels.

As soon as we reached the front gate, I showed Michael the note from the shoebox and shoved it inside the manila envelope. I handed the envelope to Michael.

"I don't get it. Why would he leave another note?" Michael asked.

"To ensure Lacy got the message." My suspicious mind was still telling me Lacy was behind both notes and knew more than she was telling. The notes could even be a distraction to divert our attention from whatever was really going on. She was a sly one.

"It must be Calvin, the stand-in," Michael said.

"This is no slam-dunk, Michael. Solving a murder is a cranky, twisty business." I told Michael about the socks. "This one's especially cranky and twisty. Take this to the officer. I'm heading to the beach."

"But—"

"When you're done, please find us transportation to get us out of here."

"Okay, but be careful, Corrie."

We parted ways, and I hopped onto the stone path running through Lacy's courtyard. It led me down to a wooden gate in the back. I left the gate propped open with a large rock and treaded through the sand.

A small, rambunctious group sat sprawled beneath the glow of moonlight on blankets near the water. A tiny barbecue hosted fiery coals, giving off wispy smoke and a biting odor.

"Party's over here," a guy called out.

"Dude, I'm looking for my boyfriend," I said. "He came

out here a few minutes ago." I edged closer. The guy's hair hung down to his elbows. He was shirtless and wore swim trunks and flip-flops. "Did you see him?"

"It's only us tonight. But I'll keep you warm 'til he shows, baby," the guy said.

My hand shot into my purse for the gun I didn't have. I swore under my breath.

"What did he look like?" A woman in a tank top and jeans got to her feet.

"Like he'd just stepped out of a Bollywood movie," I said.

"Yum," said a female leaning against a driftwood log.

"Hey, you stayin' with Lacy?" the guy asked.

So he was a local. "I'm shackin' out at her place, until I get my big break," I said. "Do you know my guy Shaw?"

"Never heard of him," he said.

A wave crashed and retreated under a growing curtain of mist. Somebody burped and the gang erupted into a laugh-fest.

I turned my head slightly. Michael waited by the gate. "See you later."

I stamped my way back to Michael. I'd almost reached him when the girl in the tank top ran after me.

"About fifteen minutes ago, I was looking at the swanky houses. A man left out that gate, the same one you used. He turned and ran down the beach." She pointed southward.

"Can you describe him?" I asked. There was enough light from most of the houses to give some illumination.

She shook her head. "He wore shorts. Dark hair. Kind of skinny. He wore a hat."

"Like a Humphrey Bogart hat?"

"Who?"

"Like Indiana Jones?"

"No, like a beanie." She stepped back. "That's all I saw." She trudged back to her sand-mates.

I turned to Michael. "Did you hear any of that?"

He nodded. "It's not our assassin unless he switched hats. That means it could be Shaw or Calvin. Or somebody else."

My mind was spinning again. "Let's get out of here," I said.

We pushed through Lacy's gate and made our way up to Coast Highway.

"Did you call for a car?" I asked.

Michael nodded and checked his smart phone. "Be here soon."

"We'll ask to be dropped off in...Westwood Village."

"You want to get a bite to eat?" Michael flipped his chin up.

"I thought you'd never ask. Call James and ask him to meet us there."

"Why?"

My insides tickled. I really didn't want to see James, but I trusted him to get a job done. "In case we're being followed. He can drive us home."

Michael stiffened and looked around.

"Let's not be obvious." I placed my hand on his arm. "We'll go to Westwood, walk in a restaurant, slip out the back and find a place to meet James."

"How about grabbing a bite?"

"Escape first. Food later," I said. "Or vice versa, depending on the timing." And any interruptions.

CHAPTER 19

The Switch

Nearly an hour later, Michael and I ducked into a small Italian trattoria near the corner of Westwood Boulevard and Wilkins, about a mile south of UCLA. We arrived thirty minutes before closing time. James was due to pick us up just after shut-down, which gave us a chance to devour garlic bread, chicken marsala and a tiramisu, the likes of which I'd never tasted before. If I hadn't been on a mission, I would have orbited in cake ecstasy right then and there. If that wasn't enough to make me declare my love for the trattoria, the door in the back of the restaurant certainly was. A dimly lit hallway led to a short, exterior staircase that would drop us off in a tidy, four car parking area, completely hidden from the street. I mentally got down on my knees and said a prayer of thanks for all the goodness. One look at Michael told me he was doing the same. Or maybe it was the tiramisu.

I watched the entry, but no one came in except for a twosome picking up a take-out order.

"Ask James to give us a three minute warning."

"What?" Michael leaned back in his chair, fingers linked over his abs. I knew the delicious dessert was being relived in his mind. "Oh, sure." He straightened and picked up his phone. He was back in business.

"Thank you," I told him, my insides aflutter. "For being here."

He leaned toward me. "There's no place I'd rather be than with you. Killer on the loose and all."

I smiled and stood, my hand brushed the top of his shoulder, and I wandered slowly to the front window. Cars whizzed by. Pedestrians slouched along the sidewalk in groups.

Westwood was one of the few places in LA where Angelenos bypassed their vehicles, unfolded their legs and actually walked. Stepping outside, I inhaled, filling my lungs with air that smelled like a dirty washcloth. I sputtered and looked both ways. Neon signs, headlights and street lamps lit up the bustling scene. The block was fully stocked with music stores, bookshops and eateries. I made a big production of checking my watch and shaking my head. I stamped my foot and returned inside, making like I was impatient for our ride. All for show, in case eyes were on me. I rejoined Michael.

"Okay," he whispered. "Almost at three minutes."

"Let's leave separately. One at a time," I said. "You first."

"Ladies, first."

"No time for manners right now, Michael, although I appreciate it. We've got to get out the back without arousing suspicion, and before they lock the front door." Two other diners remained. I figured we had a solid ten minutes.

"Okay." Michael stood, planted a quick kiss on my cheek and maneuvered toward the back.

I waited a few minutes and dropped my napkin. I reached for Michael's and dropped his near mine. I bent over to retrieve them and got on all fours, holding a folded napkin in each hand as a shield between the floor grime and my bare palms. I crawled to the back door.

"You need some help, miss?" a kindly server asked.

"No, thank you. I'm starting my pub crawl." That was lame.

He grinned while I continued on all fours. I stole a glance over my shoulder. No one else paid me any attention. This was

Los Angeles and a college town, after all. Pub-crawls were common, even if not exactly in a literal sense.

I grabbed the doorknob and rose to my feet. Pushing it open just enough to slip through, I surfaced into the backstage of Westwood Boulevard, jammed with side streets hosting relaxed apartment buildings painted in earthy tones with multi-paned windows and skinny balconies. A homeless man pushed an overflowing shopping cart down the street to find a place to hunker down for the night. I craned my neck around for Michael, and our ride. Climbing over the metal railing of the staircase, I landed in a crouched position onto the asphalt. An engine rumbled nearby. Rushing forward, I stared at the tail end of a white SUV. I glided closer; the purring motor grew louder. I made a mad dash around the rear and nearly collided with the open door leading to the backseat.

"Get in." Michael motioned me inside.

I scrambled up and slammed the door. I blew out a breath and laid my head back against a leather cushion. "Good to see you, James."

Not that I'd laid eyes on him yet, but once I did, I knew it'd be good. James twisted his head around the driver's seat and took me in with his jungle green eyes. He didn't disappoint. He clenched his granite jaw a moment before flashing deep-dish dimples in a grin that made me catch my breath. Oh why, oh why did he always have this effect on me? Me and every other female on the planet, that is. He didn't smile often, but when he did, it was a doozy.

"It's been a while," he said and faced forward again. "Tell me what happened."

Michael spilled the details, while James put the car in reverse and motored down the alley.

"Stay away from Westwood Boulevard," I told James. "Take the side streets to the 405 and be on the lookout for a tail."

I didn't need to face James to know he was probably grinding his teeth at my orders. I hadn't told him anything new. He knew exactly what to do. That's how his mind worked. Just like mine. He'd throw the tail off, assuming there was one. James was the only person more suspicious than I was, not counting Mom. Or my dad, when he'd been around.

After Michael finished his update, he sat back and asked, "Did I miss anything, Corrie?"

"I'd say you covered it all." We'd just landed onto the 405 freeway. I debated where to go. A busy hotel would be our best bet. "Let's drive to the airport."

"Why?" Michael said.

"LAX is a good place to get lost," James answered for me. "But I have a better idea." His eyes shot to mine in the rear view mirror.

I squeezed my lips together to prevent word spillage that could result in the usual oil slick that lingered between us. We'd slide back and forth over a barrage of insults, ultimately leading to mutual frustration and anger. But that was before. Things were different now. Friendlier between us. If a lion and a tigress could be chums.

"What's your idea?" Michael asked him.

"Let's lead whoever's tracking you into thinking you haven't caught on. You should go about business as usual."

I leaned forward. "Our tail doesn't know what business as usual is for us. We're recent developments in his routine. He's watching, for now."

"I say we go back to Corrie's place, like nothing's happened," James said. "Better to be on your own turf."

He was right, but I threw out my hand in impatience. "He might be waiting for us there." That might be a good thing. We could stage an ambush.

"Maybe," James said. "I'll drop you two off and park on the street." He flew down the Rosecrans exit. "I'll be watching and communicating with you the whole time."

"While he thinks he's keeping an eye on us, we'll be keeping eyes on him. Brilliant." Michael said and turned to look at me. "What do you think, Corrie?"

"What if he catches on?" I asked James, looking for an excuse not to do things his way.

"He won't," James talked in a steady voice. "I'll drop you off nearby and you'll walk back—"

"How's that going to look to our pursuer? Why wouldn't we be dropped off at my place?" Now I had him.

"He won't question it if he thinks you've been out walking on the greenbelt. He already knows you do that."

"How do you know he's not following us right now?" I asked, looking behind me.

"You'll have to trust me on that," James replied. "I don't think he's been following tonight, after he tried to run you down. We can either wait it out somewhere else…or set a trap for him."

Michael looked at James. "You think he'll be at Corrie's?"

I clamped my lips together again. My former emotions were not going to get the best of me. Besides, I was warming up to James' plan.

"That's what I would do," James said.

"And if we didn't come back to my place tonight?" I asked. "What would your criminal mind think then?"

"I'd go back to the studio and wait," James said. "I'd expect to see you there."

"How did he get on the movie lot in the first place?" Michael asked. "That's not easy, unless he belonged there."

"It would be easy for James and similar criminal minds," I said. "They'd make it seem like they belonged." I fanned myself with my hand. I was getting hot and bothered.

"Or create a diversion to get in, after which I'd look like I belonged," James said. "Point is, it's not that difficult."

James and Michael chatted for the rest of the ride, while I tried to think like the guy in the fedora. He was connected to Shaw, but he wasn't the guy I saw running. Why would he follow and try to run me down? Because he saw me with Lacy and knew Shaw lived with her for a few months. Which brought me back to the question, why me?

*　*　*

Twenty minutes later, James dropped us off on the greenbelt, near my pad, and we walked in the direction of my place. I kept an eye on the cars zipping past, just in case the guy in the hat was looking to execute a repeat performance. A light bulb suddenly burned brightly over my head.

"James is probably canvassing parked cars in my street to see which have no plates. A plateless car could belong to our scoundrel."

"Gee, that's brilliant," Michael said and turned to me. "You're both brilliant. I never would have thought of doing that."

We crossed Ardmore and turned onto Longfellow.

"Does it seem extra dark tonight?" Michael asked. "Looks like a power outage on your side of the street." He slowed his pace. "Must be our criminal at work."

I shook my head. "No, actually, it's not. I got a letter earlier this week. It's a scheduled outage from ten pm to four am."

"On a Friday night?"

"This is the third one this month. Something about faulty wiring. There are notices posted all over the place. Guess they figure people won't mind a Friday night outage." I scanned the street for James' SUV. I came up empty.

A short time later, we took the backstairs to my place and stood by the living room window. I gripped a flashlight and manned the blinds. I tilted my head. "Did you hear something?"

Michael lifted his ear and waited. "A plane's approaching."

Seconds later, the roar of a jet scattered all other sounds. I waited for the rumble to fade and perked my ears. Michael breathed softly beside me. He pulled out his knife.

"As a kid, I wished I could develop super powers, and I still do. This is sort of wish fulfillment, being with you and taking down bad guys." Michael blew on the blade and polished it with his sleeve.

"We haven't taken down anyone yet." I peeked out between the slats into the night. The fog had been settling in at Lacy's place, but no mist hung over Hermosa tonight. I opened the window an inch or so. A motorcycle whirred by. A pair of eyes glowed at me from below, as a cat tiptoed between the shrubs. A car turned up my street, lighting it up. I scanned the surrounding bushes. Still no sign of James. Or anyone else.

Always look up. Funny, how Dad's words popped into my head, unexpected like that. When I'd first heard him utter those three words, I'd thought he meant to look on the bright side of things, until I realized he meant it literally, especially during an investigation. If we always viewed a situation at eye level, we'd miss the big picture. But with the streetlamps out, there wasn't much to see, up or down.

A van turned the corner and rumbled up my street. It flashed on its brights. My gaze shot upward. A figure hugged the top of a utility pole, dressed in glowing safety hat and vest.

I moved away from the blinds. "I'll be right back."

"Where are you going?" Michael came around to stand at my shoulder.

"I want to check out the street for myself."

"I feel like we've already stumbled over this topic," Michael said. "We've got James. He'll handle things on the outside. We don't—"

"That's right, you don't," A deep, slow voice grumbled.

We both jumped and turned in the direction of the speaker. Michael's arm shot around my shoulders. The voice came from the hallway, next to my bedroom.

"Don't move a muscle," the man said.

My blood ran cold. He sounded part British, part southern twang.

"Who are you?" I whispered. My place was dark, except for strands of light streaming through the blinds when a vehicle passed by.

"Maybe you didn't understand my intent earlier tonight. I

could have mowed you down, but I didn't."

My skin crawled with imaginary insects. I stepped closer. "Why didn't you?"

"I didn't think you deserved it...yet."

I shuddered. I gripped a small flashlight that would do minimal damage. I shoved it in my back pocket and took another step. Michael matched my step.

"Did you kill Shaw because he deserved it?" I asked.

"You shouldn't be asking that question."

I edged ahead with Michael alongside. I stopped a few feet from the hallway. A light streamed in through my blinds making something glint in Michael's hand. He gripped his knife. I gulped. What if the guy saw it too?

"You should ask, how long do I have?" said the guy.

My heart was beating double-time, unleashing a throbbing in the pit of my stomach that climbed up and into my head. His voice seemed to fill the room. I inched forward.

"Alright," I said. "How long do I have?"

Michael breathed unsteadily. I lay my hand on his and took the knife. The grip was moist.

"Depends on whether you stay out of my way," the man growled.

I lifted my head. The voice seemed to come from above me.

"*If* there's a next time," he spoke slowly. "I'll aim to kill."

A tiny circle of light glowed on my Crib cam. A light that turned on only when someone was speaking through it. I'd forgotten. The camera doubled as an intercom.

"Dammit," was all I could say.

CHAPTER 20

The Visitor

I dove to the floor, sliding toward the wall, and pulled out the flashlight. I shined it on the outlet. The extension cord from the Crib cam ran down my living room wall and into a battery backup. I yanked out the plug to silence the voice that had been terrorizing us.

"I feel so inadequate right now." Michael stood behind me. He slapped his hand to his forehead. "I should've figured it out right away. These security cameras are incredibly easy to hack. All the guy needed was your email address."

"At least we know the battery backup is working." I sat on the floor leaning against the outlet, relieved to be rid of him for now. "I'm glad he wasn't here in person." I might have killed him.

Michael called James, put him on speakerphone and reported what had happened.

"He's toying with us," James barked into the phone.

"Good thing one of us was on the ball," Michael said. He slid down next to me.

"I'll call Sorkel," I said. "Go home, James. Nothing more's going to happen tonight. He's waiting for our next move."

There was silence at James' end. He was mulling things over.

"Did you see anything outside?" Michael asked him.

"No. Every single car on Longfellow was plated, all generic," James said. "No one waiting inside any of them."

"I'm betting he wasn't anywhere near here," I said.

"I'll bet right along with you," Michael said. "Hacking long distance is a cinch."

"But how did he know about the Crib cam?" I asked. The only people who knew about it were my mom and Michael...and Lacy. Was she behind all this?

"He took a gamble and scored," Michael was saying. "You're a prime candidate, being a single female, living alone. Little did he know you're no ordinary single female." He took my hand.

Michael and James continued talking about the night's events, while I called Sorkel and left a voicemail.

"She's not, but she should be carrying one all the time," Michael was telling James.

I got up and hustled to my closet. On top sat a locked metal box. I grabbed the key from the bathroom drawer and opened it. I removed a small pistol, while I replayed the creepy conversation. What had been distinctive about his voice?

"He changed accents from British to Southern. Who does that?" I asked.

"An actor." Michael stood.

"Anyone," James said. "Trying to avoid detection and spread confusion."

"James," I said, moving closer to Michael's phone. I pictured the moments before the voice came on. "Did you notice a man on the street, up a power pole? He wore a glow-in-the-dark vest. Like a *Caltrans* worker."

"I saw him," James replied. "He's still up the pole. But... there's no utility truck." He muttered the last part. His breath quickened like he was moving fast.

"There're no parking spaces on the street," I said. "Maybe they're around the corner."

"Call you back." He disconnected.

I quick-stepped to the blinds and spread them apart with my fingers. A car whizzed by, catching James in its lights. He hurried along on the sidewalk, to the utility pole, flashlight in hand. He stood two duplexes away. He tilted his head back and cupped his hands on either side of his mouth. I couldn't see very well in the dimness. Less than a minute later, he shut off his light and hotfooted away from the pole.

Michael's phone rang. He placed it on speaker again.

"I called 9-1-1," James said.

"About the phone in my place?" I moved over to Michael. "Or something else?"

My heart was pounding again.

"Is the utility guy still up the pole?" Michael asked.

"Yes," James replied. "And he's hanging at a funny angle."

CHAPTER 21

Dummied Up

Detective Sorkel never made it to my pad, but Hermosa PD did, along with the fire department and paramedics and almost everyone who lived on my street, as well as a few passers by. Turned out, none of them were needed. The guy up the pole was a dummy, and that's why Sorkel didn't bother showing up. I was not scoring any points with him.

"I actually got into my Crown Vic before I learned about the dummy," Sorkel told me when he called back. "There's not much we can do with dummy hair or dummy fingerprints." Sorkel snickered. "You sure you're related to Monty Locke?"

"What about the hacker?" I said. "He threatened to kill me."

"I suggest you contact the FBI about that," he said.

A lot of good that would do. "So they can file it away in their small time internet crime file?" I asked. "The hacker may be a prime suspect in the Shaw Kota killing."

"And how do you know that?" Sorkel asked.

"I..."

"Tell you what, I have a guy who'll pick up the dummy, as a matter of routine. Just remember, none of this would've happened if you'd stayed out of the way."

"I gave an envelope with notes to—"

Sorkel disconnected.

I shuffled over to Michael and James. It was two-thirty in the morning, which meant we were running on adrenaline fumes. They stood on the small patch of lawn near the power pole. The emergency vehicles lighted up Longfellow.

"The dummy could have come from Ameripictures," Michael whispered. "Right, Corrie?"

"Could be from the props department." I cut James a look. His arms were crossed against his chest. His jaw clenched as he watched the dummy being manhandled amid laughter from the men in black. James grunted and captured my gaze. I turned away.

"Come on, guys, these moving parts are tripping us up," Michael said to James and me. "We've got to hold steady. We'll divide to conquer. I mean, Corrie and I will." He focused on James. "Sorry, man, all we'd wanted was a ride from you tonight, not to have you mixed up in everything."

James stepped up to an officer. "Was there a utility truck parked nearby?"

The officer shook his head. "We contacted the power company first thing, and they confirmed no workers were sent to this part of the street." He pointed to the dummy lying on the ground. "Looks like local yokels had some fun with big, bend-able Gumby."

I clamped my lips together. This was exactly the response I'd expected. The murder at Ameripictures wasn't in their terri-tory, so they paid little attention. And there was no real crime committed here tonight besides the Crib cam hack. For all they knew, we were in on the prank. One thing they did agree to do was to contact the studio about the missing dummy prop. I wasn't holding my breath for that one either. The studio's checkout system wasn't foolproof.

Thirty minutes later, nearly everyone was gone, includ-ing James. Michael was spending the night at my place and had made himself comfy on my futon. It had been a long day and I looked forward to sleeping in. But it wasn't in the cards. Not the deck I was playing with, anyway.

At a quarter to eight, my doorbell rang. I grabbed my pistol and stormed to the entry. Michael got to the door the same time I did. I reached for the doorknob.

"Ask who it is first," Michael whispered.

My mind was so muddled, I'd yanked open the door before his words registered, pistol hidden behind me. I lowered my sight a good six inches. My gaze landed on a grinning octogenarian planted on my doorstep. Not one strand of coppery hair was out of place in her stylish up-do. Her face displayed enough wrinkles to populate a travel map. A lightweight pink sweater and black slacks replaced her navy-blue flight uniform. Her neck was hidden beneath a colorful scarf.

"Miss Trudy," I said, greeting my landlady. "It's so early."

She threw a hand at me. "I'm an early riser. Old habit."

Michael gave a low whistle through his teeth behind me.

For the past six decades, Miss Trudy had been a flight attendant, which worked out well for me because she was hardly ever around. She was making up for that right now.

"Did I wake you?" She leaned sideways and stared up at Michael. She gave him a quick finger wave. He reciprocated. "I arrived late last night and must've dozed off. I got up in time to see a cop car pulling away from our driveway."

I was glad she'd slept through all the excitement.

"You were back from a flight?" Michael asked over my shoulder.

"From a date," she corrected him and returned her stare to me. "I heard some guy fell off the utility pole up the street. Is he alright?"

Michael smirked and said, "Well, normally the answer would be no. But in this case, he's perfectly fine since he lacked all vital organs and had no blood pumping anywhere in his body."

Miss Trudy leaned forward and placed a hand on the side

of her mouth. She whispered to me, "Sounds like he could use a strong cup of coffee." She spoke to Michael, "Maybe it was a politician up that pole." She giggled and Michael joined her. It was too early for me to even crack a smile.

"It was a stunt dummy that fell, a joke played by a neighborhood prankster," I told her. "Well, thanks for stopping by." I started to close the door but she wedged her size six pump in the doorjamb.

"Wait a minute," Miss Trudy said. "Was there a cop snooping around your unit?"

I figured the fastest way to get her to leave was to tell her everything. "Yes, because my security system was hacked and there was a possibility the hack and the dummy in the telephone pole were linked."

Miss Trudy nodded. "Were they?"

I swapped a glance with Michael.

"Probably not, but there could be a connection," Michael said. "If there is, no one's found it yet."

"What kind of reply is that? You just told me nothing," Miss Trudy said to him. She pointed her finger at my chest. "I want to know what you think. Is there a connection or not?"

"Well, I don't think the police will be back here, if that's what you're asking," I said. That should settle any landlady anxiety she might be feeling. "Their work is done."

She settled her gaze back on Michael.

"I've got nothing to add," he said.

"Can we talk?" Miss Trudy leaned toward me again. "Girl talk."

"Oh, sure," Michael said. "I'll just be over there." He stepped into my bedroom and shut the door.

"I met a guy last night," Miss Trudy said, shuffling inside my living room. "A real looker."

I pictured a small, older man with a silvery toupee parted neatly on the side, wearing white sneakers you could spot two blocks off. Miss Trudy wouldn't have him any other way.

"I hope you two will be very happy," I said, moving closer

to the door.

"I'm talking about a guy I met after my date. He was on the street, by my duplex. The strange part," Miss Trudy said in a quiet voice. "He asked about you."

I fought back the urge to curl my lip. "What do you mean?"

"When I woke up, the electricity was back on, but I heard a noise. I came out and saw a Five-O patrol car leaving. I had to find out what was going on. I was about to call a neighbor, when this tall, broad shouldered, handsome fellow walked up to me. The hunk asked if I was okay. I told him I was fine. He had these mesmerizing eyes I could dive into." Miss Trudy dipped her chin and slapped a hand over her heart.

She could only be talking about one guy. "Was he about thirty, dark wavy hair, dimples..." I pictured James.

"What would I want with a thirty-year-old? This man was about fifty." She took a step closer. "Here's where it got a little strange. He asked how my tenant was doing."

"He must have seen the police in here and was curious. How did he know you owned the building?" I stifled a yawn.

"Might've asked around," she said.

Miss Trudy was popular among the neighbors. Plus, she'd lived in the same place since the Reagan administration.

"I said you and I hadn't talked, but you were a plucky thing, so I was sure you were fine," Miss Trudy explained.

"Okay, I think I'll go back to—"

"Not so fast. Then he asked if you were a good tenant. Wasn't that odd?"

I nodded. More than odd, unless... "Maybe he's looking for a place to rent and he likes my unit." Rentals were hard to come by in Hermosa.

"Could be. Anyway, I said yeah, she's a great tenant. I didn't tell him about the time your boyfriend broke open the door."

"That was an accident," I said. Actually, that was Miss Trudy showing Michael how to kick-in a door. "Did he wear a hat?" My heart started beating a little faster.

"Yeah, how did you know?"

"A fedora?" Now it pounded hard against my chest

"No. He wore a golfer's hat." She patted her hair.

"Like a baseball cap?"

"A white, floppy brimmed number. What are those called?"

"Bucket hat. What color was his hair?"

"It was tucked underneath so I couldn't see, but his eyebrows were kinda brownish. Didn't care much for his beard, although I wouldn't mind if everything else was in good shape. You know the guy?"

"I'm not sure."

"I didn't ask his name. But it gets even stranger." Miss Trudy shuffled closer to me and whispered. "I went back to my place, took a bath, got dressed, did my stretching exercises, and walked to my front window. And..."

"Yes?"

"...the hunky guy in the hat was standing across the street, leaning against a tree and looking right up at this building. He could've been standing there for hours. You think I have a stalker? Maybe you should let the cops know."

I bit my lip and walked over to the window. "That would be for you to do, Miss Trudy. I didn't lay eyes on the guy." I panned the street. A lady walked her Pomeranian and a man carried a surfboard to his car. No sign of anyone else. I turned to Miss Trudy. "How long was he standing there?"

"I blinked and poof! He was gone."

I wondered if she was losing her marbles. "Tell me if you spot him again."

She shuffled to the front entry. "I'll be watching for him."

I followed her to the door and opened it. "You okay, Miss Trudy?"

"Oh, sure," she said. "I've thrown guys bigger than him off the plane. But not while we were in the air." She opened the door and stuck her head outside, looking toward the street. She turned back to me and whispered, "The coast is clear."

I watched while Miss Trudy took the stairs, one foot down, two together. One foot down, two together. Now there were two men in hats for me to watch. Miss Trudy threw me a wave and disappeared inside her place. I scanned the street. The coast *was* clear. For now.

CHAPTER 22

Man of Action

"**W**hat did she say?" Michael came bounding out of my bedroom. "Was it about last night? Or are you sworn to secrecy? I'm fine with no secret sharing."

"That's what I like. A man who's perfectly capable of answering his own questions." I didn't want to worry him too much about what could be nothing. "Miss Trudy wanted to talk about a guy she'd met." I wasn't certain if Miss Trudy's encounter with the unknown man was connected to Shaw. Too much to process with too little sleep.

Michael sank onto the futon. "I was thinking about our case." He held out a folded piece of paper. "I can't help out too much this weekend, with my acting career just getting started, but I made this for you."

"Your *what* career? Careers usually last longer than a week."

Michael grinned. "Nothing like a little levity in the middle of a murder investigation."

What's this?" I took the paper and unfolded a list. "Suspects?" He'd written down *Suspects According to Michael* across the top of the page.

Lacy, Sylvia, Guy in Fedora, Guy running away after Shaw

was killed, Costumer, Caterer, Director and Security Guard

"That's a rough draft," Michael said. "We'll fine tune it as we go along."

"Thank you, Michael. A thorough list is just what we need."

"About the guy in the fedora. I still think he's an actor."

He dressed like a homeless hipster, like a lot of actors these days. "That's a good deduction."

"There's more," Michael said. "The list wasn't all I worked on while you gabbed with the landlady."

"You didn't whip up breakfast, or did you?"

"The last time I checked, your bedroom didn't have a stove."

"True."

"Breakfast is next on my list, my lady. Lacy called and said she'd set up appointments for you to meet with the costumer, caterer, director and guard. At fifteen minute intervals, starting at noon in her private office on the lot."

"I'm so ready," I said. "But why is Vanderpat on the list?"

"I also talked to Veera. She said he's only been at Amer-ipictures two weeks. According to Vanderpat, he'd worked security at Universal Studios before this job. Veera called her security contact at Universal. They had no record of him."

I sank down next to him. "Where would I be without you?"

"Probably with a really cool, smart, fearless guy who can shoot as well as you can, but has zero cooking or technical skills."

Sounded like James. I cleared my throat. "You're man enough for me, and you've got cooking and computer skills most people only dream about."

Michael blushed. "Shucks, Corrie. There's one more thing. Veera said Vanderpat has a tattoo on his wrist. She didn't get a good look, but she said it's small, dark and oval shaped."

Maybe an insect tat? A cockroach would be appropriate. "Tattoos don't mean too much. Half the studio had at least one."

I strolled into my kitchenette and pulled open a drawer. I took out a pencil and grabbed a notepad. "I'm going to try something."

"Making your own list?"

"Unleashing my inner Rembrandt." I turned to face him. "I'm sketching the face beneath the fedora." I flopped onto the futon.

"Just when you think you know someone. You're a sketch artist, Corrie."

"Not exactly. I'm going to draw and exaggerate outstanding features." I sat down and balanced the pad on my lap. I drew a diamond-shaped head. "Dark eyes, sparse, straight brows, roundish nose. High cheekbones, whiskers, narrow, pointy chin," I said, as I sketched each part. "Flowing, messy hair that ends just past the pointy chin." I showed my drawing to Michael. "What do you think?"

"Incredible."

"You've seen him before?" I asked.

"I think so. Maybe on TV." Michael's eyes darted to the ceiling before shooting back to me. "In a Charlie Brown cartoon."

"Pretty bad, isn't it?" I said.

It was terrible. It looked like an inverted triangle with dots for eyes, long, scraggly hair, a tiny hat and a small, lopsided mouth. But it was the facial hair that made him unique. A thin moustache, a patch below his lips and hair on the tip of his chin.

"This guy is real, Michael." I took a hard look at my drawing. "This is just a starting point." I continued to sketch.

"I know. I just meant...I mean, sorry, I didn't get much sleep last night. Of course, neither did you and maybe that's why..."

I pictured the guy following me on the Ameripictures' lot. "The guy was a little taller than me with a slim build. His clothes seemed loose."

"Was he in costume for a movie?" Michael asked.

"Maybe." I dropped the pad on my coffee table and padded

to my front window. I peered through the slats of the blinds. A car whizzed by, a guy walked his dog and a woman got into her Toyota coupe.

"I'm going to whip us up an omelet," Michael said.

I was about to turn away when I noticed a man standing a little ways down the street, next to the back unit of a smaller duplex. His hands were shoved in the pockets of a gray jacket. Even from this distance, he seemed tall. He wore black shades, lifted upward toward my window. His bucket hat was white, his beard dark and full. "Michael?" I waved my hand behind me.

"Not in the mood for an omelet?" Michael stood next to me.

"See that guy across the street?" I pointed. "Next to that tree in front of that brown fence."

Michael moved in a little closer. "I see. Do we know him?"

"Miss Trudy said he's been watching the duplex. Like he is right now."

"Is he the man in your sketch?"

I shook my head. "The guy following me was smaller, younger and not as broad shouldered as my latest fan." I moved away from the blinds. "Take my place and don't take your eyes off him. I'm going to find out who he is."

"Wait." Michael turned towards me. "You can't go outside like that."

I looked down. My sleep shorts and camisole might not work. I dove for my closet and grabbed a trench coat and sneakers.

"That's better," Michael said. "I'll come with you."

"No. You watch in case he leaves. See where he goes." I grabbed the pistol and my cell phone off the coffee table. "Call me if I miss his exit."

Michael stared out the window. I pulled open the door.

"Wait," Michael said. "He's gone."

CHAPTER 23

On the Job

C lues and people kept vanishing right before my eyes. After the guy in the bucket hat disappeared, I darted outside in search of him. Not a shoe print or beard in sight. I knocked on the doors of the duplex where I'd spotted him. No one admitted knowing or seeing him. I couldn't shake the feeling that there were eyes on my back, watching my every move. Of course, it could have been Miss Trudy.

I scooted back to my place and perfected my sketch while we devoured our cheese and avocado omelets. Michael peered over my shoulder.

"That's beginning to look like someone," he said.

"Snoopy?"

"Someone real. A scary dude."

I must have looked skeptical because he said,

"This time I mean it."

Mid-morning, Michael motored off to Lacy's to kick-start his short-term acting job, while I wound my way to Culver City. Lacy had called to review who I'd be meeting with and when. She'd reached everyone except Vanderpat. I was more than ready. My confidence level hit the ceiling thanks to my green silk blouse, black pants and lace ballet flats. I'd tamed my wild hair into submission, using a headband to maintain control. A short strand of pearls and matching earrings completed my low-key, I-mean-business look. I dropped pepper spray and a pistol into my purse. I would not come away empty-handed today. While the studio was in snooze mode, the crime scene at Ameripictures would be hopping, and so would I.

I accelerated onto the 405 freeway and bulldozed my way to the fast lane. TV shows and movies wanted people to think crime scene investigations involving a murder were fast moving. Not true. Everything near yesterday's crime scene would be photographed and videoed. So would all entries, exits and escape routes. My fingertips tingled, just thinking about it. Then came the up-close examination of prints, blood, hair and anything else to be sampled, measured, collected and sent to a forensics lab. Any one of those could point investigators in the right direction. Today, senior officers would roll in, along with pathologists and other experts. I wanted another look and to do that, I had to make myself useful. Otherwise, I'd be kicked to the curb again.

Forty minutes later, I'd nabbed a parking spot, and whistled my way through Ameripictures, past sound stages and the commissary, to the back lot and the crime scene. I marched past vehicles parked along the side of the road. All domestic, standard law enforcement transport, along with a late model Mercedes coupe, probably belonging to a short-tempered exec who'd been hauled out of bed to keep tabs on the troops. I trekked to the front of the brick building. Two uniforms stood by the entry. I kept my steady pace.

"Officer." I claimed a spot by the cops and handed one my card. "I'm Corrie Locke. I'm a lawyer and private..." Oops, I didn't want to go there. In case they asked for proof, I had no PI license. "...counsel to the studio chief legal officer." That could sort of be Marshall. I wasn't that far off base. "My father was a private investigator you may have heard of, Montague Locke."

"No kidding?" The older officer's brows shot up, and he bent slightly forward. His lips moved as he read my badge. He straightened and looked me in the eyes. "I met your father on a couple of LAPD cases. He was top-notch."

"Thank you." I turned my head and gazed down the road. I pictured the guy running yesterday, away from the brick building.

"I remember you working beside him. Are you here to take a look upstairs?" The officer opened the door for me, but my legs didn't play along. I'd never been given a green light so quickly. Not without Dad by my side. But still, I hesitated. A strong feeling tugged at my feet, telling me there was somewhere else I needed to be.

"Not yet, Officer." I flashed a smile. "I think I'll take a look around the lot, first."

When I'd shadowed Dad on his investigations, he'd review the facts with me and send me off to recreate them. He'd quiz me afterward, over and over, until we made sense of what might have happened. It was also to keep me out of his silvery locks while he did his own prodding.

I hurried to the place where I'd first laid eyes on Shaw's double, replaying the scene in my head. I reached the end of the fictional street and paused at the spot where the lookalike had raced past. He'd continued toward the back recesses of the lot, and that's where I headed. I'd lost sight of him when he'd rounded a corner. My bet was he'd exited out the first gate he came to. Security guards didn't care as much about those leaving the premises. Their focus was on who came in.

Rounding the same corner as the double, I stopped near the side entrance at Culver Boulevard. The wrought iron gates stood open. A security booth sporting limo-tinted windows sat off to one side. The doors to the booth were shut. My guess was the lookalike made his exit here.

I neared the booth and waved at the dark glass. The door opened and a guard stepped out. He wore a navy security polo shirt and matching pants.

"Hi there." I showed him my badge. "Yesterday afternoon, about three or so, a man exited through this gate. Do you have any record of that?"

"I wasn't working yesterday," he replied in a monotone that would put a toddler to sleep.

"You've got a sign-in record," I said. "And how about video footage of who comes and goes?"

He pointed inside the lot. "Main security office has video."

"Who worked this gate yesterday, late afternoon?" I asked.

He pulled out a chart and looked it over. "Kimika."

"Is she working today?"

He shook his head. "Not until Monday morning."

I handed him my card. "Get in touch with her please and ask her to call me. It's important."

He took my card. "I've got her on the phone right now."

"Mind if I have a word with her?"

He gave a nod before retreating back in the booth. He re-emerged with a cell phone in his hand. I took it.

"What a lucky break," I said to the guard.

I held that thought for all of ten seconds. Turns out Kimika saw no one fitting Shaw's description walking or running off. I disconnected and turned back toward the interior of the studio. There was a mini parking lot near the gate. Maybe the Shaw lookalike drove off.

"May I see a list of who left the studio around three yesterday?"

"You don't have clearance for that."

"I have a better idea," I said. "There can't be more than a handful of people who exited this gate about then." Friday afternoon meant most lot dwellers left for greener pastures earlier. "How about you read off the names, and I'll tell you if any sound familiar?"

The guard picked up a clipboard and was about to read names to me when he stopped himself. "I'll still be giving you information without permission from the security office."

"Whose permission do you need? The Chief's? I can get that for you." I pulled out my phone and started dialing. "I'm calling her, right now." I harbored the same high hopes I'd had for Vanderpat. I was banking this guard would stop me before I finished dialing. He didn't.

"Corrie? Something happen?" Veera answered my call.

"I know you're relaxing today, Chief, but if you have a moment, there's a security guard at the Culver gate that needs to confirm my access to yesterday's visitor list."

"You're having problems with another security guard? Let me at him," Veera said. I could almost see her rolling up her sleeves.

"I know." I looked at the guard. "I'm so sorry to bother you with such a trivial matter." I turned my back to the guard, but spoke loudly. "I don't have the number for the studio chief of security. You're on my speed dial. But if you give it to me, I'll call him."

"Oh, that's a good one." Veera was out of breath. "Hit him where it hurts. Listen, I called someone I know at the Security Guard Union, and he referred me to a guy working security long-time at that aerospace company, Pantheon. He said there's a Theo Wetzel works there who's a higher up. He's going to find out his position and get me his contact information, if he can. That okay by you?"

"Thanks, that'll work. I'll call right now."

The guard maintained his silence.

"What? Oh, sure." I turned to the guard. "Here." I held the phone out to him. "She wants to speak to you."

He lowered his chin and took the phone from me. I gulped. If word got out that Veera and I were impersonating the head of the studio, we'd be canned faster than a keg of beer in a brewery.

He pressed the phone to his ear. "Miss Cherie? I'll show her the chart right now. Sorry to bother you." He disconnected.

I let out a breath. Veera texted me a smiley face seconds later.

The guard handed me the chart. Three names were listed as exiting by car, between two-thirty and three-thirty. He confirmed that two were employees. But one was an outside contractor named Herman Monk.

"What kind of contractor?" I asked.

He turned to a laptop in his booth. "Landscape artist working with the gardening crew."

Was it Shaw or someone resembling him? And how did he manage the cover? The same way I managed; by making a fake phone call. "What else can you tell me about Herman? Driver's license info? Car license number? When did he arrive?"

The guard checked his chart. "About nine-thirty am."

In less than a minute, I had a driver's license number and car make and model.

"Thanks." I took off for the brick building. I placed a call to James on the way.

"What?" he answered.

"Doesn't anybody say *hello* anymore?" I asked. "I miss those simple courtesies." Everyone was so polite in the old movies. At twenty-six years old, I was becoming old school.

James snorted. "You don't call unless you want something from my bag of DA tricks. I'm cutting to the chase. I'm busy."

"Oh, right. Congratulations on your new job." Even if he wasn't courteous, I would be. "It's well deserved."

"Thanks."

"But it's Saturday," I said.

"It's Saturday for you, too, and you're working."

"Truth. And I do have a request." I reminded myself to continue the niceties out of respect for his longtime friendship with Michael. And to show our past didn't matter. I fanned my face with my hand. A fire extinguisher could have come in handy right about now. "I'd appreciate it if you'd run a plate for me, which should be connected to yesterday's homicide." I gave him the number. "A black Denali."

"I'll get to it." James disconnected.

I shoved my phone in my purse, only to have it ring seconds later. I recognized the number. "Oh, no."

CHAPTER 24

The Third Degree

"**W**hy didn't you tell me the police were swarming all over your duplex last night?" my mother asked.

"Because they weren't swarming," I said. "It was a couple of cops, and a false alarm. Who told you?" I knew the answer before I'd finished asking. She and Miss Trudy had a quaint, long distance friendship, even though they lived only ten miles apart. How they'd met, I wasn't sure. I don't think they ever hung out. Miss Trudy cut me a deal on the rent, thanks to Mom, so something was going on between them.

"Trudy told me everything," Mom said. "Honey, didn't you think I'd be worried?"

I didn't need to see her to know her right hand was pressed over her heart.

"I drove right over, but you'd already left."

I could hear Mom's heels skipping across her kitchen tiles.

"Trudy said a mysterious, good looking bearded man was watching your place."

"Well, between you and me, I think Miss Trudy has a vivid imagination." No way did I want to tell my mother anything. Who knew what she'd do in the name of motherly love?

"Trudy doesn't need an imagination. She's seen it all."

"By flying the friendly skies?"

"And she's got a great memory," Mom said. "We're talking about a woman who's memorized all her credit card numbers and the lyrics of every Simon and Garfunkel song ever written. Believe me, she's got all her marbles and they're as hard and round as ever. Where are you?"

"At the studio, catching up on some work. I'm wearing the green silk top you gave me."

"Oh, I'll bet you look fabulous. Did you get a look at the handsome bearded guy?"

"No, like I said…"

"Don't forget who you're talking to, sweetie. My lie detector works through the phone, as well as in person."

I gritted my teeth. "How do you do that?"

"Years of practice. Give me a description."

"Tall, broad shouldered…"

"Uh-huh."

"Bucket hat, sunglasses and the beard."

"You're not investigating anything, are you?"

"Of course not." I nearly ducked in anticipation of her response.

"Come over for dinner tonight," Mom said. "Bring Michael and anyone else who wants to eat. I have a sheath dress you'll love. And matching shoes."

When Mom dangled pieces of her high-end wardrobe my way, it meant she wanted something, usually a signed confession from me. Since she was the West Coast buyer of European designer clothes for Saks Fifth Avenue, it also meant I couldn't resist. "Okay, see you later." Besides, if I didn't cave, she'd show up at my place. It wasn't safe at the moment, so it worked out for us both.

I disconnected and continued my journey to the brick building. The nice officer who'd been guarding the entry was MIA. I explained who I was to the new guy.

"Can't go in," he said.

We went back and forth a few times, but he wouldn't

cave. I stormed off and landed at the back entry. Officer Ramirez stood by the door.

"Hello," I said to him.

"Hey. Are you looking for Detective Sorkel?"

"I'd like to go upstairs. I think I might have left something in one of the rooms."

Ramirez' face fell. I could see the gears turning in his head.

"I'll be quick," I said.

"Give me a minute," he said and disappeared inside.

A moment later my phone rang again. I answered on the first ring.

"Mom, I really—"

"A hello would be nice," James said in a low voice.

"Oh...hello...how's...hi." I spoke with the calm of a monk in meditation who suffered from a slight stammer now and then. "I'm...I guess, I'm glad... it's you." I meant that last part.

"I'm glad it's you, too," he said in the same, low voice.

It was as if he stood next to me, gaze boring into mine. I cleared my throat. "Thank you." Then I realized why he was calling. "You have information on the plates?"

"Belongs to a Sergio Rivera who lives in Santa Monica. He reported it stolen a few days ago."

"Did you tell the cops about the stolen plate?" I asked.

"Before I called you."

"I appreciate your help." My self-possession had returned. James couldn't yank my chain like he used to do.

"You're at the studio investigating," he said.

"Where else would I be?"

There was a moment of silence before he spoke. "I can be there in thirty minutes."

Ramirez returned with another officer.

I whispered, "I'm with a cop. Talk later." I disconnected.

"I'll escort you upstairs," Ramirez said. "What did you lose?"

"What?" I asked. Then I remembered. "Oh my...a bracelet."

The other officer stood watch by the entry, while I followed Ramirez inside.

"I'll help you search," Ramirez said.

He looked so earnest in offering to assist that I felt guilty about lying. That lasted a whole three seconds. Lying was indispensable for survival and progress in the PI world. I was not the harmless butterfly with "eyespots" on my wings to confuse predators into thinking I was a tough owl. I *was* the tough owl.

Ramirez led us to the room where Sorkel held the crewmembers and me for questioning. It was pretty bare, so we swapped it out for the room where Shaw's body had been found. As we neared the door, I noticed something was off.

I pushed past Ramirez. A cop and two plainclothes officers stood near the window. The room was clean, like nothing had ever happened. "Where is everybody?" I asked.

"We're done here," the uniform said.

"So quickly?" The two in plainclothes tossed me a glance and exited. "Crime scene investigations involving homicides take days."

"The investigator worked through the night," the cop said. "She and her team got everything they needed. They did the scene briefing and walk-through. It was signed off by the lead investigator thirty minutes ago. All and all, pretty straightforward. Clean-up'll be arriving soon. You with the force?"

I shook my head. "The studio."

He nodded to Ramirez and left the room.

I stared long and hard at Officer Ramirez. His sincerity didn't waver. The only time a murder is straightforward is when the killer is caught in the act. "Where's Sorkel?"

"Headed for that actress's home. The one the deceased lived with."

I took a slow spin around the room.

"Cause of death?" I did a visual of the ceiling.

"Multiple stab wounds," Officer Ramirez said. "Should we be talking about this?"

"Probably not." My gaze collided with Ramirez' large

baby browns. "Why the hurry to get the crime scene unit out?" I stepped to the window. The Mercedes I'd seen earlier was gone.

"I'm not sure."

"Was there a studio executive here this morning?" I opened the top drawer of the desk.

"I don't think so."

"There was a Mercedes parked outside." I shut the empty drawer. "Earlier."

"Oh, that belonged to Burton Kramer. He left before you showed up. We forgot to look for your bracelet." He crouched and peered around. "Was it silver or gold?"

"Why was Burton here?"

"To prepare to resume shooting on Monday. I guess they found a replacement for Shaw Kota. Maybe your bracelet was bagged and removed by the CSI unit."

"Oh, yes. I'll check with them," I told him.

Ramirez straightened. "That's not really why you came, is it?"

"I'm here to piece together what happened."

"Isn't that our job?" Ramirez asked.

"Since this scene was shut down so rapidly, I assume evidence was found leading to a possible suspect. Is that true?"

"I really can't say."

"Who is it?" I asked.

He clamped his lips together.

"This is getting old, Officer Ramirez. I'm going to find out soon enough. Why not save me the trouble? Please?" I smiled.

He shook his head.

"Don't you want me to quit bugging you?"

"You're not bugging me. I like your company."

"Why can't—"

My phone chimed to indicate a text from Michael.

Lacy's in trouble. Please come.

I looked up at Ramirez. "It's Lacy Halloway, isn't it?"

CHAPTER 25

She's Done It Now

I arrived at Lacy's house to find police vehicles had claimed the spots in the driveway, leaving me to hunt one down through the thicket of cars parked on Coast Highway. Finding an empty spot on a summer afternoon was like detangling knotty hair with a mascara wand. I finally managed to squeeze my BMW into a slot newly vacated by a motorcycle. I hiked along the highway, one eye on oncoming traffic and the other nabbing snippets of beach life between the ritzy houses. Sand and sea teemed with Gidgets, Moondoggies and families who'd braved traffic and crowds from inland LA to sample a bit of smog-free, salty air.

Fifteen minutes later, I'd stepped through Lacy's front gate and crossed the threshold into the whiteness. Sorkel was suited up as before, but this time in a light gray number with a navy tie. Men in black loitered at the top of the stairs. Lacy sat in the middle of the sofa, arms crossed against her chest, lips pressed together. Michael perched on the armrest by her side.

"What's new?" I asked Sorkel.

"I've never understood why muzzles aren't part of standard law enforcement gear." He whirled around to face me.

"A janitor claimed he spotted Lacy in the building where

it happened." Michael stood. "Right about the time of the murder."

"That's it?" I cut a glance to Lacy. She rolled her eyes. "She wasn't the only one in the building at the time of death. Motive?" I asked Sorkel.

"How about this?" Sorkel said. "Shaw was holding up production and racking up the costs, which made her furious."

"That made Burton Kramer furious, too," I said.

"And we found this," Sorkel held up a black feather. "At the back entry. She admitted she has a black ostrich feather boa."

"Who wears a boa to commit a crime?" I asked. "They're always shedding."

Lacy hissed out air between her teeth. "*If* I wanted to kill someone, there wouldn't be a stitch of evidence left behind. I was there, but it was later... Mister Bean here..." she flicked her gaze to Sorkel. "...isn't taking the timing into account. I got there after it happened." Her voice dropped to a whisper at the end.

Despite the warm weather outside, Lacy wore a black, long sleeved dress with a sheer tropical cardigan. Red lipstick tried to liven up the straight line of her mouth. She scratched the side of her lip with a pearly pink fingernail. A half-filled bottle of white wine sat on the table in front of her, so did an empty glass.

"What about the note Lacy received in the manila envelope?" I asked him. "We gave it to an officer sitting across the street."

"A forgery," Sorkel said.

"What about Calvin? Has anyone found him yet?" I asked. "Maybe he wrote it."

"Why haven't I thought of it?" Sorkel turned on me. "You'd go really far...if you could curb your adolescent instincts."

"May I speak to you in private, detective?" I folded my arms against my chest.

"Why would I—"

"Thank you." I turned and made my exit. I waited by the tree fountain. Sorkel joined me moments later. "Was there anything in the kill room linking Lacy to being in there when Shaw climbed inside?"

"I'm sure as heck not sharing police evidence with you," Sorkel said. "How do you like that?"

"I dislike it very much," I said. "I'm going to guess the answer is no since she's not been arrested."

"I think Miss Uncongeniality is highly capable of murder." Sorkel shook his head.

"I was in the front of the brick building, as you know, before and after it happened. I would have seen something." I knew Lacy had been near enough to play a hand in the murder. But was she quick enough to change her clothes and return to the stage? "Did you find a hair sample, prints, anything?"

"Everything's been collected and sent to the crime lab," Sorkel said.

"Corrie?" Michael joined us. "There's something I think the detective should see."

"Did you find a clue?" I asked.

"No, but you did," Michael said to me. He held a large manila envelope in one hand. He opened it and slid a piece of paper out.

"Michael, no," I said. "You shouldn't—"

"This was the man following Corrie on the lot yesterday." Michael showed Sorkel my sketch. "He tried to run us down in Hermosa Beach, and he hacked into her home security camera last night."

I mentally braced myself for the well-deserved criticism of my artistry by Sorkel.

He grabbed the paper and looked up at Michael. He cocked his head. "Remarkable. You drew this?"

"No, she did." Michael pointed to me.

Sorkel placed his index finger against his thin lips and gave a headshake. "I had no idea."

"Pretty good, huh?" Michael grinned.

"I didn't know you were a stick figure artist," Sorkel said to me. He puffed out his cheeks. "Listen, I want you two back at the country club or whatever cocoon you emerged from—"

"One more thing…" Michael dug into the envelope.

I had to tip my hat to Michael in the persistence department…even if it was slightly misplaced.

"You're kidding me. I should lock you two up for impeding the lead detective's investigation of a homicide."

"Wait a minute," I said to Sorkel. "You know very well that the point of a sketch is not to make an identical match, but to offer particular features, or a resemblance. To jog a witness's memory."

"There's nothing unique about that sketch," Sorkel said.

I held the sketch up. "Note the facial hair. Patchy around the mouth and chin."

"You may not know this at your tender age, but facial hair is easy to eliminate," Sorkel reminded me. "That's not going to help."

"What about facial shape? Kind of like a diamond. He can't get rid of that. Or the pointy chin. Or the gaunt cheeks."

"You do realize you're going nowhere with this?" Sorkel said. "Look, I'm not just criticizing your artistic skills. Because they are terrible." He shrugged. "But how close were you to this guy? Fifty yards?"

"About twenty to thirty paces," I said.

"That's close enough," Michael added and held out another sketch. "What do you think of this one?" he asked Sorkel.

"Not bad," Sorkel said. "Not bad at all. He bears a striking resemblance to…a guy I saw on the street." He gave a slow nod. "What street was that?" He snapped his fingers. "Sesame Street. He's a muppet." Sorkel snickered. "Is that chia seed grass growing on his head?"

"He does look like a muppet." Michael peered closely at the drawing. He turned to Sorkel. "What's really incredible is that this sketch was used by police in Texas to apprehend a guy on charges of aggravated robbery and burglary. Does the name

Gerry Manderling ring a bell? Look him up. Or better yet, check with El Paso PD."

I stared at the El Paso sketch. It made mine look like Da Vinci had gently taken my hand and guided my pencil stroke.

"That's a joke," Sorkel said. "There are no brows or lips on this guy."

"Please note mine has both," I said.

"There's something to these sketches, Detective, like Corrie said." Michael held my drawing up. "It's the outstanding features that matter."

"Those lines by the way…" I pointed to two slants representing the hollows in the cheeks. "…are his prominent cheekbones."

"Give me that." Sorkel grabbed the two sheets of paper and took off.

"I scanned and sent a copy to James as well," Michael said. "To circulate around the DA's office."

"You did?" How embarrassing.

"You're a woman of many hidden talents," Michael told me.

If only this one had been left hidden.

✳ ✳ ✳

Since the police had no hard evidence, Sorkel and his team took off, and I joined Lacy on the sofa. Sylvia leaned against a kitchen counter. Michael and Basil kept her company.

"What else?" I asked Lacy. "Anything about Shaw you want to share?"

She poured herself a glass of wine. She took a sip and spoke slowly and softly, "He played small parts in a few Indian films, but acting wasn't his passion. He'd been working on a science project, an important one. Shaw created a special type of protective clothing. He didn't say too much about it."

And neither would she until she felt like it. All was quiet

for a few beats.

"That explains the science magazines in the closet," Michael said.

"Any more ideas on the notes?" I asked her.

She chugged down the rest of the wine in her glass. "*RA* could be a research assignment that somebody thinks I know about," she said. "But I don't."

"What if *sit-O* referred to a place Shaw like to sit and ponder?" I asked. It was a stretch, but I needed Lacy to continue talking. I was hoping she'd say more with a little help from the wine. "Was there such a place? Maybe under an oak tree?"

"Maybe *RA* stands for rest area," Sylvia said. "He liked to sit on the bench by the fountain in the courtyard. The fountain looks like an oak tree."

"Maybe something's hidden there," Michael added.

"Let's go see." Sylvia hurried to the door. "I'll get a shovel."

Michael followed her out the front door. Basil and I slid closer to Lacy.

"What if *RA* stands for really alive?"

Her head snapped in my direction. "Is this some sort of revenge for something you imagined I did?" She rose, swaying a bit, and glared down at me. "You're stooping."

"I'm trying to help." While she was trying to drive me nuts.

"By torturing me? Don't make up things you think I want to hear. Even if I'm not always the easiest person to get along with." She burped.

I stood. "I need the truth…"

"Ask and I'll tell."

She poured more wine and reclaimed her spot.

"Why did you bring Shaw over? Why him?"

Lacy closed her eyes. "1978. He reminded me of an Indian youngster I'd met in New Jersey that year. The boy had invented something useful that I didn't take seriously. Credit for that invention ended up going to somebody else. The youngster got nothing." She flipped open her eyes. "Shaw was my second chance to make sure a contribution to humankind didn't get lost in the greed of others."

"You brought Shaw over with his invention to…?"

"Meet with the right people. Which he was about to do, before he was killed." Her glittery gaze locked on mine. "Now you're all caught up."

"Who was he meeting with?"

She shook her head. "He'd signed all sorts of confidentiality agreements. He'd met with a representative in India. The company was—"

"Pantheon."

Her gaze narrowed. "You do know something. Why are you peppering me with questions when you already have answers?" Her voice was on the rise again.

I took my place next to her. "Your answers help put the pieces I have together. It's called teamwork."

She turned her head away. "I'm result oriented."

"Burton Kramer was at the crime scene today," I said.

"I sent him there to keep an eye on things. Tell me something I don't know."

"I was there, too."

"Moving right along." She sipped her wine.

"Someone exited out of the Culver gate in a car with stolen license plates, right after Shaw was killed."

Lacy raised her brows. "And what are you going to do with that vital piece of information?"

"Give her a break, Lacy," Sylvia ambled through the front door, winding her way toward the kitchen. She fanned her face with a hand.

Michael plodded in after her, beads of sweat dotted his face. "Nothing is buried anywhere near the fountain. Except…" he pulled something out of his back pocket that squeaked. Basil scampered over to him. Michael knelt and gave him the chewed-up dog toy. "The gardener may have to do some patch work out there. Sorry, Lacy." He straightened.

Lacy turned back to me. "What about the stolen plates?"

I brought Michael up to speed, and said, "The guy I saw running away from the brick building could've used the car to make the getaway."

"Did you tell the police?" Michael asked.

I shook my head. "But I did let a certain ADA know about it. James told the cops."

"Why involve an assistant district attorney?" Lacy asked.

"He's my best friend, besides Corrie. He's been there for me ever since I can remember," Michael replied.

"And he's an incredible...resource," I added.

"We're still getting nowhere. You..." Lacy waved a hand my way. "Go away and make progress. You have meetings, starting at three pm, in my private office on the lot. Security will tell you where to go." She turned to Michael. "Back to our lessons." She headed for the stairs.

"On my way," I said and headed for the door.

"I'll be right there, Lacy," Michael said and turned to me. "I'll walk you out."

We stepped into the bold-faced summer day, full-blooded and hot. I dove into a patch of shade and updated Michael on my day.

His hazel eyes lit up. "I just thought of something. Lacy's put the word out that production's moving forward. Isn't there a small chance Calvin could show up to resume his stand-in role?"

Something in Michael's words nudged my little voice into talking, but I was a little hard of hearing. "Not if he was involved."

Michael walked me to my car and stared after me when I pulled out onto the highway. I threw him a backward wave and motored toward Ameripictures. I'd nearly made it before my little voice spoke again. This time I heard it loud and clear.

CHAPTER 26

Following Me

I trekked along the mostly deserted main drag of the Ameripictures lot. It was nice having the place to myself, if I didn't count a small crew of maintenance workers and a casually dressed executive. I wandered past soundstages and stucco buildings with chrome accents before landing in front of a grand, three-storied Art Deco structure. The building once housed legendary movie mogul and founder of Ameripictures, Otis T. Morton, original studio chief. Why Lacy liked to lurk among the relics in her spare time, I couldn't figure.

There was my little voice again, nipping at my ears, telling me Calvin played a starring role in Shaw's death.

An aging security guard unlocked the double glass doors and escorted me into a foyer with walnut colored walls. My heels tapped along terrazzo floors, composed of chips of marble, granite and glass. I glided past six polished Oscar statuettes, representing Best Picture awards won by Ameripictures back in the day. We paused in front of crystal-paneled elevators while the guard used a key to unlock the elevator panel. He pressed a button.

"213 is your destination. Door's open and your first appointment's waiting." He waved a white glove and shuffled off.

Moments later, I stood in an empty corridor with high

ceilings and white walls that showed no signs of aging. Tall, lush potted palms stretched their leaves outward. Natural light poured in from windows at either end of the hall, giving the place a cheeriness that made me want to skip my way to Lacy's office. A security camera faced an emergency exit on my right.

I entered an office mirroring the whiteness found in Lacy's home, except for the movie posters on the walls, and the woman sitting in an armchair across from the entry.

"We meet again." I strolled and took a seat on a small white sofa.

"What's the point?" Debbylynn planted a pout on her black lips. She wore a dark gray T-shirt over a puffy skirt and ripped fishnet stockings. Black army boots completed her weekend attire. "I told Lacy I had nothing more to say."

"Why did you come?" I asked.

Her gaze flickered sideways and back. "I have a job to keep. Lacy said filming resumes on Monday. She's found a new lead."

"How does that make you feel?" I asked, channeling Sigmund Freud.

"Glad for me, sad for Shaw." She hiccupped a sob.

"We can talk freely. I'm no cop, but I can use information you provide to determine what happened." I spoke quietly and even-toned. Any display of emotion was not coming from me. That was not the way to squeeze out answers.

"You're Lacy's private investigator. That's cool, but who cares? It's the cops' gig. And I know you'll report back to them if you discover anything." She reached into a large black handbag covered with spikes and took out a can of diet soda. She popped the tab open and took a sip. "Besides, I don't have to tell you anything."

"I thought you had nothing to tell," I said.

"If I did, I wouldn't." She put the can down on a side table.

I stood and slipped behind Lacy's desk. "How's Lacy going to take it if she finds out you wouldn't talk?"

She stopped drinking.

"I hear Shaw was more than just an actor," I said.

Debbylynn gripped the armrest tightly. "I don't know about that," she said quickly. "He didn't tell me anything."

"About what?"

Her face twisted. "I don't know."

I'd rattled a nerve. "What color socks was Shaw wearing when you found the body?"

Her eyes darted from side-to-side. "I wasn't looking at his socks."

"Lacy said he always wore patterned socks. He climbed in the window wearing argyle socks. He wore black ones when he was killed."

Her eyes widened. She crossed her legs and circled an ankle. "Well, he was nervous yesterday. He must have changed them after he climbed inside."

"There's something you're not telling me."

She shook her head fast. "No, there's not."

"Just how close were you two?" I asked.

She stuck out her lower lip. "He broke up with me, like two days ago. I was hurt and...angry." She wiped an eye with her finger.

"And now he's dead. Did you have anything to do with that?"

Her mouth dropped open, eyes slanted upward.

There was a loud rap on the door. It opened and Burton Kramer stared at Debbylynn and me.

"Am I interrupting?" He sauntered inside, lifting his chin by way of a greeting.

"Take a seat," I said and turned to Debbylynn. "I'll walk you out."

In the hallway, I shut the door to the office and headed toward the elevator with Debbylynn. "What do you know about Calvin?"

"Nothing."

"When was the last time you talked to him?"

"I don't remember."

The elevator door slid open. Debbylynn stepped inside.

She stared at the floor. "I told you everything."

"Good because you don't want to be responsible for anything else happening." The door slid shut. I spun on my heel and headed back.

* * *

"So," Burton rubbed his hands together. "Been to any basketball games lately?" He stood at the back of the room, next to a small bar.

"Did Lacy tell you why we're meeting?" I asked.

"I've got nothing more to say about Shaw, if that's what you mean. I'm just indulging a former studio star."

"Who's producing your latest film. I'd say you'd better do more than indulge Lacy."

He scratched the back of his head and opened a cabinet behind the bar. He took out a glass and a bottle of port. "I'll indulge myself in the meantime."

"Was Debbylynn temperamental?" I asked.

"All I care about is if she gets the costumes straight," Burton replied.

"Know anyone who might have had it out for Shaw?" I asked.

He held out the glass and swirled the liquid. "Lacy. She's got killer written all over her." He smirked and took a sip.

"She hand-picked Shaw to star in her new film, moved him into her home, and then killed him? Motive?"

"Maybe he turned down her advances. Happens all the time. Females in the same position as Shaw cave-in to unwanted advances by powerful, alpha Hollywood males, but when we men are harassed, we stand our ground. And we don't wait twenty years to whine about it. We act now. Shaw could've complained about Lacy, and the old bag killed him. Everyone knows she's hard to get along with."

If I wore gloves, this is the part where I'd take one off,

fill it with marbles and slap him hard across the face to knock some sense into him. As it was, I didn't have gloves or marbles, so I used my words. "I'm going to recommend Lacy replace you. Effective immediately."

"Good luck. She'll never find anyone else. And I've got a contract."

"Did you notice how quickly Shaw was replaced?" I asked.

"Yeah, but I'm still alive."

I slid in behind him before the sentence was finished. I grabbed his wrist and twisted his arm behind his back. In one quick move, his wrist was touching the opposite shoulder blade.

"Hey, what're you doing? Owww! You're hurting me."

"If you land in the hospital, Lacy'll need to replace you."

"You can't threaten me."

My grip didn't budge. "What do you know about Calvin? Did he get along with Shaw?"

"They were buds. Owwww."

I loosened my hold and pushed him forward. He rubbed his wrist and tripped back to the door. "We're done, right?"

"Have you spoken to Calvin?"

"No."

My eyes flicked to the door and he scooted out, nearly colliding with Rhoda. He backed off and raced down the hall.

"What's wrong with him?" She pointed her thumb over her shoulder.

"He's allergic to the cologne he's wearing," I said.

Rhoda was outfitted in a loose fitting chiffon dress that skimmed her ankles. She grinned. "I wish he wore it more often. He didn't say a word to me."

I didn't bother taking a seat. "What can you tell me about Lacy that you've not told the police?"

She took a tour around the office. "I don't like this room. It's cold, inflexible and filled with sharp corners. Just like Lacy." She covered her face with her hands. "I can't get the picture of Shaw out of my head—" Rhoda looked up and sank onto the armchair.

"How well do you know Debbylynn?"

"We met on the set. We're friendly, sometimes."

"Do you think she killed Shaw?"

"That was my first thought when I saw her kneeling next to him."

"Go on."

"She's got a God awful temper and..." she leaned into me. "I saw them arguing the night before, right behind the brick building."

I was beginning to think Debbylynn played a hand in the murder. "Any idea why?"

"I'm guessing she was mad about the break-up."

Mad enough to kill? "Tell me about Calvin."

She jerked her head up. "How did you know?"

My stab in the dark wasn't so dark, apparently. I sat across from her. "You talked to him?"

She nodded and wiped her nose with the back of her hand. "He rang early this morning. He sounded scared about a man that had been following Shaw and him."

"Did he tell the police?" I stood.

"No. He's hiding, but I don't know where."

"Why would he be followed?"

She shrugged.

"Did Calvin get a look at the guy?" I asked.

Rhoda squeezed her lips together.

"This is not the time to keep secrets. The killer could strike again. If he thinks you know something..."

"I...I don't, except..."

"What?"

"Calvin said the guy'd been hanging around the studio the day before Shaw died, and to watch out for him. The man has long hair and wears a hat. Cal hung up after that."

An icy stream trickled down my spine. "Did you try calling Calvin back?"

"Went to voicemail, every time." Tears welled in her eyes.

"Do you think I'll be next?"

"Call Detective Sorkel and let him know. He'll make sure you're not."

Rhoda sniffled and shuffled out of the office a minute later.

It was becoming obvious the guy in the fedora had been keeping an eye on Calvin as well as me. What did he think we knew? And how did Debbylynn fit in?

CHAPTER 27

Mistaken

I motored down Palos Verdes Drive West past Malaga Cove Plaza, a majestic, Spanish style building with stone walk-ways and brick arches galore. I whizzed along the winding curves toward Mom's house with the guy in the fedora on my mind. It was true; I'd not seen him up-close. It was possible he was in disguise to make it harder to ID him. I dialed James.

"Is there a fast way to do a background check on someone from India?" I asked him.

"Someone by the name of Shaw Kota?" James said. "Already done."

"Really? When?"

"Right after a certain sleuth threw logic out the window by mentioning she'd seen a Shaw lookalike leaving the murder scene after the real Shaw was killed," James spoke quietly, like he wasn't alone. "There needed to be an explanation."

"Sorry," I said. "For interrupting your weekend."

"You never interrupt me."

There was that flutter in my chest again, like butterflies flitting around. Fluttering feelings belonged to Michael, not to James. "Thanks for looking into Shaw's background. Any thing of note?"

"Not yet. I'll be in touch." He disconnected.

I rolled down my window and let the sea air rush head-long into my face. I closed it and called Michael.

"Please ask Lacy what she knows about Calvin. Where did he come from? We need details."

"Details are my specialty," Michael whispered. "Lacy's napping on the sofa. I'm memorizing my lines. How did the interviews go?"

"Calvin's been talking to Rhoda."

"What?" he raised his voice. I heard Lacy in the back-ground.

"For God's sakes, can't a woman get a little peace and quiet in her own home?" she said.

"I'll call you back." Michael disconnected.

❋ ❋ ❋

Twenty minutes later, I sat on a leather stool at Mom's kitchen counter, cramming tortilla chips dipped in guacamole into my mouth. In between crunches, I told her about Shaw, leaving out the part about my investigating.

"Oh, honey, you got it all wrong." Mom was gussied up in a blue and red floral print dress with elbow sleeves. Wedge sandals adorned her feet. "One of them is a diabolical twin who was insanely jealous over his brother's blossoming film career. He followed him here in secret after stealing airfare from a poor elderly couple on their way to temple—"

"Temple?"

"As in Hindu temple. The evil twin made it all the way to LAX for the sole purpose of knocking off the talented brother and taking over the starring role."

"But wouldn't he have knocked off the brother in secret and pretended to be him? That way there'd be no investigation." Listen to me, falling for her hypotheticals.

"Sweetie, there are no secrets these days." She plopped a scoop of chicken salad onto my plate. "I'm surprised the police haven't thought of that theory." She stared off into space. Her hair was pulled back with a black headband. "Maybe they already know about the brother."

"Did you ever offer theories like that to Dad?"

"All the time." She sat next to me. "Monty always said the same thing."

"That your theories belonged in old Hollywood movies?" Dad was a professor of Motion Picture History at UCLA before he switched careers.

"That I had a terrific criminal mind."

I bit my tongue. That was as far from the truth as the earth's core was from the sun. My mom did have a suspicious mind, at least when it came to me, but that was all she had.

"If I wasn't in the fashion business, that's where I'd be."

"In jail?" I asked.

Mom slapped my arm. "No, silly. In law enforcement, handing out speeding tickets left and right. I'd love that job."

This was the first I'd heard of it. "Is this about me? Because I haven't been busted…I mean I haven't gotten a ticket in a long time." Nearly six months was a long time. That was a record for me.

"What do you know about the bearded guy on your street?" Mom asked.

"Not enough," I replied.

"You're investigating this studio murder, aren't you?"

Here we go again. Mom was dead set against me doing any PI work, ever. Better come clean now before she found out later. "Mother, I've been focused on legal work and contracts. Then along comes our division's star performer demanding I investigate Shaw Kota's death. He was an actor in India and her godson, sort of."

Mom frowned and stared my way. "What star performer?"

"Lacy Halloway."

"The woman who says she was a tortoise in a former life?" Mom said.

"I told her I was sticking to my lawyer guns—"

"You turned her down?"

"Not exactly."

Mom crossed her arms and moved closer.

"It's not like I went out looking for criminal activity. It practically crawled up to me on its hands and knees."

"You should help her."

"I tried to get her to back off, I really did...what?" This was the last thing I expected from my mother. She'd been firmly steering me away from anything remotely resembling PI work ever since I'd assisted Dad on his cases.

She put up her hands. "I've accepted the fact that you're good at investigating. There's no denying it. You're a natural. Which makes it your civic duty to help the police in capturing the degenerate who took out that poor Bollywood actor. Be sure you cooperate with the police. Your father always did."

"Mom, are you all right?" I put a hand on her forehead. She felt cool.

"Of course, I'm all right." She pushed my hand away. "What I'm *not* is predictable."

"Is that what this is about?" I asked.

"It's about using your talents to help people who need your help."

Something was up. I stared at her long and hard. She plucked up a grape and popped it into her mouth. She avoided eye contact.

"Have a grape," she said.

"Look, I know all about it," I said. "Michael's been snooping around." I had no clue what was up with her, but she didn't need to know that. But if she thought I knew something, she might fess up.

Mom stopped, arm frozen mid-air with a grape between her fingers. Her eyes locked on mine. "Snooping around what?"

"Do you want to talk about it?" I asked.

"Not really," she said.

"When did you find out?"

"You first," was her reply.

I was stuck now. "A few days ago. You?"

"Last week."

"And you didn't tell me?" My blood started to simmer over a topic I knew nothing about.

"I wasn't sure," she said. "Until yesterday. I kept thinking it would turn out differently."

"How did you feel when you found out?" Gee, I sure hoped we were going somewhere with this.

"Angry, at first. Then strangely, relieved."

What the heck was she talking about? What big secret was she keeping from me? It could only be one thing.

"Just like I thought," I said. "Dad's alive, isn't he?"

CHAPTER 28

Fresh Starts

"Don't tell me you're back on that 'Dad is alive' kick again, because he's not. What does losing my job have to do with your father?" Mom's hands shot to her hips.

"You lost your job?"

Her mouth dropped open. "I thought you knew. You tricked me." She sank onto the sofa. "Technically, I was laid off. Who'd have thought after all these years…"

"I don't believe it. You okay?" I plopped onto the cushion next to her and took her hand.

"Sweetie, I made peace with my situation. After I gave them a piece of my mind." She grabbed a pillow and held it to her chest. "No more fashion week parties, no more front row seats at private trunk shows, no more nabbing designer clothes before they hit the rack."

I stood. "It's high time for a career change."

She stood and faced me. "That's exactly what I said."

"But not in law enforcement, right?" Not at her age.

Her eyes darted to one side and returned, attached with a smile. "I was thinking more like undercover work."

"Like a secret shopper?"

"Like a secret agent."

I snorted and stopped. "Like in the CIA?"

"That would be dangerous. Although, I wouldn't mind the travel. I meant, I could help you with your work."

"Seriously?" My legs tried to run, but my shoes had sprung fast growing roots securing me in place.

"No one would peg me for being a PI in training. I'd be undercover without even trying. You know, your father gave me quite a few pointers." She turned toward the window.

"Mother, I'm a lawyer, remember?"

"I'll help with your side jobs and watch your back. Then I'd never have to worry about you again. It's a win-win situation. I've got skills no one knows about yet. I'm discovering them myself."

No way was the one and only original helicopter mom going to be working with me. I'd go berserk. "Thanks very much for the offer." I uprooted my leaden soles and hustled to the front door. I'd expected Mom to follow, bent on convincing me about the PI work. But when I turned, she stood where she was, chewing on a fingernail and staring out the window.

"Thanks for coming by," she said. "I'm sure I'll find other meaningful work."

I slid closer. "You divorced dad because of his private investigator work. It makes no sense for you to travel that same road."

"I see things differently now." She left the window and glided over to me.

"I'll consider your offer. But I've got everything under control." I pulled open the front door and stepped outside. "I'm working with the police on this one."

She followed me up the cement walkway, past the rose trees, and strolled ahead to my car. I'd backed in, and the nose tilted slightly upward on the short-sloped driveway. "Thanks for feeding me, Mom." I caught up and turned to give her a hug.

She stared down the hilly street leading to the quiet cul de sac.

I joined her. "Are you expecting someone?"

"Huh? No." She tilted her head and gazed past me. "That's strange." She pointed to the hood of my car. "Why is it open?"

I turned. A small gap kept the hood from shutting properly.

She walked up to the front end of my BMW. "Why is the hood not down?"

I strolled over. My heartbeat took up a faster tempo.

"When was the last time you opened it?" she asked.

I stopped. "Never. It must have come loose." Or someone had been inside. "I think I left my sweater in the living room, Mother. Mind getting it for me?"

"You weren't wearing a sweater." She took a step back. "Call the police."

I removed my cell phone from my purse. "Why were you looking down the street?" I asked. "Did you see anyone?"

She grabbed my arm and pulled me away from the car. "Well, I did see—"

"Wait," I said. "Follow me." We padded over to a stucco wall that sprung up between mom's place and the next-door neighbor's. "What?"

"When we were eating, a car drove up the street. A black SUV. Very slowly. It's a hill, but come on already. A kid could ride a trike up faster. Either the driver was lost or up to no good."

"Or visiting a neighbor." Or fiddling with my engine. "And?"

"He took too long to leave, but too short for a visit. So I figured, he'd stopped, did something and left."

"Did you see him park?"

"Across the street," she whispered. "He got out and walked to my driveway. I couldn't see him after that."

My gaze landed on my BMW. "What did he look like?"

"Long hair. Tanned face. He wore loose clothes like he'd gotten them out of his grandpa's trunk."

"Not bad." Her observation skills were spot on. "No hat?"

"No. But he had sunglasses. Aviators."

I gulped and stepped away from the wall. I headed for the car, but Mom grabbed my arm.

"Don't go near that ticking time bomb," she said.

"I have a strong feeling this guy's just trying to scare me."

"And if he's not? You think I'm going to let you get blown to smithereens right in front of my eyes?"

"You can always go inside. Or we could both blow, if you prefer."

"Be serious. I'll check under the hood." She stepped out in front of me. "Make that call."

I grabbed her arm. "No, I've done this before. Plus, home-made bombs do very little damage. At worst, I'll receive a mild concussion." I moved forward.

She held me back. "I don't want my daughter getting any kind of concussion."

"You think I want my mother to have one? Now stand back." I took a step forward.

"No." She pushed in front of me. "*You* stand back."

"Mother..." I caught my breath. A tall, broad-shouldered man had strolled up the hill. One minute there was no one, and the next minute, he stood in front of the BMW wearing a white bucket hat.

"Step away from the car," he said in a hoarse voice.

CHAPTER 29

The Hoarse Whisperer

"Who are you?" I asked.

He wore big, black shades that nearly wrapped around the entire top of his face, shielding his eyes. The dark beard was the only visible hair. The rest was hidden beneath the bucket hat. He was dressed in a blue button-down shirt and black jeans. This had to be Miss Trudy's stranger. What was it about men in hats and me?

He reached a hand to his neck and yanked out a long, silver chain from inside his shirt. The end was attached to a black badge holder displaying a shiny, silver shield.

"Department of Justice, special agent?" I read. He seemed kind of old to be a special agent. Fifty at least.

My mother stepped forward. "Check under the hood of my daughter's car, Officer. Make it fast, in case it blows." She grabbed my hand. "Come on, honey." She pulled me away, tottering off onto the street.

The agent hung around the front of the car a minute, listening, touching and eyeing the hood, before he lifted it easily with one hand. I stopped and dug in my heels. Mom threw out her anchor next to mine. The man fiddled beneath the hood.

"Well?" Mom said.

He turned toward us. He held a brown fedora. "This was

under the hood."

I stepped forward and looked up at the agent. "Pretty harmless, right? I mean, nothing's ticking. Must be some kind of a joke." I didn't want to worry Mom.

"Maybe he was scared off by this helpful officer." Mom stepped forward. She turned to him and smiled. "You arrived in the nick of time." She craned her neck around. "Where's your car?"

"I'm on foot," he whispered. "Didn't want to attract attention."

Mom whispered to me, "Meanwhile, he's got a beard that belongs on one of the Three Wise Men. As if that would go unnoticed."

"Do you know anything about the man wearing a hat like this one?" he asked me.

"He's been following me," I said.

"Because?" the man continued to whisper.

"I'm not sure," I said. "Why are you whispering?"

He faced me and pointed to his throat. "Laryngitis."

"You should see a doctor. But in the meantime, are you sure there's nothing else in that engine?" Mom asked him.

He nodded.

"You were in Hermosa last night staring at my duplex," I told him.

"I was called in to find a connection to a case I'm working," he continued in the same whisper.

"Did you find a connection?" I asked.

He shook his head.

"Yet, you followed me here." As soon as the words slipped out, I knew he didn't tail me. I would've spotted him before. That meant he knew where to find me.

"Still looking for that connection," he said.

"Would you like to come in for some coffee?" Mom asked him. "I can fix it to go."

He turned to Mom and stared at her for a while. She held his gaze until he finally shook his head. "Not while I'm working, thank you, Miss." He looked back at my car.

Mom whispered to me, "You'd think I was offering him bourbon."

"Do you have a card so I can call you?" I asked the man.

He tipped his bucket hat and walked off.

"Your name?" I called after him.

He took long strides down the road until he disappeared around the corner.

"I'm beginning to re-think my career change," Mom said. "Not that I don't want to watch your back." She straightened. "I'll keep watching."

I walked over to my car, knelt and ran a hand along the back bumper. I did the same with the front bumper. "Bingo." I pulled off an active GPS tracker in basic black, about the size of my palm. The device had been slipped into a sleeve containing magnets stuck to my bumper. I stood and Mom joined me.

"He followed you here?"

"Looks like it." I bent over and examined the engine.

"What are you looking for?" she asked. "You think he was lying?"

"I need to see for myself."

"Since when do you have any mechanical skills?"

"Since…never," I replied.

"Then how would you know if something was wrong?" Mom asked.

I dropped the hood. "I wouldn't. I was looking for traces of something that didn't belong. Like a piece of wire, a thread…" I moved closer to the driver's side. "I'm going home." I dropped the hood and brushed my palms together to dust off the engine grime.

"Give me a second to grab my purse."

"You are not coming with me," I told my mother.

"Never mind, I don't need my purse," she said and hot-footed it to the passenger side.

"Michael's got my back. So do James and Veera."

"Okay." She marched over to my side and placed a hand on

my shoulders. "You got this."

"Wow. That's a first. Thanks, Mom."

"But I'm still coming."

I blew out a puff. "I'm going home and staying put. I'm not going out again this weekend. If I do, I'll check-in."

"Having a special agent involved bothers me," she said.

"If you want to help, I have an assignment for you," I told her.

Her brows shot up. "You do?"

"Call the Department of Justice and find out whether the agent was for real."

"I'm on it." She gave me a quick hug and took a few steps before stopping. "It's Saturday. They won't be open."

"You'll find a way. Start with the public safety department."

She nodded and tottered to the front of her house.

* * *

I checked my place thoroughly for signs of entry when I got there. I'd locked it up tight when I left, and Michael had rigged booby traps to alert me to uninvited guests. No signs of any intruders, lucky for them.

I kept the blinds closed that night and the next morning, taking peeks outside periodically. Not that I'd spot the special agent or the fedora guy unless they wanted me to. But if I did it enough times, I'd be bound to see something, like when I spotted the agent yesterday.

Michael called to give me an update.

"We were working on my lines when Lacy decided it was bath time, for her, not for me," he said. "That's when I asked about Calvin. Stand-ins are hired through central casting. They choose someone the same height and look as the lead, but that's not what happened with Calvin. Shaw brought him in, with no background check. Lacy said Calvin followed directions, and that's all that mattered in a stand-in job."

"You'd think she'd have something more important to share about Calvin," I said.

"If she wanted to," Michael added.

I updated him on what happened at Mom's.

"I'm coming—"

"Don't you worry about me. I'm armed and dangerous. Plus, that special agent has eyes on me."

I convinced Michael, by promising I'd check in periodically. I disconnected and slipped into my pistol-toting bra, strapped on my shuriken belt, and inserted the artillery. I dared any one with criminal intent to cross my path.

Mom called to tell me she hadn't made progress yet, but she had an idea of how to speed things along.

"It's a trade secret I picked up from my ex-trade. Tell you later." She disconnected.

I surfed the Internet for information on Shaw Kota. I had zero luck. But I had a surprise visitor.

The doorbell rang when I took a break to watch Bogart in *The Petrified Forest*.

"Open up, Corrie. It's me."

I hopped up and yanked open the door. James stood there in all his handsome glory. I stepped back, leaving the door ajar.

"Are you coming in or just decorating my doormat?" I turned my back and pictured Michael. The good, kind, exceptional safety net of a man who was always there to catch me, and who'd honed practical talents I lacked. I glanced over my shoulder. James stood pinned to the doorstep.

"Do you have information for me? Or are you checking in 'cause Michael asked you to?" I fixed my gaze on my laptop where Bogart was preparing to make a run for it in the desert. I paused the flick and cut my stare to James.

He stepped inside and tossed a paper onto my coffee table. "I've found our man."

"Which one?" I picked up the papers. The page was a scan of an article from the *Mumbai Economic Times* with the headline, *Pantheon signs MOU with Tutu Advanced Technology to Jointly Make Anti-radiation Components.*

"I'm sure this is going somewhere," I said.

"Keep reading 'til you get to the quote," James said.

I skimmed the piece and stopped at the fourth paragraph. I read it out loud,

"Our agreement with Tutu Advanced Tech deepens our industrial partnership with a global technology leader in India. We are joining forces to achieve a vital vision." I caught my breath when I read the name, "Theo Wetzel, Pantheon Vice-President of Intelligence."

"Don't stop there," James said, breathing slow and steady.

I dipped in some more until I reached the next quote, "The collaboration with Pantheon is in keeping with our other partnerships in the defense sector, said Anil Kota, Vice President, International Relations of TAT." I looked up. "Holy what?"

"I'll let you know if I find anything else." In three steps James was out the door.

"James." I scooted to the open doorway.

He turned to look at me over his shoulder, which made me a tad self-conscious. Had I even brushed my hair today? It was in its wild state, half up and half down, spilling just past my shoulders. I tucked a stray strand behind my ear.

"Thank you, " I said. "This must've taken a while to unearth." I touched his shoulder and he pulled away.

"The good stuff's always buried." He continued to stare with his jungle green eyes. But there was something different about him.

"You okay?" I asked.

He pressed his lips together. "I'm fine. I'm..." He took a step closer.

"Yes?"

He dropped his chin and flicked it up moments later, his eyes watchful. "I'm not doing this anymore."

I felt a declaration coming on. Did I want to hear it? "Doing what?"

"Going to be involved in your investigations."

"Fine," I said.

"I've got a new job and with a little luck, I'll be more than just an ADA in the very near future." He shoved his hands on his hips. "I don't need to get mixed up in any more off the grid activities. I'm done with distractions. Understand?"

"You're cutting me loose." No problem.

"I'll answer questions when I can." His mouth softened slightly.

"Appreciated."

"You and Michael seem...happy," James said.

"We are."

"I'm glad," his voice dropped a notch.

And with that as his parting remark, James slogged down the short staircase. I closed the door and leaned my shoulder against it. There was a time he'd given me so many goose bumps, it took days before my skin lied flat again. I had no goose bumps today, just a deflation, like a helium balloon hovering between sinking and flying. No sinking for me today. I had work to do.

In two strides, I landed on the futon and studied the paper. I debated calling Lacy, but decided against it. I needed facts, not fiction. I slipped behind my laptop and cruised the Internet for news about crime in India, using Shaw's name. I came up empty. So did my other searches.

I lay on my side and dozed off. When I woke up, it was morning. I took a quick shower, towel dried my hair and resumed my surfing. This time I threw in Shaw's name and *engineering*. Still nothing. I added the name, Anil Kota. More nothing. If James could dig deep for facts, so could I.

I whiled away an hour or two until I tried an uncle and nephew search. Lacy had mentioned protective gear. I added those terms to my search. That's when I hit pay dirt.

CHAPTER 30

The Con

B uried on the sixth page of my internet search was a piece
from an online publication, *Delhi News,* featuring a photo
of a quartet of men standing together, all eyes aimed
at the lens. Two smaller guys sporting facial hair and button-
down shirts stood to the side of a man wearing what looked
like a space suit. But it was the fellow standing next to him that
made me sit up. Taller, younger, and slimmer than the rest of the
men, he was Shaw right down to the V-neck pullover sweater
and Chuck Taylors, not to mention the silver cuff he sported on
his left wrist. The caption read:

Con Men Use Space Age Technology to Scam Investor

The article was dated six months ago and mentioned an
uncle and nephew that scammed an investor to the tune of...

"Fourteen million rupees?" I read out loud.

Ten seconds later, I'd discovered the scam amounted to
nearly half a million in U.S. dollars. The men included an uncle
and nephew who'd feigned discovery of protective clothing.
The names of the con artists were being withheld pending investigation. Maybe Lacy had been Shaw's ticket to the US to
escape the police. Was she part of a new con? I shut the laptop
screen and paced the hardwood floor. The Shaw I'd witnessed
seemed to be a pretty good actor when it came to looking

scared. Unless, of course, he really was scared. I kept my head down and continued pacing. Someone had followed him to Los Angeles. Someone he'd stolen money from. Likely, the guy in the fedora. He could have been the investor, or hired by one, to find Shaw, get back the money and knock him off. With Shaw dead, why would the guy in the fedora hang around? Maybe Calvin was in on the scam and the fedora guy was after him now.

I resumed my spot behind the computer and studied the photo. I couldn't see the face of the person in the space suit. He could be Calvin. How did the uncle fit in?

A loud pounding shook my front door.

"Let me in," Mom said. "I've got news, sweetie."

I yanked off my shuriken belt and hid it in the closet. I didn't need any conversation starters with Mom. I pulled open the door, and she scuttled inside.

"You're not going to believe it. Good, you've got the blinds shut. You never know who's watching. Why are you still in your pajamas? It's nearly eleven."

"These are my workout clothes." I looked down at the drawstring jogger pants and V-neck tank top, both in light pink.

She threw a hand my way. "You should throw on some real clothes and some blush." She trotted to my kitchenette. "I was careful driving here. Instead of taking Coast Highway—"

"Mom, what's the news?"

She yanked open the fridge door. "After you left, I tried calling the Department of Justice. No emergency number, no weekend help at all. Then I remembered one of my clients, Hazel...I mean one of my former clients..." Mom bunched her lips. "...I still can't believe it. Anyway, she's the wife of a UN ambassador." She bent over and peered into my refrigerator. "You've got enough to feed...a gnat in here. When was the last time you went grocery shopping?"

"What about your client?" I grabbed her arm and led her to the living room.

"I told her about the guy at my house, and Hazel said she knew exactly who to call at the DOJ. That's what you get when you do a ton of schmoozing. She texted me twenty minutes later and confirmed no special agents were on assignment in the South Bay."

I couldn't help but be impressed with Mom's speedy information gathering on a weekend, no less. "What if it's a clandestine mission? No one would know, including an ambassador's wife."

"I didn't think of that."

"What country did Hazel's husband represent?" I asked.

"A few..." she chewed on the tip of her nail. "Morocco, I think. Before Hazel's husband was an ambassador, he was a political officer at U.S. embassies in Istanbul, Rabat and the Maldives."

My jaw must have dropped because she placed the tips of her three fingers under my chin and pushed it upward. I'd never even heard of Rabat.

"Any of those places near India?" I asked.

"Good thing I have a globe in my office. *Had* a globe, I mean." Her eyes shot sideways. "Rabat is the capital of Morocco. Istanbul is in Turkey and the Maldives are these beautiful islands right near—"

"India." I knew it. The universe was on my side on this one. "Would he happen to know anyone on the police force in Delhi?"

"I'll ask. Wait." She put up her hands. "Was the special agent from India? That could explain the beard."

"No, but the victim, Shaw Kota, was, remember? I found a photo of him in a Delhi newspaper."

"Why would he be in the paper?" Mom asked.

"It was a story about a possible con. I need to get the information verified. That's where your contact can help."

"See how much we can accomplish together? I'll call Hazel again." She sat on the futon and pulled out her cellphone.

"Mom, I've got things to do."

"I'll call now, and you'll have the answer in real time."

"I was going to go grocery shopping," I said.

"Good. We'll shop together."

I stifled a sigh.

"I'll go home eventually," she said, fanning out her hair. "You didn't have any plans tonight, did you?"

"Just a quiet dinner at home with my mother."

"Good girl." She pushed a button and placed the phone to her ear.

While Mom talked to Hazel, I texted Veera.

Meeting early Monday in our office. Can you be there at seven?

The answer arrived a minute later.

I'm nearly ready to go now. See you bright and early.

"Hazel's source called back," Mom said. "Word on the street is an agent or two connected with covert activity are in this vicinity. It's all hush-hush."

I was speechless. How did my mother go from fashion expert to federal agent tracker?

"Mom, you really are good."

"Oh, honey."

Fifteen minutes later, she literally held my hand in the supermarket, pulling me along as she replenished my food supply, giving any men crossing our path the evil eye.

It was a relief to return home. My paranoia piqued when I was with her. She cooked up a storm and my phone rang. It was Veera.

"I got news," she said. "Theo Wetzel is not just any high level executive at Pantheon. He's the head of Intelligence Services on the West Coast. His projects are usually done on the down-low. That's all I've got, for now."

"That's a lot, Veera. Thank you."

Mom did all the talking while we ate. Good thing because my mind was on the case. Most of the kernels of relevant info had originated in Shaw's bedroom, which reminded me that one item from his room needed closer examination: Shaw's little red notebook.

CHAPTER 31

Stepping Out

After I convinced Mom to leave, I thumbed through the red notebook Michael and I'd found in Shaw's room. Notes were scribbled in the first few pages. What had made him stop?

I eventually conked out on the futon and woke up just in time to slip into a pinstriped wool jersey dress. I added a few essentials to my handbag: a small pistol and pepper spray, disguised as lipstick.

I hustled to Ameripictures and blew into my suite five minutes before seven. Veera leaned against my office door in a lemon yellow skirt suit. Her hair was in loose curls, her lips bathed in pink gloss. The sweet aroma of warm butter and caramelized sugar escaped from the small cardboard box she cradled. Just what I needed. Saliva pooled in my mouth.

I held out my palm. "Hand it over."

"Are we meeting in here?" She looked around. "No telling when Marshall'll show up."

"We'll lock ourselves in." I unlocked my door.

Veera followed and set the box down on my desk. She removed the lid to expose four moist and gooey cinnamon rolls with a thin glaze of white frosting.

I gave Veera a run-down of the weekend and polished off a

roll. "I'm planning to tell Marshall I'm working on a project with Lacy."

"He's not going to be happy." Veera licked a finger. "No sir-ree. Lord knows he deserves it, always taking credit for all the work you do around here. Just promise me I can be here when you break the news. I want to see the look on his face."

"Maybe we should sell tickets," I said.

Veera burst out laughing and we bumped fists. She licked another finger and reached into a pocket. She pulled out a sticky note.

"I got a phone number for Theo Wetzel. In case you wanna call."

"Sounds like a job for Michael, a fellow intellectual." I texted the number to Michael, and asked him to call and find out about Shaw and Wetzel. "I need more help," I told Veera. "Do you think the head of studio security would let me view tapes of the Culver gate from Friday afternoon?"

"Don't the police have access already?" Veera asked.

"They're not going to share anything with me. I need to figure out a good reason to ask to see the tapes."

"Child's play, C. Tell him a black Denali dented your car door and drove off, and that your DA friend says the Denali plates were stolen. That's nearly all true."

"Veera, you make a better PI than I do."

"I learned from the best," Veera said.

I leaned forward for another roll, but Veera yanked the box away.

"Leave some for Marshall. He's going to be mad when he finds out about all this. We'll need to settle him down."

She had a point.

Veera flipped around, box in hand, and opened the door. She headed for her desk. I followed her to my doorway, just as Marshall popped inside.

He strolled into the suite wearing a mushroom colored suit; his gray-streaked hair carefully parted to one side, his bloodless face clean-shaven, as always. He aimed his dark beady stare straight ahead.

"Good morning, boss," Veera greeted him.

Had he already spoken to Lacy?

Marshall paused by my door. "We need to talk," he told me and continued on his gloomy way.

I dragged myself into his office. Veera followed and paused in the doorway.

"I brought cinnamon rolls for you," she said.

Marshall landed in his seat, turned on his television screen and pulled a file out of his briefcase. He slapped it on his marble-topped desk.

"Sit," he said, without raising his head. "Step out and close the door, Veera."

The door skimmed shut behind me and I took a seat.

"Did you...?" I started.

"I'll do the talking." He cut a sharp glance my way. Lacy hadn't wasted any time. He caught my stare. "Why were you in so early?"

"I didn't get much done on Friday, thanks to—"

"I know. I was here, remember?" He reached down and pulled open a desk drawer. He rummaged around and extracted a folder, which he slammed on top of his desk.

"Have you talked to Lacy?" I asked.

"Briefly. She'll be needing your services for a new project." He rummaged through another drawer.

"Are you okay with that?" I asked.

He straightened and gazed up at the TV screen. He grabbed the remote and switched channels. "You have my blessing."

"Great." I stood. "Thank you. I'd better—"

"And Adam's blessing."

"Who's Adam?"

"Didn't I mention him? He's the new hire. The new V.P. We needed someone since I've been promoted to senior V.P. and you're...occupied these days."

"Did all this happen over the weekend?"

"Irrelevant," he replied.

"Does Adam have a lot of experience?"

Marshall shook his head. "He passed the Bar a few years ago. He's been working for his family."

"In the entertainment industry?"

"They run a yogurt business."

If I were a geyser, this is the part where I'd blow my top, erupting scalding hot water four stories high, but mostly onto Marshall. "How can he be promoted over me before he's even started?"

"He's older. Just turned thirty."

"But I have more industry experience." I wasn't a newbie anymore.

"He's not as easily distracted."

My inclination was to grab the folder out of his hand and slap him over the head with it. But that's exactly what he hoped for. The man lived for drama like a seasoned theater critic. "Lacy is not an outside matter. You told me to keep her happy."

"I need someone whose full attention is on this job," Marshall said.

"If you didn't want me to work with Lacy, you could have said so."

He caught my eye and gave a weak grin. "Is something the matter?"

Damn straight, there is. I'd love to shove my shuriken into his button-sized butt. I stifled a scream and stormed out.

Veera waited in my office. I slammed the door behind me.

"Was he mad about Lacy?" she asked.

"Nope. He handled it well. By hiring my replacement."

"Your what?"

I should have known Marshall couldn't stand a decision he hadn't made. Even if it came from our top star.

There was a rap on my door. Veera opened it.

"Veera," Marshall said. "I'll expect you to work for Adam while Corrie's on loan to Lacy Halloway. Adam's our new V.P. He'll be here soon. I'm going to a meeting." Marshall left our suite.

Veera sucked in her breath and turned my way. "What's he talking about, C?"

"He's hired a new lawyer with zero experience." I grabbed my handbag.

"As a vice president? We'll see about that."

"Not today. I'm going to track down the security chief. I'll text you when I have information. Thanks again, Veera."

"You can't leave me here to work for Marshall and the new guy. I've got a bad attitude. No good ever comes from that."

"We can't let a highly objectionable situation shape our attitudes if we want to make progress. We'll hang in there. I've got a homicide to solve and we don't want to risk losing our paychecks yet."

"Corrie, when you coming back?"

I paused in my doorway. "I don't know." At that moment, I wasn't sure if I was ever coming back.

❉ ❉ ❉

The cool morning air and the bustling racket of morning traffic were welcome diversions from the office drama. I made a bee-line for security and nearly made it there when I got a text from Michael.

At stage ten, rehearsing. Not as bad as I thought. I left a message for Wetzel and he called back right away. Call when you can.

I switched direction. I had a quick stop to make before heading to security.

CHAPTER 32

Talent Scouts

I slipped into the soundstage and spied Lacy chatting with Burton Kramer. They stood redhead-to-hardhead in a dim corner. Lacy did all the talking. I scanned the room for Michael and spotted him slouched in a director's chair off to one side of the main shooting area. His hair was slicked back, his beard trimmed. He looked down at a script with a big smile pasted to his lips. I sauntered over to him.

"I'm not the guy you're looking for," he was saying over and over in different tones.

"You fooled me," I said.

"What?" He straightened up when he saw me and smiled broadly. "I'm having a great time. I'm so honored to be part of this cast. These are my people, my thespians. We're dreamers trying to build three-dimensional characters from scratch. Did I ever tell you I played a rooster in my kindergarten nativity pageant? Who knew? Cut me off please, or I'll just keep talking."

"Here you go, Mr. Parris." An intern handed Michael a steaming ceramic mug and a small bag before dashing away.

Michael held the cup out to me and whispered, "I asked for a hot chocolate with marshmallows, and a gingersnap cookie. Here they are. So unbelievable."

I surveyed the surroundings. "Everyone seems over

Shaw's death."

His grin vanished. "I know." He leaned closer. "Every time I think about Shaw, I feel terrible. He should be here, not me. I've been asking around. Shaw kept to himself, especially recently, but everyone says he was basically a nice, friendly guy."

"Anything else?" I asked.

"Yes. We're all grateful production's moving forward. We need the jobs."

"Michael…"

"Just playing my role." He grinned. "See, I'm a pretty good actor, after all."

I took a sip of hot chocolate. The sweet warmth swam down my throat stroking it along the way. My sugar high was going strong. "Did you make any headway?"

"You mean besides getting Wetzel to return my call?"

"How'd you do that?" I asked.

"Asked a senior faculty member at LA Tech who used to work at Pantheon. He gave me Wetzel's personal line."

"You're the man," I said. "What did he say?"

Michael lifted his lips to my ear. "He confirmed he had a meeting with Shaw about a project he'd worked on in India, but he had to cancel last minute. Then he wanted to know why I called. I told him about Shaw's death and that I'm helping on the investigation. Wetzel said he never wanted to hear from me again and hung up. You smell nice."

"Any chance you can make him talk some more?" I asked.

"I can try. Here's something that doesn't fit. Debbylynn hasn't shown up yet. We were supposed to discuss my clothes. I mean, my character's wardrobe."

"No one's heard from her?" I handed the hot chocolate to him.

He shook his head and took back his drink.

"She could just be running late. You've only been working an hour."

"An hour? Gee, more like three hours. I've been here since five. How's your day so far?"

"Oh, the usual." I didn't want to relive my meeting with Marshall. I updated Michael on my internet findings and reached into my handbag. "Don't know if Shaw's activities with Pantheon are part of a con or the real deal." I extracted the little red notebook we'd found in Shaw's room. "Here." I handed it to him. "Take a closer look. It's odd Shaw took the time to write details and then stopped." I looked around and whispered, "Can you figure out why? I'm heading to security to get some tapes."

"Maybe you should ask Lacy to go with you."

We both turned to look at her. She was done with Burton and was barking orders at two guys repositioning furniture. The scene was set for the interior of an office.

"You might be doing the set designer a favor," Michael said.

I gave Michael's hand a squeeze and aimed for Lacy.

"What the hell do you—?" She was in the middle of slamming a fist on a desk when she noticed me. "Take five," she told the guys. They dropped the desk and scuttled off. She planted her hands on her hips. "What have you got?"

"It's what I'm about to get. I'd like you to join me."

"Where and what for?"

"Do you know the chief of security?"

"Why?"

"I need to watch some videos," I said.

"I know someone better." She picked up her blue suede loafers and headed toward the nearest exit. "The security chief hardly ever gets off his butt. But the director of security coordinates red carpet events and keeps an eye on all surveillance cameras positioned around this septic tank."

I nipped at her heels. "We only need footage from the cameras around the brick building and the Culver gate."

"That'll make his job easier," Lacy said.

"Also..." I took bigger strides to keep up with her. She may have had a few decades on me, but she hadn't slowed down one bit. "...I need to know if a dummy is missing from the props department."

"Because?"

"One ended up on my street and I think it's connected to the Shaw case," I replied.

Her eyes darted from side-to-side. "I'll find out," she said quietly.

We stepped out under the cheerless summer sky. Dull clouds had suffocated the sun with no hint of a break-through. Lacy blazed a path for the commissary.

"Are we stopping to get breakfast first?" I asked.

She ignored attempted greetings from passers-by, except for one from an older man riding past in a cart. She threw him a head toss.

"Security is back there—" I said.

"Dan should be getting a bagel and cream cheese right about now."

"Do you keep up with everyone's schedules?"

"I'm the original busybody. How do you think I stay in shape?"

Lacy halted by the main entry. She checked her watch, but couldn't tell the time without her reading glasses, so I did the honors. She planted herself next to the door and stared at it until it burst open. A tall, fit guy strutted out, early forties or so, wearing a white dress shirt and dark slacks. His alert eyes and mild grin hinted at the Boy Scout he once was. Lacy responded to his greeting with a quick hug. It was surprising to see her touch another human.

"Dan, this is my..." she pointed to me and followed up with a questioning look.

"Girl Friday," I said. "Even though it's Monday."

Dan cut a stare to Lacy and clasped her hand in both of his. "Sorry about Shaw. How can I help?" He turned to me. "Nice to meet you, Miss Locke."

"How did you..." I started.

"I know all persons of interest on the lot."

"Person of what?" First the cops and now him?

"Do as she says," Lacy told him and turned to me. "Meet

me back here in an hour." Lacy took off.

With Dan's help, I had the information I needed in less than an hour. I also discovered that studio dummies often went missing. I waited for Lacy in the commissary at her usual private table. Veera texted me while I was waiting.

Adam is a dweeb. I don't even know what that means, but I know that's what he is. He gave me the third degree about you and asked how much longer you'll be working here. I didn't reply, but my paperweight accidentally fell on his foot.

I grimaced. Veera kept a large paperweight on her desk. It was shaped like a screw going through a ball.

I don't know how that hunk of metal fell. ☺ I can't work with Adam. This is one time I'm unable to embrace what I've been handed. Hurry up, will you?

I gripped my bouncing knee, bringing it to a standstill.

"What did you find out?" Lacy waltzed in and took the seat across from mine. She was about to clap her hands when a server showed up with a Bloody Mary and a basket of fresh rolls. After he left, Lacy sipped her drink and grabbed a pumpernickel roll. "Talk."

"A black Denali drove into the lot Friday morning. A camera followed the occupant as he got out, but lost him after he entered the recording studio."

"How do you lose someone with cameras everywhere?"

"Cameras aren't posted everywhere. If you know what you're doing, they can be easily avoided. Plus, the visuals aren't usually clear in videos. All I could see was the guy had dark, longish hair."

Lacy slathered butter all over the roll. She broke it in half and put one on my plate. "I'm not impressed. What else?"

"At about three, another camera showed somebody entering the brick building where the body was found. He'd entered from the back door and ran out about twenty minutes later."

"That's what I saw." Lacy sniffled.

"No way to make a clear ID using the tapes. It was a male

with dark hair. No one admitted seeing anyone out of place near the building."

"We need to talk to the pinheaded detective," Lacy said. "Snorkel. I had a dream he was withholding important information from me."

"The police don't usually share facts to outsiders in the midst of an investigation."

"Your father would never say that. He'd march inside the station, grab Snorkel by the collar, and find a way to get it done." Lacy gulped down more of the Bloody Mary. "And that's what you're going to do."

"Dad would never do that. And why would Sorkel share information with me?" I asked.

She stuck her neck out. "Wrong question. Anything else?"

"The Denali exited and made a left, which means he wasn't headed for the freeway."

"Maybe he needed gas first." Lacy grabbed another roll. "Or a donut."

"He'd want to dump the car and lie low. That SUV would be easy to spot."

"Okay, smarty pants. Where did he go?" She buttered the roll and ripped off a piece with her teeth.

"I'm going to try to find out."

"Try? Erase that word from your vocabulary."

"Have you always been this difficult?"

"I'm being easy on you, kiddo." She leaned across the table. "You want to see difficult?"

I leaned back. "Some other time. Any more ideas on what the notes meant?"

"Notes?" Lacy stopped mid-bite.

"*RA sit-O*. In the shoebox and on your doorstep."

"Meaningless!" she practically shouted.

"What about the Lacy Jean part? Is it true that's what Shaw called you?"

"A lot of people heard him call me that. Anyone could have written that note. His writing was easy to copy."

"Why would they?"

"To throw us off-track. Your father—"

"I know. He'd never ask such questions."

"No. He wouldn't waste time tracking the SUV."

"Why would you ask me to help when I waste so much time?" I asked.

"That's what I want to know." She finished the last of her drink.

"Tell me about Debbylynn."

Lacy dropped her head and scanned the room. "She's a Republican."

"Any information more relevant to our case?"

"I don't know every member of the cast and crew." She blew out a long huff.

"I found a newspaper article on the internet with a photo of Shaw. He was involved in some kind of a con," I said. "What do you know about that?"

"He was framed." She rubbed her temples and dropped her voice. "Shaw and his uncle invented protective gear for highly hazardous work. An Indian investor convinced Shaw to sign the rights over to him, for a tidy sum." She hiccupped. "The uncle refused. He wanted to partner with Pantheon. Shaw, being the honest boy that he was, told the investor about the competition. A story was planted in the press accusing Shaw and his uncle of conning the investor. They were arrested, but eventually released. Pantheon had backed off by then. I met Shaw just after his release."

I was speechless for a moment while the wheels in my head cranked. "So you brought Shaw over to meet with Pantheon again. Acting was his cover, so he'd go unnoticed. But the Indian guy did notice."

Lacy put out her hands and slowly clapped. I couldn't imagine a person more impossible to like. Except Marshall.

"It was a good cover. Shaw had acting experience."

"The investor's been trying to strong arm Shaw into turning the gear over to him," I continued. "Shaw didn't. That's the motive for the murder."

Lacy sucked in her cheeks. "Took you long enough. Where's the killer?"

"If you'd bothered sharing this information sooner, we'd be moving along faster." Assuming it was true.

She leaned in close. "I had higher hopes for you."

"You're impossible." I stood and left the commissary without another word. I didn't stop until I reached the Culver gate. I leaned against a wrought iron post and shook my head for a while. There was a good chance Lacy'd get rid of me before the day was done. Then what? I'd be saddled with Marshall and Adam. Steam jetted out of my ears. I was stuck. My compass lacked an arrow.

My phone rang from inside my handbag. I pulled it out.

"Hi, Mom," I said.

"Can you talk?" Her voice was muffled, like her lips were pressed to the phone. "I've got news about the victim, Shaw Kota."

"Go on."

"There was an actor by that name who had supporting roles in two Bollywood movies a few years ago. Both films tanked."

So he really was an actor? "Any background info on him?"

"You mean like a dossier?"

"That'll work."

"This is so exciting. It's like sitting on the edge of your seat all the time. But with meal and bathroom breaks."

"Sure, Mom. Thanks a million. Let me know what you find out." I disconnected.

I debated my next move until I spotted a female security guard slinking near the security booth. A passerby might've viewed her as just another guard. I viewed her as an opportunity to gather intel.

CHAPTER 33

All About Looks

T he shoulder of her bomber jacket displayed the studio guard patch. Her name was printed on the badge around her neck. I couldn't have asked for a better opportunity. She planted herself near the booth and stared down at a clipboard through her sunglasses. The guy in the booth poked his head out to talk to a driver of a vehicle trying to get in.

"Kimika?" I said.

She lifted her head. "Do I know you?"

I raised my badge and showed it to her. "We talked on the phone over the weekend, about activity at this gate, Friday afternoon."

Her dark hair was pulled back in a ponytail; her lips outlined in scarlet. Her eyes shot from my badge to my face. "This isn't a main entrance. It's not used much, 'cept for people who work this end."

"You let a black Denali onto the lot that morning. I'm interested in the driver."

"Can't remember all the faces coming in and outta here." She pivoted toward her booth.

"This driver was unusual."

She stopped and looked at me. "He got horns on his head?"

"It's related to the murder."

She exhaled and faced me. "I already talked to the cops."

"I spoke to Dan today and viewed the tape." The truth felt good. Like it belonged on my lips. It wasn't all that long ago where the opposite was true. "But my involvement is at the request of someone at the top. She wants her own take on what's going on." Kimika might think I referred to the studio chief and that was A-okay. It worked before.

Kimika waved a food truck in. "Why don't you just tell me what you want? Save us some time so we can get back to what we should be doing." She faced me, head on.

"How's your memory?" I asked her.

"Good. Really good."

"The Denali had tinted windows and a Herman Monk at the wheel."

"Okay."

I waited for her to elaborate. "And?"

"Just saying, I remember him."

"Remember any details?" I said.

Kimika moved away from the booth to the side of the entrance, and over to a patch of dirt where baby succulents were roosting. "He seemed uneasy. Out of breath. Overly nervous."

"You're aiming for the police academy."

She nodded.

"You're going to be just what they need. You're thinking like a police officer." I scanned the area around us. A camera from a nearby building pointed at the booth. "I think you may have seen the killer."

"This same Denali drove up earlier that day, and the guy inside barely rolled down the window to slip me his license. His name's on the list, so I let him through. Didn't think nothing of it. We get odd visitors. Eccentric, some might call them. At least he wasn't rude."

"Description?" I asked.

"Skin about the same shade as mine."

Like the color of the pumpernickel bread Lacy had nibbled on.

"A mess of black hair and aviator sunglasses," she added.

"Did you notice any tattoos? Earrings? A hat?"

"No, I didn't. But he wore gloves. And…" she stared past me. "…I remember a hat on the seat next to him. I bent real close 'cause I couldn't hear him through the crack. It was brown and made from felt. Like an old guy's."

There was that chill along my spine again. "What about when he left?"

Her gaze drifted along Culver Boulevard, tracing the cars shooting back and forth. "It was nearly the end of my shift. This time he rolled the window down 'bout halfway. He looked straight ahead, while the gate opened."

"Anything distinctive?"

"Both hands gripped the top of the steering wheel. He didn't wear gloves this time."

"Anything else?" I reached into my handbag and removed a piece of paper. I unfolded it. "Did he look like this?" It was the drawing I did of the guy in the fedora.

She started to laugh and stopped to look at me. "You're serious?"

I nodded. "Focus on his unique features."

She made a face. "He did have high cheekbones, like the face in the drawing. Yeah, this kinda does look like the driver. Never saw his eyes though."

I thanked her and left. I'd made a little progress, but had nowhere to go with it. And no office to retreat to. Which left me with only one destination. Back to the scene of the crime.

CHAPTER 34

The Revisit

I had no trouble getting into the brick building today. No one was posted inside or out. A guy whizzed past in the foyer, coffee cup in each hand. If I didn't know a murder had been committed, I'd never have guessed it. Business as usual...until I got to the office where Shaw was found. Vanderpat sauntered along the hallway, pausing next to each door, before moving on. The kill room itself sat dark and empty.

"Why are you here?" I asked him.

"Like I'd tell you anything." He stared at me with eyes so narrow they looked like cracks in old leather. His rough hands were balled in fists. He was the only leftover from the day of the murder.

"What's the matter, Vanderpat? Have I gotten into your head too many times?"

"You wouldn't last two minutes in my head." Vanderpat turned his back to me and swaggered away.

I watched until he rounded the corner toward the back stairs. I slipped into the kill room and was stalled by the biting odor of cleaning fluid. I held my nose and flipped on the light switch. I knelt and examined the floor where the body had rested. Then I slid to the desk. I stared through the window, picturing Shaw racing for the fire escape. Someone had been waiting for him. Maybe not inside this room, but just beyond the entry. I inspected the hardwood floor. The position of the body had indicated Shaw's back was to the door. I stepped near the spot and sat cross-legged. The hard, coldness seeped through my dress and stockings. Vanderpat stuck his head inside the doorway.

"You appeared out of nowhere that day," I told him. I'd watched the entry. One guard came running, but Vanderpat showed up almost instantly. "You were inside the building when it happened."

"That's right. I had to use the john."

We locked eyes and would still be staring if Vanderpat hadn't gotten a call. He moved away and answered. I crawled to the doorway and listened to a few grunts and one-syllable responses before his voice faded down the corridor. I resumed my sitting position and closed my eyes. Shaw, or whoever, had lain facedown, back to the door, meaning he was likely taken by surprise. Or someone he knew had entered, and he'd turned to grab something. There'd been an awful lot of blood. The guy I'd seen running afterward would've had no chance to change his clothes. There'd be blood on his hands, not to mention his face and shoes. But the runner was blood-free.

A snort came from the doorway and my eyes flipped open. Vanderpat stood in front of me.

"Find anything?" he asked.

"Like what?"

"Who did it?"

"That's the burning question," I said. "In the meantime, where are the restrooms?"

"One stall upstairs and two down."

"Any showers?"

"This isn't a gymnasium," he replied. "What I want to know is why the big hurry by the police to get this place spic and span?" His ferret like eyes swept the room. "You know anything about that?"

I shook my head.

"Makes no sense." He turned back around.

So he was human, after all. I'd mistaken him for a block of cement.

"Any theories?" I called after him.

"None," he replied from the hallway.

I picked up my phone and placed a call. Would he talk to me?

"We're done, remember?" James answered.

"My memory's short," I replied. "Besides, I really need professional help. That would be you." I waited for his reply. When there wasn't one, I continued, "Why would a murder scene be cleaned up quickly?" I could almost see him tapping his fingers on his desk.

"It's a movie studio. Could be politics, could be because the show must go on. Time wasted burns holes even through the deepest pockets." There was silence for a few moments. "Or, there could be a blood or air-borne pathogen involved. If word got out, that would cause widespread panic, which could shut down not just the production, but the whole studio operation. Clean-up would need to be speedy."

I shuddered. "Okay. But there could still be DNA lying around," I said. "Isn't that worth further examination?"

"Are we done now?"

That was a loaded question. "No, we are not." I just gave him just the answer he was looking for. "We're talking about a murder, James. I'd understand if the killer was caught and the law had all the evidence needed, but that hasn't happened."

"You sure about that?" James asked.

"Is someone in custody?"

"I meant, are you sure we're not done?" James asked. His voice turned low.

I was anything but sure at the moment. I gulped. "I… how can I find out?"

"About the clean-up?"

"Yes."

"I'll check with the coroner," he said.

He disconnected.

Why was I flirting with Michael's best friend? I had a history of falling for the wrong guys. Hot and unsteady types. The ones in James' category. Here, I had the man of a lifetime, Michael, at my fingertips and I kept pushing him aside. Why?

Because you don't think you're good enough for him.

Little voices could be so irritating. "That is not true, any-more," I said out loud.

"Out of my way," A woman's voice rang out.

Muffled talk responded to her command. I rose and hur-ried to the top of the staircase. I peered down the bannister. I should have known. It was only a matter of time before she came here.

CHAPTER 35

Identity Crisis

"I was getting nowhere on the set," Lacy said when she reached the top of the landing. Vanderpat waited downstairs. Lacy's orders. "Nincompoops. All of them."

"What about Michael?" I asked.

"He's a natural." Lacy slowed down. "That apple pie sincerity of his would make anyone confess." She stopped and asked quietly, "Which room?"

I pointed. "In there."

"Where's the police tape?"

"They're done."

"Bullcrap. You uncover anything?"

"Not yet."

She flicked me a killer look and headed inside. She paused after she'd entered, eyes circling unsteadily around the room. She ambled toward the window.

"They cleaned the place in a hurry," I told her. "I'm trying...I'm going to find out why."

She wheeled around and faced me, cheeks flashing red. "You damn well better." Lacy turned on her loafers and stomped out.

I reclaimed the spot by the window, picturing Shaw

stumbling in, out of breath. Someone at the door had spooked him. Maybe he'd turned to dive back out the window and...too late, he was stabbed.

"No, that's not right," I said. The body lay close to the entry.

Plus, if someone had been waiting, someone Shaw didn't want to see, he would have turned around sooner and escaped.

Taking a giant step forward, I planted myself on the spot I'd seen Shaw laying, face down. I knelt, fought back a wave of nausea and unfolded into Shaw's last position. I lay on my stomach, resting my cheek on one hand, and faced the bookcase. Had Shaw died instantly? He didn't stand a chance if there were multiple stab wounds.

I stared up at the white bookshelves. The blood-mottled books had been changed out for a new batch that lined up neatly on each shelf, propped up by bronze bookends shaped like stars. I blinked and raised my head, zooming in on the inside of the bottom shelf. I shifted to a sitting position to get a better look. "What the—"

A floorboard creaked loudly outside the entry, intercepting the quiet. I twisted toward the doorway. A man stood there.

"You don't scare easily, do you?" he said.

I shot to my feet and faced the visitor. A pin-striped baker's cap replaced the fedora, but he'd stuck with the blue aviators. A nasty grin played between his hollow cheeks. Up close, his chin was more chiseled, his hair hung more wildly.

"What do you want?" I asked.

"To talk." He slowly circled around me.

"What a coincidence," I said. The hairs on my arms stood on end as he slunk behind me. I'd snatched a glance at a small tattoo on the inside of his wrist, shaped like an eye. An evil one.

"Who are you?" I asked.

"Introductions aren't necessary when two people aren't going to be friends for long."

Where the heck was Vanderpat? He'd been so accessible when he wasn't needed.

"Good to know you'll be leaving momentarily." I linked my fingers.

He continued his stroll and stopped in front of me. There was something dirty about him, like he'd crawled out of a shower drain.

"I'm not leaving until I receive what I need," he said.

You could cut the tension with a surgical knife.

"Why do you keep returning to this room?" he wanted to know.

"I'm attracted to places I shouldn't be in. You killed him, didn't you?" I hoped I sounded braver than I felt. There was no friction between my palms, thanks to all the moisture. I tensed my legs to keep them from shaking.

He reached a hand inside his jacket. Before it slipped out, I'd pulled my lipstick out of my purse and yanked off the cover. I aimed for his face and sprayed, tipping the lipstick so it hit beneath the shades, while I stepped back.

"Argh!" His hands rushed to his eyes and he pulled off his sunglasses. His head rocked from side-to-side.

I raced past him and torpedoed through the door, slamming it shut behind me. Stopping at the top of the stairs, I yelled for Vanderpat and texted Sorkel. Pepper spray should be good for a solid twenty minutes, but I wasn't taking a chance on this guy escaping.

Vanderpat stomped up the stairs. "What is it?"

"Call for backup. There's a man in there that tried to attack me."

Vanderpat pushed past me and opened the door. He gasped and rocketed out the door in reverse, as the guy in the baker's cap head-butted him in the chest. Vanderpat hit the floor hard, spread eagle, with the guy landing on top with a thud, a bandana wrapped around his eyes. He pummeled Vanderpat in quick succession.

I reached into my purse and pulled out my gun while the guy stumbled to his feet. He groped his way to the stairs. He'd made it to a few feet of me when I lifted my gun and bashed it against his head. He cried out, arched his back and toppled onto the floor. I shoved the gun in my purse and ran over to Vanderpat. He was leaning up on an elbow.

"You okay?" I asked.

He managed to haul himself up, head swiveling from me to the guy. "Took me by surprise."

"Ever see him before?"

"Never. You?"

"At the studio, last week. He followed me from the commissary to the Producer's Building. Don't know who he is."

Vanderpat shook his head. "Me neither."

Finally, Vanderpat and I had reached an understanding, upping our non-existent relationship a notch. The guy lay still for a minute, before lifting his head. He stretched out a hand, bracing it against the wall. I raced over and he froze, ear lifted in my direction. I tiptoed closer. He began a slow rise to a sitting position.

"You made a big mistake," he spoke breathlessly.

"You're the one who made the mistake," I told him.

The wail of a siren interrupted our debate.

"She's right, pal." A vein in Vanderpat's neck pulsed through his thick skin.

The guy in the cap braced his back against the wall and dragged himself up with a low moan.

"Who is he?" Vanderpat planted his hands on his hips and his squint on me.

The door of the building busted open downstairs. Footsteps tramped up the stairs, Detective Sorkel in the lead.

"We're about to find out," I said.

CHAPTER 36

The Color Red

The next forty minutes were a blur. Medics arrived and treated the guy in the hat. All I got from Sorkel was a snarl and a smart remark, "Why are you always in my face?"

"This is the guy who—"

"I can't play with you today. I'm taking this parasite to the station." Sorkel shot off with the guy in tow.

Vanderpat was briefly interrogated, but I was barely questioned, which is why I kept the clue I'd uncovered to myself. After the cops left, I took off, only to circle my way back to the building and sneak in through the rear entry. I padded up the narrow stairs and worked my way to the crime scene.

Vanderpat had locked the door to the room, but that only slowed me down. The door's old school lock easily clicked open with a pair of paperclips on loan from an office down the hallway. I straightened out the clips, jiggled them around in the lock, and in less than a minute, I was in. This time I locked the door behind me.

I hustled to the bookcase and knelt beside it, pulling out my cell phone from my purse. I lay on my side, gaze inching up to the top inside corner of the bottom shelf. And there it was. A small, oval shaped spot with spattering the color of blood.

Bright red blood. A remnant from Shaw's stab wounds the cleanup crew had missed. I took a few pictures and sent them to James. At this moment, he was the only ally I had with experience and know-how. I crossed my fingers that he'd find time to help again.

You're just using him, my little voice said.

"Not true. If it turns out to be related to the case, it could be a feather in his cap, and he's a big fan of feathers. It'll be good for both of us."

And where does Michael fit in?

"He fits in just fine." I huffed out the last word to push away the ridiculous thought flow in my mind.

Meanwhile, the light bulb burned brightly above my head. Blood is red...until it mingles with the open air for a short while, after which it gradually turns darker, usually a rusty shade. The blood on the bookcase was still bright, over forty-eight hours later. Real blood would have turned color by now. The blood was fake. Had all of it been fake? And who'd been lying in the pool of blood? Was that real?

I scrambled to the door and pressed my ear against the cold wood surface. Muffled voices floated through from a distance. I cracked the door open. The voices drifted along the hallway. I leapt out, closed the door behind me and made a beeline for the back of the building, keeping my head down and my heels quiet.

I tore down the rear stairs, casting a glance behind me. I pulled open the backdoor and smacked into something solid.

"Where you been? I've been looking for you."

"Sorry, I didn't mean to...it's you." I stared up at Veera. "Shouldn't you be in the office?"

"A girl's gotta eat, and this is my lunch break. Late, as it is."

I checked my watch. One-fifteen. "I lost track."

"Meals are one thing I never lose track of," Veera said. "Especially today. I'd been counting the minutes. Marshall took the new guy out to the commissary. Thought I'd look around for you first. The police let you in here?"

"No."

"You're snoopin'. That's the only way to do it. I saw old Vanderpat around front. That man has no personality. I'd rather have a split personality than none at all. Find anything?"

I took her arm and navigated away from the building. "Yes. But let's not talk here."

"I brought lunch." She leaned her head down to mine and whispered, "I got enough for the two of us and even Vanderpat, if he had something to offer."

"That's not going to happen."

"That's what I'm saying," Veera said.

"Memorial Park is a few minutes away," I said. "We'll go there."

"I like that place. All the trees and benches make it peaceful. Which means no one from the studio ever goes there."

We aimed for the Culver gate and were nearly there when I pulled Veera behind a tree. I pitched my chin toward the Otis building. Vanderpat lurked beside the side entrance. He turned his back to us and bent over. His arms moved like he was working the lock, or using a key. We watched until he slipped inside.

"What's that man doing now?" Veera whispered. "He's got no business in there."

"It's not easy getting inside without permission," I said. "Maybe he's got a key."

"Unless he's senior security, which we know he's not, he shouldn't have a key." Veera pulled out her phone and sent a text. "We'll get his butt kicked out of there."

We waited and watched until Vanderpat left the building, escorted by another security guard. We high-fived each other and exited out the Culver gate.

Ten minutes later, Veera and I planted ourselves on a park bench beneath a tree filled with leafy branches that twisted skyward in different directions.

Veera flipped open a large plastic container. She placed five heaping spoonfuls on the container lid and passed it on to me. "Cranberry chicken salad." Veera smacked her lips.

"Did you make this?" I asked.

"Last night."

I took a bite. "Delicious."

Minutes later, we were both done and licking our spoons.

"Next comes a combo dessert and fruit dish. It's part of my diet of having fruit with every meal." Veera opened another container. "Homemade funnel cake with strawberry sauce."

"Veera, I'd be starving without you."

"Good thing you've got friends and family who cook. Your mom, Michael, me...does James cook?"

"He sure does. But not with food."

Veera slapped my arm. "I know it."

James and Veera had met during my last investigation. Being a full-blooded female, she'd not been immune to his charms. I cleared my throat. We were way off track, like in the middle of the Indian Ocean. I told Veera about the guy in the hat and the attack. "I found something at the crime scene today. Leftover blood."

A body shiver ran up and down Veera. "That's no surprise. That was one gruesome scene."

"Except, it was fake."

"What was?" Veera asked.

"The blood."

She shook her head. "Looked pretty real to me. I get sick thinking about it."

"The blood spatter I found wasn't real," I told her.

"Did you verify that?"

"Real blood turns color after exposure to air. This spot was still red. It was in a hard to view place unless you were lying down close by. I'll show you." I pulled out my phone. "Uh-oh." My battery was dead.

"You were lying down? In that room? I don't believe it." She scratched her chin. "Could be the blood reacted with the material of the bookshelf. That's why it stayed red."

"Not likely. It was wood. Maybe...there's a chance...it was Shaw running away afterward."

She bit into a chunk of funnel cake and slowly shook her head. "That's far out, C. There were crime scene experts there, an ambulance, police...someone would have to know if something fishy was going on."

"The scene was cleaned in record time."

"You're saying..."

"It could've been staged," I said. Saying it out loud made it seem less possible.

"Have you ever solved a fake murder before?" Veera asked.

"This would be my first."

"I'm not saying I believe this theory, but if I did, how can a body be still for so long? That body looked real."

"Easy," I said. "There are muscle relaxants that can last hours, slowing down the pulse and heartbeat. There was one case where a man was pronounced dead and almost cut open at the autopsy before the ME realized he was alive." More tidbits learned from my father.

"Damn."

Veera's cell phone played a tune and she grabbed it. "This better not be Marshall." She stared at the number. "Michael. Now why would he be calling me?"

"My cell has no juice." I held up my phone.

Veera pressed the phone to her ear. "Your summer gig going well?" Veera sliced into another piece of cake with her fork. "We're sitting here bouncing around way out theories." She waited a beat. "Her phone's not working, as usual." She lifted the fork to her mouth. "What?" The fork dropped onto the ground. Her gaze caught mine. "Lacy just got a call from that detective. There's been another murder."

CHAPTER 37

Killer or Not?

"What murder?" I grabbed the phone from Veera.

"Corrie, where've you been?" Michael asked. "I've been trying to reach you. I'm still at the soundstage."

I could barely hear him with the commotion in the background.

"Someone killed—" he started.

His next words were drowned out by a voice on a loudspeaker, telling everyone production was wrapped for the day.

"What did you say?" I said.

"I said..." Michael raised his voice. "Someone killed Calvin." The background went quiet. "Really sorry, everyone." Michael spoke to the people around him, then lowered his voice and said to me, "Hold on. I'm moving outside." Shuffling, static and loud breathing were all I got until he started speaking again. "They found Calvin's body in a car in his sister's driveway. He'd been staying at her house. Lacy went to the station to see for herself. I told her I'd find you."

My fake blood theory was fading fast. Faking one murder was possible. Two? Not so much. My stomach clenched at the news. "That's terrible."

"There's more," Michael said. "They found the murder

weapon inside Calvin's apartment, the knife that killed Shaw."

"He just left it out in full view?" I asked. That couldn't be right.

"Inside a bucket. They think Calvin killed Shaw and then killed himself. They don't know for sure."

"Give me a little time to process this, Michael. Talk later." I disconnected and gave Veera back her phone. I stood and told her what Michael had reported. "Thanks for lunch, Veera. Gotta go."

Veera shot up. "I'm coming with. There's been another murder. I can't be babysitting those two self-important, stuffed suits."

"You've got to keep up our presence at the office, and keep an eye on Vanderpat. He's been sneaking around way too much for a studio security guy."

"You think he's the killer?"

"Let's see. He exited the brick building right after the murder, so it's possible, but why would he still be hanging around?"

"He's missing something he left behind," Veera said.

"Or something Shaw left behind." Finally, things were beginning to make more sense.

"What about the fake blood?"

"That could've been leftover from a previous scene filmed in that room," I said. Meanwhile, my little voice was screaming, *if Calvin killed Shaw, who's the guy in the hat?* I dug in my purse and unearthed a folded piece of paper. "I made a sketch of the guy in the hat." I opened it. "Find out if anyone's seen him."

Veera took the paper and blinked a few times.

"I know it's not the best—" I said.

"I saw him this morning when I drove in. He was leanin' against a pillar in the parking lot, trying to look like he belonged."

"Really? That means other people saw him, too." Veera was a great friend. She didn't even question my artistic ability.

"I'll get on it, boss." She placed the folder into her lunch bag. "You be careful."

"I will." I took off for the studio and wound my way back to my car, only to find a tall, hunky guy leaning against my door.

CHAPTER 38

Surprises

"You're the last person I expected to see," I said.
Even in a standard navy, two-piece suit and tie,
James looked like he'd climbed off the cover of a romance novel.

"You text me for help, and leave no way to contact you."
He reached out and yanked my handbag out of my hand. He unzipped it, and grabbed my phone. He pushed the unlock button.
"Dead."

"You're supposed to be working." I yanked back my purse
and phone. "Not hanging around a film studio."

"That's right. But a so-called friend asked for help."

"Which you said you weren't giving." Yet, he was here
even after I'd exasperated and frustrated him. "Why do you
bother with me, James?"

"Where're you headed?"

I unlocked my door. "Culver PD." I opened my door. "I
shouldn't be long. If they throw me out, it'll be really fast. We
can chat while I drive, if you're game, that is."

With James beside me, I recharged my phone and
motored toward the police department, a hop, skip and a jump
away from Ameripictures. It should've taken five minutes, but
with traffic, it stretched to twenty.

"How did you get on the lot?" I asked.

"My best friend is an actor, remember?"

"Oh yeah."

"The studio demanded the fast cleanup," James said. "They stand to lose big bucks every day a production is shut down. In this case, multiple productions were affected because the enclosed area was large."

"Just like you'd said." I started to update him about Calvin, but he already knew.

"I talked to a cop on the scene. They're looking at suicide." He turned on the radio, switching channels before turning it back off. "A few days ago, Calvin told his sister he bought a vial of poison, from the dark web."

"And she didn't question it?" I asked.

"She said it wasn't the first time he was morbid. She didn't take him seriously."

"What about the photo I'd sent you with the fake blood?"

"Could've been from another movie set."

"Did anyone besides Lacy ID Shaw's body?"

"Where are you going with this, Corrie? There's a possibility you've got this all wrong." He shook his pretty head. "I could get a line-up of five men that could easily be mistaken for Shaw Kota. You got a fast look of the guy running past after the murder, which isn't enough for a foolproof ID."

I eased into a spot a half a block away from the station. James was right. I held out my car key. "Go back to the studio and get your SUV. I'll collect my car later." I stepped out.

James joined me. "I'm not going anywhere. If Calvin killed Shaw, he could have had an accomplice who'll be prosecuted by my office."

"Fine." I hustled toward the station. "You're here to get a jump on the situation, I know that." I slapped him on the arm. It was like hitting a steel baseball bat. My palm burned. "Always looking out for number one, aren't you?"

"I'm looking out for what matters." He stared past me.

Why had I brought James along? I marched through the

front entry, over to the desk officer. "I'm here to see Detective Sorkel."

"He expecting you?" The officer asked.

James appeared by my side and flashed his ID. "I'm here on behalf of the DA's office."

The guy nodded and buzzed him in. I followed.

"Not you," the officer said to me.

James stopped and I smacked into his back.

"She's a colleague," James told the officer.

"ID?" He held out his hand.

I flashed my state bar card.

The officer nodded and waved us in. James paused and motioned me ahead.

"Stop it," I said. "I shouldn't have brought you with me."

James slowed and bent to place his mouth to my ear. "Tell me what you want me to stop and I will."

"Pretending to help," I said. "All you do is get in the way."

The station went quiet. An officer sidled up to me. "Is this a domestic situation, miss?" he asked.

"Hardly," I said.

"She's not domesticated," James added. "She's feral."

I faced the officer. "I'm looking for Detective Sorkel or Officer Ramirez. I'll take either."

"Well, you're in luck. They're in meeting room three. Follow me."

A minute later, we'd entered a small conference room with a long wooden table, matching chairs and a corner mounted TV screen. Surveillance equipment took up most of the table. Sorkel was on his feet staring at his reflection in the window while he adjusted his tie. Ramirez sat near the equipment, laptop open. Sorkel spun around and scowled when he noticed us.

"What's a girl have to do to get a cup of tea around here?" I said.

Rodriguez stood.

"Earl Gray with a splash of milk, please," I said.

"Sit down," Sorkel told Ramirez and aimed his glower my way. "What are you doing here? Why am I always asking you that? And who's he?" He flicked his chin toward James.

"ADA James Zachary, here on behalf of the district attorney's office." James extended his hand and introductions were made. "I understand there's another death connected to the Shaw Kota case."

"Nothing's been concluded yet," Sorkel said.

"Except that it's no longer our case," Ramirez added.

Sorkel turned the scowl up and on him.

"What does that mean?" James asked.

"Who's taking over?" I asked.

"Not that it's your business, but I'll tell you if it'll get rid of you faster. This case is out of our jurisdiction, which…" Sorkel turned to James. "…means it's out of your jurisdiction, Mister *Assistant* District Attorney. We're turning the body…bodies…over to a federal agency."

I took a step closer to Sorkel. "What kind of evidence do you have that Calvin killed Shaw, besides the knife in the apartment? And what about the guy that attacked me at the studio?"

"Who attacked you?" James said, sliding next to me.

"She's the one who attacked him," Sorkel said.

"That would make more sense," James said.

"They brought the guy in the fedora to the station," I told James. "After he attacked me." I took a step toward Sorkel. "What can you tell us about him?"

"This is not show and tell," Sorkel said.

"I want to see Calvin," I said. "His body, I mean. I need to know if he's the one I saw running."

"That's seems fair," Ramirez said. "But—"

Sorkel shot him a nasty look. "I say what's fair, Officer." He flicked his gaze my way. "No, you can't."

"She was an eyewitness, Detective," James said. "If she can confirm it was the man she saw running away from the scene of the crime, it'll only bolster the case you're handing over to Homeland Security."

"We've already got confirmation." Sorkel's scowl switched over to Ramirez. "Get out. You can finish up, later."

"Right away, Sir." Ramirez vacated.

"Who said anything about Homeland Security?" Sorkel's droopy eyes shot to James.

"Why would Calvin be regarded as a terrorist?" I asked.

Sorkel threw up his hands. "No one said anything about a terrorist."

"If Homeland—"

"They're not involved," Sorkel said.

While Sorkel and I argued, James leaned over to view the screen of the open laptop. He slid away just as Sorkel pivoted around to him.

"Don't you want to know if I can make a positive identification?" I asked Sorkel.

He turned back to me. "I do not. And to make sure you don't, I'm going to personally escort you out." He marched to the door and held it open. "Like I escorted the batty actress out."

"But what about the guy in the hat?" I asked. "He hacked my home security and he was the driver that tried to run us down—"

"No one saw him attack you," Sorkel told me. "Or try to run you down or anything else. We had to let him go."

"But I—"

"Saw him from a distance the first time. Through tinted glass the second time, while another eyewitness identified a woman as the driver of the car that nearly hit you. And today, no one witnessed the attack." Sorkel planted his hands on his hips. "You're lucky he didn't press charges."

"It was self-defense," I said.

"He wasn't armed," Sorkel added.

"What was he doing at the studio in the first place?" James wanted to know.

"In the room where a homicide had been committed?" I asked.

"He's representing a financier that invests in movies, including *Bullets Flying*." Sorkel leaned in closer, shifting his torso forward. "He was there to protect his interest and to ensure filming resumes. Bottom line, we're done."

I dragged myself out the door. James came in a close second. Sorkel pushed past us to take the lead. I shuffled through the lobby, turning my head to the side to allow my peripheral vision to view people coming in from behind. James grabbed my arm, pulling me forward.

Sorkel stopped and rolled his eyes. "Pick up those feet." He waved us in front of him.

"Who ID'd Calvin Singh?" I asked Sorkel.

"His sister." Sorkel bit his top lip and turned to us. "Look, you were right. There was someone running after the murder occurred. Someone resembling the victim. A federal agent obtained video footage."

"Video footage from the studio?" I asked.

"Very good, Miss Locke." Sorkel held out a hand. "Let's proceed."

"That's not possible," I said.

"Yes, it is. The door is twenty feet away and if you put one foot in front of—"

"I reviewed the videotapes. The runner wasn't on any of them."

"Maybe not on the tapes you saw." Sorkel marched toward the entrance.

James walked beside him. "Why are the feds involved?" he asked Sorkel.

"Not that you need to know, but they've reason to believe Calvin Singh was a foreign national wanted for a string of break-ins. And now murder." Sorkel squinted so fiercely, he nearly squeezed his eyes shut. He opened the door for us to step through. We did, and he swiveled and stormed away.

We continued our trek onto the sidewalk. I stopped by an SUV parked in a green zone. The windows sported a dark tint. James appeared next to me.

"I'll bet this belongs to the feds. We can follow undetected." I met James' gaze.

"Shouldn't be a problem. Assuming the agents are blind and comatose."

I caught my breath and blew it out between my teeth. "I can't believe they released the guy in the hat. I don't even know his name." I had no idea where to go from here.

James took my arm and pulled me past the vehicle. "He was released before we got here," he told me.

"How do you know?" I asked.

"It was on Officer Ramirez' report. I took a peek at the laptop he left behind."

"Did you get a name?"

"Deepak Nangia," James replied.

Now I was impressed. James got the name of the guy posing as a landscaper at Ameripictures, and with the stolen license plates who left the lot shortly after the murder, not to mention my attacker. Deepak had to be the man in the fedora.

"His address is in Culver City."

Minutes later, I was aiming for Deepak's street.

CHAPTER 39

The Plan

"We should come up with a plan before barging in anywhere," James said.

I pulled over into a strip mall and put on the brakes.

"That's a first." James dropped his chin to his chest and stared my way.

"What is?"

"Doing what I say. You feeling alright?"

"We'll wait and re-group, like you said." We were making progress. "I'm glad—"

"Let's go back to the studio," he said.

"Why?" I stiffened.

"To come up with a plan, after which, I'm out. Like I said, I'm not getting involved this time."

Yet, he was here with me now. What the heck was going on? I flipped a sharp U-ey. "You know what? I don't need you to come up with a plan." I stepped on it and switched lanes. "I can do that much myself."

His head turned to me. "If cases didn't fall into your lap, you'd never need me."

"That's not—"

"Save it."

I stomped my left foot. Sounded like I wasn't the only one that couldn't make up my mind. Being with James was part thrill, part torment.

We didn't speak again until the Ameripictures sign loomed over our heads.

"I'll get out over there." He pointed to a red zone near a side entrance. "There's an even more important reason I'm leaving."

"No need to explain. Thanks, James." I kept my face forward.

He opened the door and stepped out. One hand held the door open while he bent down, sticking his head into the car. "With a federal agency involved, the odds in favor of getting caught are higher."

He referred to my past and present penchants for bending the law now and then. "I haven't broken any laws in this investigation." That was sort of true.

"Unlike local law enforcement, the feds won't let go. Shaw Kota wasn't killed over something trivial. And with the second murder, this is beyond your usual PI work. If your dad was here, he would've backed off."

"Well, he's not, is he?" We locked eyes. A firecracker lit up my insides and burned through my veins.

"How long do you think your luck will last?" he asked.

"I'm going to find out." I slammed my foot on the pedal, barely giving him time to shut the door. I'd never left a job half-done and I wasn't going to start now. I buzzed through a yellow light and slowed. I slapped my palm against the steering wheel. My hand stung from the blow. "Dammit." Why did I behave so badly around him?

Correct your mistakes and move on, my father used to say.

"That could take a while." I exhaled and pulled over. I sent off an apology text to James. My foot hit the gas and I peeled off.

* * *

The address for Deepak turned out to be the Starlight Motel, a shabby inn jammed onto a shabby street in the shabbiest part of town. The single story motel wore a peeling coat of pink paint. I drove by a few times before squeaking into a parking spot a block away. I hurried along the sidewalk, scanning vehicles that could belong to Deepak, but he wouldn't be around. Either he was using the address as a cover or stayed only as needed.

I pushed open a wooden door and entered a lobby the size of a large bathroom stall. It had the odor to match. A small guy in a tank top sat behind a clear, plastic partition with a slit at the bottom, like the kind used in a drive-through bank or theater box office.

"Oh no, girlie, you don't want to stay here," the guy behind the partition told me in a sing songy voice.

"I don't?" I replied.

"Nuh-uh, it's not for you. We got sketchy wi-fi and it gets crazy noisy at night."

"I'm looking for a man."

"You a hooker?" He winked.

"Is there *anything* about me that resembles a hooker?" I asked.

"Maybe a high class one, huh? We had one dressed like a librarian last week. A hot one. You a hot business lady? What do you charge? Fifty an hour?"

I opened my mouth and snapped it shut again. I did not want to have this conversation or the guy could end up in the hospital.

"Deepak Nangia," I said. "What room's he in?"

The man rose to his full five feet four inches. "What do you think? I give private information about my customers freely? This is a respected establishment..."

I dropped a ten-spot on the desk.

"Are you insulting me? Because I insult easily—"

I slapped my State Bar card on top of the ten. "I'm an attorney investigating health code violations."

"What department you with?"

"I work freelance. I find violations and report them to County Health, to the Attorney General, to Consumer Affairs—"

The guy in the tank top slipped a door key through the slit. "You get rid of this violator?"

"That's the plan."

He nodded. "Room 227."

A minute later, I stood in a dingy room with bubbling wallpaper and carpet that smelled like the ashes of a thousand cigarettes had been rubbed into the faded red diamond pattern. A leather duffel bag balanced across a small, cracked sink in the bathroom. In the bag were men's toiletries, underwear and a change of clothes. No form of ID.

I peered inside the mini fridge and the microwave, and was about to make my exit when an ironing board snagged my attention. The board leaned against the wall in the corner, next to the double bed, but instead of leaning straight, it tipped at an angle. The bottom portion was hidden behind the table. I stepped over and patted down the end near the floor. My heartbeat pounded in my ears as my fingers rested over a square bump in the cloth. I pulled off the cover and removed two passports held together with a rubber band. One was a British passport issued to Herman Monk. The other was an Italian passport belonging to Deepak Nangia. I shoved them into my handbag and hightailed out of that dump.

I dove into my BMW and peeled off, running a red light in the process. I didn't stop 'til I'd reached the executive parking lot of Ameripictures. Marshall's spot was empty, so I took possession. Grabbing the passports from my purse, I called Sorkel.

"Sorkel," he answered.

"Corrie Locke here. What kind of movie investor has counterfeit passports?"

"I'll call you back."

Sorkel was true to his word. Less than a minute later, my phone rang from a restricted number. I answered.

"Hold on," Sorkel said.

The tap, tap, tap of footsteps padding along told me he

was on the move. In a few moments, a siren wailed and horns honked. Why couldn't he talk inside the precinct?

"Listen close," he said in a low voice. "I'm only telling you this because of your dad, and because I read up on your past work. I took the guy into the station after your incident. Deepak Nangia's the name."

"And?" I said.

"I couldn't hold him. He gave me the name of a production company and it turns out, he's acting on behalf of a foreign fund investing at Ameripictures. We checked it out, and I let him go. Next thing I know, a DOJ agent shows up and takes over the Shaw Kota investigation."

My mind raced. "Justice Department?" I wasn't sure if I'd spoken out loud. So the guy in the bucket hat *was* connected to the Shaw case.

"I suggest you back-off. There's no way we can gather enough facts to figure out who killed anyone on a case we're no longer investigating. And, after the Calvin Singh discovery, the case should be closed soon."

"I have two passports." I scanned the area around me. "One British passport issued to a Herman Monk, which looked pretty credible, and the other's an Italian passport belonging to Deepak Nangia. Did you verify his ID?"

"Yes, using passport number three, which was a French one. Where did you get your information?" Sorkel asked. "Someone feeding it to you?"

"I can feed myself fine, thanks very much."

Sorkel huffed into the phone. "I suggest you return to lawyering and leave this mess alone. It has nothing to do with you or me."

"Wait." I wasn't sure what to do next. "Where's Shaw Kota's body? And Calvin's?"

"At the coroner's office, as far as I know."

"Don't you want to—"

"No, I don't. Either bring the passports to me or turn them over to the Justice Department yourself."

He disconnected. I pulled out my phone and called my mother.

"The dossier is partially done," Mom said by way of answering.

"I'll take whatever you've got," I said.

"Make sure you eat—"

"We're on an assignment, remember?"

"Lost my focus for a minute. My routine's been disrupted. I haven't even done my makeup yet."

"What about Shaw?"

"Bollywood is not where he spent most of his time. He worked for his uncle's science and engineering firm on a team designing protective clothing."

"Like in hazmat suits?" So far everything was consistent with Lacy's story.

"Sweetie, Hazel didn't elaborate. All I know is he disappeared a few months ago, and there's been no word since."

"What about his uncle?"

"I'm new at this dossier stuff. Should I find out about his relatives, too?"

"Only the ones involved in science related projects."

"I hope Shaw didn't have a lot of relatives. Should I make enchiladas for dinner?"

"After this job is done. Thanks, Mom." I disconnected and rested my forehead on my steering wheel. I needed to talk to Michael. My phone chimed. A text rolled in from Michael.

We have to talk! I found a break in our case.

CHAPTER 40

Puzzling

"**A**s a kindred nerd spirit, I tried tapping into Shaw's mindset while reading through the magazines. Of course, the sticky notes he'd used to mark articles were a huge help," Michael was saying.

We'd strolled over to the back end of the studio near an old-time barbershop. I sat on a metal bench beneath a magnolia tree. A barber pole swirled red, white and blue stripes behind us. The shop was closed and foot traffic was scarce on this section of the lot.

"What do the articles have in common?" I asked.

Michael pulled out a magazine from the bag he cradled under his arm. He opened to a page with a yellow sticky note. "*How Radiation Threatens Health*." He dropped the issue back in the bag and removed another, opening to a page with another sticky note. "*Radiation Levels Explained*. And the radiation list continues."

"Like the press release with Wetzel and the uncle. It mentioned radiation components. Why would Shaw be interested in radiation?"

"It must have to do with his project and Pantheon," Michael said.

"Why rely on magazines? Why not books?"

"I've been seesawing back and forth with that myself. Magazines pop up faster with the latest information. But personally, I think he read everything and anything. Magazines, journals, the internet, science and comic books..."

"Okay, let's reel it in a little," I said. "What about the notebook?"

"Alright, let's go there." Michael reached into the magazine bag and pulled out the little red notebook. "Just when you think you've seen it all, there's something you didn't see the first go around."

"A code to crack?" I took the notebook from Michael and thumbed through while I spilled the beans about the latest events. Michael sat down next to me.

He gazed off. "This is so much bigger than we imagined. For the federal government to be involved, Shaw must've been onto something huge. What do radiation, protective gear and aerospace companies have in common?"

There was that brightly burning light bulb over my head again. "Anti-radiation clothing."

"Wow! If he created that...it would be amazing. You think Lacy knows?" Michael asked.

"Hard to say."

"Time for my zinger." He took the notebook and opened it midway. "Mostly empty, right?"

"I didn't find anything."

"This was in the back." Michael removed a small photo and held it out to me. "Taped to the last page. I missed it the first time I went through the notebook." It was a photograph of a box next to a small gooseneck lamp, both sitting on a bookcase. The box displayed a picture of a light bulb.

I caught my breath. "The photo was taken on the lot."

"How do you know?" Michael stood.

"The background. It's the room where his body was found."

"Whoa, I never would have—"

"Why would he take a photo of a lamp in that room and

keep it in this book?" I asked.

Michael stood and paced the sidewalk in front of us. He paused and held out his arm. "Shall we?"

"Unless this photo was randomly placed in the notebook, which I doubt, the lamp in the crime scene could give us an answer." I linked my arm with his.

"An answer we don't even know we're looking for," Michael said beaming. "I'll race you."

* * *

Ten minutes later, Michael and I had climbed the backstairs and headed for the room where Shaw's body was found. The building was quiet except for the buzz of conversation from a downstairs office. Michael kept watch while I worked the lock.

"Not to alarm anyone, especially me, but I hear footsteps downstairs," Michael whispered. After a beat, he added. "Now they're on the stairs. That's fate telling us we need to be somewhere else." He breathed over my shoulder.

The door clicked open, and we tumbled inside. Sunlight streamed in through the only window in the chilly room. It smelled damp. Michael shut the door.

"I am so glad to be in here right now," he whispered.

"Let's get to work."

I scanned the space for the lamp. Michael peered inside the drawers of the desk.

"Shaw held on to this for a good reason." Michael shook the red notebook in his hand and opened a bottom drawer. "Hey, this looks familiar." He removed a small, brass, goose-neck desk lamp. "It's a handsome lamp."

"Sure is. If you're Mister Cleever and your sons are named Wally and Beaver." Growing up, I watched more than my fair share of old TV shows. Mom didn't want me to miss the good stuff. "May I see it?"

Michael handed the lamp to me. "Maybe you should turn

it on. It's kind of gloomy in here." He sank into the chair next to the window and held the notebook up to the light.

"There's no bulb." I opened another drawer in the desk.

"Corrie," Michael shot up, his back to the window, open notebook in his hands.

A hundred watt bulb appeared in the back of a bottom drawer. "I've been looking for you." I screwed the bulb into the lamp socket and turned it on. "Much better."

"Come take a look," Michael said.

I strolled over and peered at the pages he held. Faint markings appeared where there was nothing before. I took the book and held it beneath the lamplight. Page after page displayed drawings and notes. The empty notebook was now full. Michael leaned over my shoulder.

"How is this possible?" I asked.

"It's written in strokes, like with a small paintbrush," Michael said.

"Secret writing." I stared up at Michael.

"AKA invisible ink," he said. "I played around with it when I was a kid, after I spent a summer reading the *Hardy Boys*."

"How did you make it visible?" I asked.

"Sunlight. But to give the pages full exposure..." He regarded the lamp. "...that's what Shaw was trying to tell us with the photo. We needed to view the pages under a light bulb." Michael wet his index finger and touched it to the words on a page. He placed the finger on his tongue. "Lemon juice. Perfect for writing in invisible ink. Who did he expect to find this?" Michael straightened. "Not us, that's for sure."

"Had to be Lacy. But look." I flipped through pages filled with drawings of sleeves and pant legs, and notes on NTP studies and RF energy and similar items of which I was completely ignorant. "Do you understand any of this?" I asked Michael.

"Not yet."

I handed the notebook to Michael. "Shaw Kota was a lot more than just an actor."

"Kind of like me." Michael grinned.

"Yes, like you. If *you* had a secret you didn't want everyone to know..."

"I'd go with the invisible ink and leave a clue that only a good, caring friend would understand," Michael said. "Like you. Or James."

I didn't like being back to the friend category, but I wasn't up for that kind of discussion right now. "Or he figured Lacy would get help to figure things out. She's still holding out, I'm sure of it. She likes to dole out facts in bits and pieces with fabrications in between. We need to find those facts."

"Exactly how are we going to do that?"

"I have an idea on how to get her to talk." I tapped my fingers along the bookcase.

"One that doesn't involve loss of limbs or organ damage, right?"

"We're going to feed Lacy false information and watch how she reacts." I turned and paced the floor. "We'll set a trap."

"What kind of trap?"

"You're using Shaw's dressing room, right?" I asked.

"I am."

"Think of a place to plant a note or something from Shaw. Maybe in a drawer or the pocket of a piece of clothing."

"Too cliché," Michael said. "Geeks are creative." He joined me in pacing the floor. "There's a small collection of eighties films on VHS tapes in the dressing room. I'll dissect a tape and hide something inside. We'll convince Lacy that Shaw left it for her to find."

"That could work. We'll take a page from the notebook and plant it in the tape. Only it won't be an actual page. We'll recreate it so we don't mess with evidence."

"Like we haven't messed with evidence yet."

"Trying to keep it under control, Michael," I said.

"Okay. I'll copy his handwriting..."

"You won't have to. We'll type it out." I headed for the door.

"But everything's handwritten in the notebook." Michael

followed me.

"Lacy doesn't know that."

"Where are we going?"

I opened the door and stepped outside, Michael at my heels. I padded down the hallway.

"To find a computer to use." I paused by a door and rapped my knuckles on the hard wood. There was no response, so I turned the knob. It was locked. I pulled out my paperclips. "You know the drill," I told Michael.

He stuffed his hands in his pockets and stood guard, patrolling the hallway.

In less than a minute, the lock clicked open. I stuck my head inside the room. The scent of minty air freshener seeped into my nostrils. The office was dark, the blinds drawn. A brown velvet sofa rested beneath movie posters on the walls. An L-shaped desk faced the door. Sitting on the desk was exactly what we needed.

"Come on," I whispered to Michael.

"Whose office is this?" he asked.

"Somebody that could be back soon." A dent on a sofa cushion told me the office was being used. "We have to hurry."

Michael slid behind the computer.

"I'll stand watch," I said. "If you hear two raps, it's me warning you—"

"To scram, I know." He wiped his palms on his pants and glanced over his shoulder. "I've always wanted to speed climb down a fire escape and crash land. I don't suppose they've got safety pads at the bottom?"

"We're on the second floor. You'll be fine."

His gaze caught mine. "Hurry up, will you?"

"You're the one who's got to be quick. Type and print a note that looks like it came from Shaw."

"I have to get into the system first," Michael said, pounding a few keys.

I stepped back into the corridor, shut the door and locked it. I looked both ways and tiptoed toward the front of the building just as the main entry door slammed shut. Laughter bubbled upstairs cutting through the quiet. I flattened my back against the wall, ears perked. The one-sided conversation told me the chatterbox was alone and on the phone. Footsteps pounded along the floor, growing fainter as the voice faded down a corridor. I edged forward to peek over the landing. The front entry was closed.

A minute later, I stood at the opposite end of the corridor staring down the back staircase. A woman stood at the bottom. A woman with hair the color of hell. Her glittering gaze was pinned on mine. She swayed slightly.

"Why do I always find you doing nothing?" Lacy asked.

"It's what I do...least." My swagger down the stairs would have made a swashbuckler proud. Phone in hand, I texted Michael to let him know I was with Lacy. "I came across some interesting—"

"I don't care," Lacy said.

I reached the bottom and faced her. My phone vibrated. It was a text from Michael.

I can't get in!

"Is that my fake actor?" Lacy wanted to know. "I've been looking for him, too."

"He's been looking for you," I said. "He's got something to show you."

"That's a crock of...I can't take this anymore!" She yelled so loudly, the door to a nearby office opened and two heads peeked out. They retreated the moment they spotted Lacy.

I pushed stray hairs away from my face. "There's more to Shaw's case than we figured. Michael found something important that can prove that."

"The way I see it, neither of you have uncovered a friggin' thing." She turned her head to the side and lowered her voice. "Calvin is dead. Do you know how little sense that makes? This whole thing has spun out of control." She shook her head and stumbled backward. "I pretty much killed a bottle of wine today. You think it helped?"

I grabbed my vibrating phone. It was Michael.

I'm in!

"Answer me." Lacy inched closer.

"Wasn't that a rhetorical question?"

"Is that all you've got? Fancy talk, fancy schmancy clothes and..." Her eyes rolled over my face. "You're stalling, aren't you?" She leaned her torso my way, and I caught a whiff of alcohol, strong enough to light up a wet rag. "You lawyers are so good at stalling." She hiccupped and wobbled.

"Did Debbylynn finally show up?" I asked.

She shook her head. I linked my arm with hers and led her to the back door. Calvin's dead, and Debbylynn is MIA. What did it all mean?

"How well did you know Calvin?" I asked.

"He and Shaw...they were cousins."

What? "Did you bring both over?"

"Cal came later. Shaw needed Calvin...for support."

I tried to get her to talk more after that, but she kept shaking her head.

"Michael will meet us in the dressing room." I propped her up against a wall and sent off a text to him. I grabbed Lacy's arm again. "I'll fill you in on what I discovered today. Maybe you'll have a few things to add."

I led Lacy out of the building, along with dragging feet and a tirade of nasty comments. We took it slow, partly because she tripped most of the way, and to give Michael time to head out.

"Detective Sorkel's turned the investigation over to a federal agency." Maybe that would make her talk some more.

"Feds. Stink. They threw me in the slammer for protesting in front of the Federal Building."

"Really?"

"Ha! You don't even know when someone's lying. Your father would be so disappointed in you. Only suckers go to jail. I've never been caught."

Was she unstable enough to hire someone to kill Shaw?

And then to hire me and feed me indigestible clues? She could easily hire people to fake a death or two. I deposited her near the commissary.

"You're not surprised about the feds," I said.

She pressed her lips together.

"Did you mess up Shaw's room to make it look like he was a slob?" I asked.

"Wrong." She hung her head and dragged her feet forward. "I ransacked it looking for the plan."

"What plan?"

"To finish the..." She clamped her lips shut.

"Yes?"

"Never mind."

Lacy was trying to throw me off the scent of something, even in her drunken state, if she was really drunk. "I'm going to find out what went down," I told her. "Why don't you save us the time and trouble? That way I can track Shaw's killer. If you still want me to find him. Or her. Or am I talking to her right now?"

"Open your eyes. If I'd knocked him off, why would I hire you?"

"To do what you do best. Put on a good show. The caring benefactor, benefactress, whatever you are. When in reality..." My anger and frustration runneth over. It was my turn to shout, "You've been wasting my time." I turned on my heel and strode away toward my office, chin up, head high...for about twenty paces. Then I thought of Marshall. I tucked my tail between my legs, wiped the grimace off my face and slowed down. I should have practiced the major butt kissing I needed to convince Marshall to take me back. A shudder ran through my spine nearly paralyzing me from moving forward. My gaze flew skyward. "Please God, don't make me go back to work for Marshall. Isn't there somewhere else I'm needed more?"

"Corrie! Lacy!" Michael stood outside soundstage ten, waving his arms above his head. "You won't believe what I found."

I threw a glance over my shoulder. Lacy swayed right

where I'd left her, face and shoulders drooping. I retraced my steps and bent my elbow. I held it out to her. "Coming?"

CHAPTER 41

No End in Sight

L acy followed Michael into his dressing room. I trailed behind.

"Ladies," Michael was saying. "When I came back here and—"

"I searched everywhere for you," Lacy said.

"You did? I was just a text or phone call away," Michael told her.

"You're missing the point. Stars don't disappear during filming." Lacy extracted a tissue from her pant pocket and blew her nose. "Unless they're dead," she lowered her voice. "That's a legitimate excuse." She raised her voice and said, "Where were you?" She sat in the middle of a ten-foot long leather sofa built into the trailer, eyes glued to Michael.

"Looking for clues." In one long stride, Michael stood opposite the sofa, in a kitchen with a stainless steel microwave and mini fridge. He reached into a cabinet, grabbed a cup and poured hot coffee from a small coffee maker.

I leaned against the entry. The compact dressing room was outfitted for a ten-year-old fixated on *Transformers* and *GI Joe*, if the wall posters and accent pillows meant anything.

"I left to find Corrie, then came back here." He handed the steaming mug to Lacy.

Lacy took it and slurped. "Well?"

Michael strode to a shelf below a flat screen TV. A batch of videotapes leaned against each other on the shelf. He removed one from the sleeve and showed it to Lacy.

"I've already seen *Weird Science*," Lacy said.

"It's what's *inside* the tape you need to see." Michael cradled the black cassette in his hands and pulled apart the top portion. A small piece of paper was wedged between the spools. "I was looking for a movie." He looked up at us. "And found this." He held the slip of paper out to Lacy. "Maybe you can make sense of it."

Lacy fluttered her spidery lashes and took the folded paper. She opened it and read out loud, "What is the impact of low dose radiation on human health?" She jerked her chin up and stared at Michael. "Is this a joke? Because it's in very poor taste. Shaw never would have written this...he knew all about rad—" She snapped her mouth shut.

I slid between Lacy and Michael. "What does radiation have to do with Shaw?"

Lacy lowered her voice. "The plan...it doesn't matter now, does it?" She shot up, spilling her coffee onto the floor. "Think I'm blind?" She spun around to Michael. "Think I didn't see the screwdriver by the sink? You planted that note." She shook her head and stood. "Amateurs." She cut a glance to the shelf holding the tapes. "That cassette is the only one without any dust on it. I noticed that, too."

Michael's jaw dropped and his eyes widened, like he'd been caught stealing a copy of a master exam before finals. And me? Well, I straightened my slumping shoulders only to have them slump again, moments later.

Lacy shuffled for the doorway. She whirled around again and threw us a look that would have scorched a gallon of ice cream.

"Who's Deepak Nangia?" I asked.

"Never heard of him."

"Didn't Shaw tell you he was being followed the day before he died?"

She shook her head. "He seemed distracted. I figured it was because he'd broken up with Deb." She turned and shuffled out the door.

Michael and I locked gazes.

"Sorry, Corrie. If I hadn't been in such a hurry, I would've noticed—"

"Never mind. We got what we needed."

"I could have done without the scolding. Wait, what did we get?"

I glided over to the shelf holding the videotapes. "Lacy told us Shaw understood radiation. He was *involved* in radiation protective gear, either as a con or for real. Why can't she just tell us?"

"But she said he'd never have written the note."

"Because he knew enough about it already. She also said the tape you pulled out was the only clean cassette on the shelf." I eyed the twenty or so cassettes bunched together. "She didn't notice this one." I tapped my finger on a tape and pulled it out.

Michael cocked his head to read the title. "*Better Off Dead.* Creepy, considering. But it's not dusty at all. Is it new?"

A tingling sensation tickled my stomach. "Maybe. But couldn't there be another reason this tape isn't dusty?"

"Either it was Shaw's favorite or it's a new addition."

"Try again." I handed the tape to Michael. "Being a nerd, it's possible your kindred nerd spirit hid something inside."

Michael slapped his hand to his forehead. "Am I always this slow?"

"Open it, please."

Michael unscrewed the top and pulled it apart.

"Whoa," he said.

I picked up a small piece of paper folded in half. I read out loud,

RA sit-O

"There's that message again." It was something vital Shaw didn't want missed. I felt so close.

Michael ran a hand through his hair. "Royal Academy. Rental Agreement."

While Michael rattled off all things with RA as the acronym, I nosed around the dressing room. I opened drawers and found nothing unusual, until I reached one in the tiny bathroom. In it sat another red notebook. This one was smaller and thinner. Not surprisingly, the ten pages were empty until I held it under a desk lamp.

"Michael!"

CHAPTER 42

Corrie's Little Helper

"Take a look." I handed Michael the notebook. He flipped through the pages under a lamp. "There's a number on each page, on ten pages. Which means..." He lifted his gaze to mine. "...it's not a social security number."

"It's a phone number with a coastal area code."

Michael caught his breath. "A South Bay telephone number." Michael lit up. "It's the number in El Segundo. Wetzel's number." Michael looked at the back page. "There's a date here."

"Two dates," I said. "One for last Friday, late afternoon. That was when Shaw was meeting with Wetzel at Pantheon."

"It's crossed out." Michael looked up at me. "Wetzel called to cancel. And the other date..."

"Is tomorrow at three." I stared up at the ceiling. "Meanwhile, we still need to determine what Lacy's not saying."

"But maybe she doesn't know anything else."

"Go back to your temporary acting job and find out," I told him.

"That's a tall order after that awkward encounter. But I can do it," Michael said.

"Show her the red notebooks." I handed the first one to him. "Listen to the tone of her voice. When she drops it, she's sincere. If it's raised, she's acting."

"How do you know that?"

"Trust me, I've been around her enough," I said.

"I don't need to tell you, but I'm totally impressed. And to impress you right back, I'll convince Lacy to talk," Michael said. "And if I can't, I'll tell her I'll remove every negative review she's ever received on the Internet, if she's straight with me. She won't turn that down."

"Not bad," I said.

He stepped closer to me. "Have I redeemed myself?"

"You were never unredeemable."

"Like a coupon that never expires."

"I'm a big fan of coupons," I said.

We locked gazes until my phone vibrated. I glanced at the screen. I answered, "Veera? Everything okay?"

"No, it's not," she said. "The new guy's back."

"Sorry, Veera, I can't come—"

"Fine with me, as long as you don't mind him sitting in your office, behind your desk, going through your files. I wouldn't be surprised if he slips on your blazer."

I disconnected, blew Michael a kiss and darted off.

Minutes later, I barged into the suite and zipped into my office to find a curly haired guy sitting behind my computer, just like Veera said. I slapped my hand onto my desk. Good thing I'd calmed down or I would have manhandled him out of my chair.

"Freeze, Mister," I told him.

His dark eyes nearly popped out. He opened his mouth and stammered, "I was...Marshall suggested..." He stood, hand outstretched, "Adam Allenby."

I could tell Adam had about as much backbone as a jellyfish. "Get out," I said.

Veera peered in and stepped into the room. "She wants you out, Double A," she said.

"You've got a nickname for him already?" I asked Veera.

She leaned in to me and turned her head away from Adam. She whispered, "I figured if I gave him a nickname, it'd take my mind off knocking his block off every time he opened his mouth."

Adam pointed to Veera. "We're getting along really well."

I tossed him a killer look and turned to Veera. "Where's Marshall?"

"He dropped his little buddy off and left without a word."

"He's meeting with a production head." Adam side-stepped his way to the door. "Is now a good time to talk, Corrie?"

"Man." Veera clicked her tongue.

"No, it isn't." I pivoted around to make sure he stayed in full view at all times.

"Wh...when would be...can we speak—" Adam stuttered.

"Never," I said, "step into my office again, unless I invite you in here."

"Pick up those Hush Puppies," Veera said to him. "You should be getting to your desk."

"You have a desk?" I asked him. "What were you doing behind mine?"

"His desk is two suites away. The spare office hasn't been furnished yet," Veera replied.

"Out you go," I said to him.

Adam rushed off and into the hallway.

"Veera, why on earth did you let him into my office?" I asked.

"Just followin' orders, C," she replied. "I couldn't lock him out."

"You should've told him to leave."

"I would've if you didn't get over here," Veera said. "Any breaks in our case?"

I leaned against the wall. "A lot of small cracks that could turn into big breaks. I need time to figure out what's relevant."

"Speaking of...I've been checkin' Vanderpat some more. Seems he's worked overseas mostly. But get this, he's been spending time in that brick building even when it's not his shift."

"How did you find that out?" I asked.

"From the same person who gave me this." She rushed to

her purse and pulled out a videotape. "Straight outta security."

"Already been there. Security didn't have much to show me. I talked to a top dog."

"Why waste time with the higher-ups? I got this from a sharp-eyed woman aimin' toward moving up. Follow me." Veera locked the door to our suite and hurried into Marshall's office. He had a combo DVD-video player, along with a cassette deck and a projector. Veera slipped the tape into the player.

"Take note of the date." She pointed to the numbers at the bottom.

"It's from Friday, the day of Shaw's murder." I squinted at the screen.

Someone dressed like Shaw and resembling him raced at high speed on the lot toward the Culver gate. It lasted all of four seconds.

"This must be the tape the fed saw," I said.

"That's what I was told. The camera was mounted outside a window pointing to the street."

"Play that again," I said.

Veera rewound and played the short scene. I peered closer at the screen. The scene was blurry. All that showed was the back of the runner. How could anyone make a positive ID?

I crossed my arms and tapped my fingers against my biceps. "It seems like I'm the only one who's not lying these days."

"That's what I call progress," Veera said.

A rapping outside interrupted us. Veera fumbled with the tape player and ejected the tape in a hurry. We ran to the front entry. The doorknob was jiggling. Veera turned the lock and pulled the door open. Adam stood there gaping, key in hand.

"Why was the door locked?" he asked.

"So we could get some work done around here," Veera replied.

His gaze swung between us, then shifted past. "Why is Marshall's door open?"

"We don't have to explain each move to you," Veera told him.

"Does he give you free use of his office?" Adam asked me.

"I'm working on a project that requires the use of Marshall's...video player," I said. If Adam shared that tidbit with Marshall, he'd realize it was something for Lacy.

Adam continued to stare my way. "Can you bring me up to speed on what goes on in here?"

"I'm busy," I said and turned to Veera. "I'll be in touch."

"Okay, boss," she said.

I scooted past Adam and out the building.

I'd nearly made it to my car when I got a text from James.

I'll pick you up in thirty minutes. We're going to visit the coroner's office.

I caught my breath. How did he know? That was exactly where I'd wanted to go. It was time to view the two bodies. I texted back.

Goodie!

CHAPTER 43

In Sight

PIs usually don't visit a crime scene until after law enforcement is done scrutinizing, and the scene is reopened to the public. But reopening the scene didn't always mean all evidence had been collected. To make the best use of my time until James' arrival, I headed to what was becoming my second office. Every visit to the crime scene held the possibility of unearthing something new, like the fake blood and Deepak. I dashed for the brick building when my cell phone vibrated in my purse. It was Michael.

"Are you back on the set?" I asked.

"It's like I never left. Or more like that awful dressing room scene never happened. Production's in full swing. Lacy said work'll get our minds off the terrible events. I'm back on her good side, by the way," he whispered.

"If she has a good side."

"She even hugged me."

"That's suspicious," I said. "Don't let her manipulate you into doing something you don't want to do." I may have been on the phone, but my neck was craning in all directions to make sure I wasn't being followed.

"I've stuck a piece of caution tape on my sleeve as a reminder."

"Funny."

"But get this. She invited me for a drink after we wrap today. Do you think she's trying to make amends?"

"No." Lacy wouldn't waste time without a good reason. "Did she invite anyone else?"

"I don't think so," Michael said. "I'll let you know what I find out."

"Please do." I stepped into a narrow concrete walkway between two sound stages. "Any news on Debbylynn?"

"No one's heard from her."

It looked like she could have played a hand in the murder or...she was another victim. I shuddered.

"You know I'll do everything in my power to help, within reason and as long as it doesn't involve bullets, knives with big blades or tear gas," he said. "Unless you're being threatened by any of those, then reason is hurled out the window."

"I'm meeting James." No big deal, right?

"Oh, that's fine. Because?" Michael's voice inched up a notch.

"To visit the coroner's office."

"You sure? I mean...want me to come? I'm an expert hand-holder."

"I appreciate that, but I'll be fine." I slowed. Dad and I made many a field trip to the morgue and coroner's office. It got so a dead body was just another dead body. "Gotta run." I disconnected and picked up the pace.

A man in dark shades, red beanie, black coat and slacks had cruised around the corner, drifting in my direction. His dusky skin and lean frame reminded me of Shaw. Head bowed, he pounded the keys on his phone and lifted his face. Our gazes collided.

The guy took two big steps back, turned and bolted. I did what any hot-headed, tender-footed PI would do. I dashed after him.

CHAPTER 44

A Hunting We Will Go

T he man I chased looked a lot like the guy sprinting past me the day of the murder. I had no intention of losing him this time, until I barreled around the corner.

"Drat!"

He'd disappeared. Leaning against a large planter box was a studio bicycle, practically begging to be taken for a spin. I hopped on and pedaled straight ahead. I stood on the pedals, legs pumping up and down. The wind rushed against my face, and the lower half of my dress puffed out as I whizzed past buildings, a water fountain and a theater, leaving dust in my wake. I pedaled away from the fake city street, and there he was, reeling around a corner, down a studio alley. I flicked the handlebars to the left, stomped my shoe on the pavement and pivoted, switching direction. I darted off again, stray strands of hair whipping across my face.

Small shops peddling ice cream, ladies hats and antiques flanked the road. I zipped past an old-fashioned drug store and paused, stopping next to the ice cream parlor. I dropped the bike on its side. My target could be hiding anywhere. I checked the doorknobs on each fake storefront, hurrying along while loose bricks clinked an uneven melody beneath my soles. All doors were locked. The road ended at Main Street, which led back to the sound stages and the real office buildings. I straddled the bike and pedaled toward Main. A cyclist on a cruiser slowly rode past, and I turned in his direction. I caught up and asked,

"Did you see a man in a red beanie running down this street?"

He slammed a sneaker on the ground. I stopped as well.

He pointed a thumb over his shoulder. "I almost crashed into the idiot back on Main and Fourth."

"Thanks." I pumped the pedals toward the sound stages and sat upright, steering with one hand, while my other hand pulled off the purse strapped across my torso. I unzipped it to grab my phone and call Michael for backup. The bike wobbled, but my speed stayed the same. I leaned sharply into a curve and cut a glance down an alley in time to see the guy running around another corner. Before I could make my turn, a construction worker in a hardhat popped out in front of me.

"Hey!" Gripping both handlebars, I hit the brakes. The bicycle stopped, but I didn't. I flew over the handlebars, over an orange work-zone cone and crash-landed into nearly six inches of fresh cement. Landing on my palms and knees, I shook my head, wet dog style. Most of the thick stuff scattered off my clothes, but no luck with my hands. It was like being dipped into a thick gray milkshake filled with jalapeno pepper seeds. My skin stung. "Yuk."

"You okay?" The guy in the hard hat pulled me up and out.

I stepped onto the fake cobblestone road. Onlookers assembled around us, along with a couple that aimed their smartphones, and took pictures. Humiliation pinched my cheeks.

"Brace yourself," the guy said, gripping an industrial strength hose. He switched it on, full blast. The gush of cold water blasted my chest, pressing my clothes against my skin, nearly sending me reeling.

"Stop!" Water filled my mouth and I gagged. Another blast rolled over me, from head to toes, before the hose shut off.

"Had no choice." The construction worker wore a small grin on his sun-parched skin. His work vest, T-shirt and jeans were drenched.

Meanwhile, small puddles formed around me. "You could have...given me ...more notice." I panted.

He leaned forward. "You don't want cement on your skin. It's corrosive. And..." he leaned further and lowered his voice. "...I wanted to send a message to the guy and gal taking photos."

I swiveled around. The couple snapping pictures were nearly as wet as me. I turned back toward my cleaning man.

"Who knew you'd be a sight for sore eyes once you were cleaned up," he said. "You're a pretty woman underneath the concrete."

"Thanks." I scanned my front. Barely a trace of concrete remained on the soggy dress. I flipped damp strands out of my face.

"Better go to wardrobe and change," the guy said. "I apologize for getting in your way."

"Sorry. My fault for being careless," I said. "Thanks again."

He threw a hand at me. "Don't mention it. Good use of our time."

"What time is it?"

"Just past five."

"Oh no." I turned to run.

"Slow down," he yelled after me.

I eased up. Where'd my purse and phone go? The bike was leaning against stage nine, my handbag draped over a handle; the phone perched on the seat. "Thank you," I whispered.

I trotted to wardrobe, only four soundstages away when a text rolled in from James.

Running late. See you in twenty minutes.

"Perfect." I sent a text to Michael:

Please find out if anyone saw a guy in a red beanie and black coat. He resembled Shaw.

I texted Veera next.

Can you keep an eye on Michael? He's on stage ten. He's meeting Lacy after filming. Follow please.

Both Michael and Veera texted back in the affirmative. I

didn't garner much attention walking through the studio in my disheveled state. Passersby assumed I was an actress in character. By the time I arrived, my clothes had gone from sopping to damp.

The entrance to wardrobe sat wide open. A bottle blonde in stilettos, jeans and a fitted white blouse stood in the doorway.

"What set are you from?" she asked.

"I'm not an actor."

"You fall in a pool?"

"Wet cement."

"You're not the first. Haven't gotten cement in a while, but I've gotten a vat of grapes, a tub of mud and a few shady substances. I'm Flicka. Yeah, my mom named me after a horse." Flicka turned toward a long metal rack of clothes behind her and parted them with her hands. "I get requests for a wardrobe change all the time. Some exec doesn't like what she wore to the office or another spills coffee on his pants and needs a new set of undies and trousers."

"You have undies?"

She gave me the once over. "You've got a wild look. You related to any gypsies?"

"Not that I know of."

"I see you in a pumpkin colored get-up, tambourine in hand, steppin' out in a groovy flowing, almost sheer skirt." She grabbed an off the shoulder, see-through chiffon mini dress, and held it out to me. "What do you think?"

"I'm not going out in public in that. Don't you have something similar to what I'm wearing?"

"That gray dress is dullsville." Flicka turned and faced the rack again. She pulled out another get-up. "How about this? You'll have the guys on the set saying, 'hubba, hubba'." She held out a body conscious red dress with a thigh high split up the seam and low V-neckline. Cutouts on either side provided waistline ventilation.

"You're getting closer. I'm a real-life lawyer in the business affairs department."

"Huh." She slapped the back of her hand against my arm. "You'd get people to sit up and pay attention in this puppy. You in TV or motion pictures?"

"Animation."

"Cute." She turned toward the rack. "How about this?" She dangled a Bo Peep costume at the end of her fingers and burst out laughing.

My arms crossed my chest. I opened my mouth, but Flicka put out a hand.

"Just joshing. Let me see." She flipped through the rack and pulled out a silk dress. A sleeveless, black and red floral number with a crewneck.

"Now you're talking," I told her.

Flicka worked her magic on me, and presto! I was dressed and almost dry. She touched up my makeup, pulled back my hair into a loose bun, threw in a blazer, and I was rarin' to go.

"Come again, ya hear?" Flicka said and waved me off. "I'll handle your wet duds."

"Thanks..." I started off and stopped. "Do you know Debbylynn Diamond? She's a costumer—"

She shook her head. "Isn't it awful?"

"About Shaw Kota?"

"That, too. But I mean about Deb. The good news is they think she'll pull through."

I froze. "What happened?"

"She was getting into her car this morning, right in front of her apartment, when some maniac ran up and grabbed her. He pulled her out and started beating on her. An off-duty cop was driving past and saw. She's lucky. I hear she was knocked around pretty badly."

"Did they get the man?"

"The bastard's still running loose. Deb's in the hospital. Got a call from her sister. Think I should be treated for PTSD or something." She spread her feet and crossed her arms, staring skyward. "At studio expense."

Debbylynn *had* known more than she said, like I thought. If she'd only talked to me...

"You okay?"

"Fine. Thanks again." I turned on my heel and stomped off in my wet pumps.

I called Michael and told him about Debbylynn.

"That's terrible." He lowered his voice.

"Stick close to Lacy. I'll join you as soon as I'm done." Deepak wouldn't strike again so soon, right?

"I will. And no sign of the guy in the red beanie. Be careful. I heard some woman got into a tussle with a construction worker near stage nine. She went berserk and had to be hosed down."

"That's not exactly true." I didn't have time to fill Michael in on the facts.

"Before I forget," Michael lowered his voice. "Lacy's office is where we're headed after we wrap."

"In the Otis building? Do you have your knife on you?" I asked.

"Never leave home without it, especially during an investigation."

Which was nearly every time we were together. "Good work. Talk soon."

Five minutes later, I stood outside the main gate. I didn't wait long before James pulled up. He parked and I jumped in.

His stare rolled over me and he leaned in closer. "You didn't have to dress up just for me."

"Best I could do on such short notice."

"Like I said."

"I was in hot pursuit of Shaw or someone resembling him."

James faced forward and merged into traffic. "I forgot who I was talking to. What happened?"

I gave him a quick rundown. "I'm hoping the visit to the coroner might provide more answers."

"You should be prepped for disappointment. We could

end up with nothing. What are you expecting?"

"That the coroner won't be dressed nearly as fashionably as I am."

CHAPTER 45

Mission Unaccomplished

T he Culver coroner's office had a high turnover of chiefs, so my father once told me. He'd also added the tidbit that at least two dozen bodies a year couldn't be identified. And then there were those that were misidentified. James must've heard similar stories.

The office was only eight miles from Ameripictures, but snarling LA traffic ate-up thirty minutes. Securing a parking spot two blocks away sucked up another fifteen.

We trekked across graffiti-packed sidewalks and streets, past high fences topped with a roll of barbed wire, and landed in front of a broad staircase leading to a three-story, brick building rising up from a sea of cracked asphalt. The neoclassical façade was to die for...maybe fifty years ago. Low relief carvings showed off elaborate curlicues. The place must have been a head turner back in its day. Now it resembled an aging actress wearing a fancy girdle on the outside of a faded gown.

I beat James to the door and held it open. I wasn't great at expressing myself, but I needed to show him I was capable of more than bad behavior. He eased inside, and I followed.

The dimly lit lobby threw us into a foyer with an old-world, low dome ceiling and white granite walls. Red and white fabric chairs tried their best to distract visitors from the morbid work done inside the place. James exchanged a quick greeting with a guy at the reception desk, and we headed for the elevator.

"We have an appointment with Doctor Paco O'Malley," he said.

"Can't ask for more than that," I said. "Except, to see the body with my own eyes."

"We'll make it happen."

We stepped into the elevator and the door slid shut. Since it wasn't my first visit, hanging out with dead bodies didn't bother me. But still, I anticipated a small wave of nausea followed by numbness.

"It's a little toasty in here," I said.

"Enjoy it while you can. It's going to be thirty-nine degrees downstairs."

The door to the basement whimpered and slid open. A sobbing woman pushed between us, clutching a large manila envelope. James and I exchanged a glance and stepped out.

A minute later, frosty air slapped my cheeks, and the smell of rotting fish invaded my nostrils. We met up with an elfish looking guy with graying hair and a trim white moustache. He sat on a stool, squeezing a small upside-down trashcan between his knees. He was tapping it with pencils in each hand. He wore blue scrubs and matching rubber gloves. Sinks, scales and stainless steel instruments littered the room. Metal cabinets hung on the walls. I held my breath while James made the introductions.

"That's me. Paco O'Malley, deputy ME, no rhyme intended, don't you see?" the man rapped, hands out, pencils stuck between his fingers. He grinned. "I write lyrics in my spare time." The grin vanished and he focused on James. "Like I told you on the phone, we showed the photos to the decedent's boss, that actress with the red hair and great legs. What's her name again?"

"Lacy Halloway." My teeth were starting to chatter.

"That's her. She positively ID'd him. Done deal."

"She..." James pointed to me. "...is an eyewitness to the murder."

"I have reason to believe Ms. Halloway, in her bereaved state, didn't examine the photos closely," I said. "It could be someone that looked similar." I exhaled. "We need to confirm."

The guy's shoulders touched his ears before slumping. "I knew this one could be problematic. Being so new to this country, and from a small village in India. The deceased, I mean. Not me." He leaned forward and whispered, "But, like I said, the actress confirmed, so it's all good."

James and I swapped glances.

"Did he have any unusual markings on his body? Birthmark? Tattoos..." I asked.

"No, none. Would you look at that?" Paco held up the watch around his wrist. "I'm on the night-shift, but it's my break-time right about now." He stood, dropped the pencils on a counter and pulled off a glove. "Nice meeting you."

"Not so fast." I placed my hand on his arm. "I need to see the corpse first."

Paco froze. "You two are barking up the wrong crypt."

"We need to re-confirm." James held up his hands. "It's fine if you take your break. I know the County Coroner. I'll just call her—"

"Okay, you want to see the dead guy?" Paco stood, sucked in his gut and opened a large metal door behind him. "I thought I'd spare you."

Even colder air blasted my face and hands, and now I was shivering. I zig-zagged around the room to warm myself up. Paco waved a hand toward an oversized walk-through refrigerator.

"I've got bunks full of corpses. But most..." He stuck his neck out in my direction. "...are gruesome cadavers." He pointed behind him. "You don't want to faint in there. The floors are nasty."

"I'll let the Coroner know," James said.

"I'm joking, come on." Paco hurried into the giant cooler.

"You could eat your dinner off the floor. Although I don't think it would be very appetizing."

I made my way inside, strolling between the toe tags. I gritted my teeth and rubbed my hair, hoping the friction would provide some warmth. James hovered near the entrance. Bodies beneath white sheets were stacked two high on each side, lying on metal bunk after metal bunk.

Paco strolled deeper into the refrigerator and removed a clipboard hanging on a wall. He peered at it and looked up.

"We have a little problem, Houston," he said.

"How little?" I asked.

"You're not squeamish, I'll give you that," Paco said. "I'd let you see the body. But it's not here."

"How can it not be here?" I asked. Two possibilities crossed my mind: because the feds had it...or because Shaw was still alive.

"I contacted you over an hour ago," James said. "What's changed since then?"

Paco trekked out of the refrigerated section, back into the office. I followed.

"According to this chart, the body was transferred yesterday. For a separate probe. I was never updated."

"Who made the request?" I asked.

"Doesn't say." Paco's gaze rolled down the chart. "We don't get transfers too often. The last time was two weeks ago, a police sergeant was involved. His family requested an independent exam by an ME."

"What about Calvin Singh?" I asked. "His body was found in the past twenty-four hours. Was he brought here?"

Paco put down the chart. "We were expecting him, but the stiff stood us up." He grinned. "Can't help myself. It gets pretty grim around here."

"Do you know where he ended up?" I asked.

"Beats me. We got a call from local PD telling us he was rerouted."

"What about the stab wounds on Shaw Kota?" I asked.

"There were a lot, weren't there? I think he set some kind of record," Paco said.

"Did you confirm the blood type matched?" James asked.

"No question about it."

"Are you the one that conducted the exam on Shaw?" I asked.

"Actually, no," Paco said. "I reviewed it, but it was an outside contractor. We're understaffed here."

"We're done." I stood to leave when I got a text from Michael.

Lacy and I are going to the Otis building so I can meet someone. She wouldn't say who. Any ideas?

I texted back:

Why can't she just tell you like a normal person?

That would be the day.

CHAPTER 46

Uncertain Death

I waited until James and I stepped into the elevator, and the door slid shut before I told him about Flicka and Debbylynn.

He chuckled. "At least her mother didn't name her after Secretariat or Seabiscuit." He wiped the dimples off his cheeks. "Too bad about the costumer. Both victims must have had access to the same information."

"Seems like everyone has access to the information, but me."

The door slid open and we stepped out into the mausoleum of a foyer.

"Meanwhile," I added. "Why would the feds claim the body?" If there was one. "I'm assuming that's what happened." My feet didn't move fast enough. I wanted to sprint out of the place.

"If they've got their own separate case, they need to make their own positive ID or conduct an autopsy, if one's needed," James said.

We pushed open the doors and stepped outside. The odor of car exhaust never smelled so good.

"Fed involvement could mean there's something of large monetary value or a federally insured bank is involved," James said. "Or local police are deemed incompetent."

"Or..." There was that light bulb again. "...if it's a technology-based investigation, the feds would be on it."

James shot me a glance. "Probing the dark web would be another reason. Calvin was on the dark web."

"True." I'd made more progress in the last few minutes than in the whole day.

We dashed across the car-lined street and headed for the SUV. Industry rose up on our left, and small yardless bungalows huddled together on the right. James marched toward the SUV, parked between two hybrid vehicles. I waited by the passenger door, scanning the neighborhood. James paused when he passed the front headlight on the driver's side. His Adam's apple bobbed up and down.

"Step away from the car," he spoke quietly and stared down at the hood. "Do it slowly, without catching attention. Point your finger behind you. Like you forgot something."

I opened my mouth and pointed toward the coroner's building. That's when I spotted him. The guy in the fedora. His torso stretched out from behind a small warehouse. He disappeared. I bolted off and waved to James.

"It's Deepak Nangia," I said.

James quick-stepped behind me. Seconds later, an eardrum-shattering boom rattled the scene. I flew forward and landed flat on my stomach against the rough asphalt. All air escaped my lungs. My ears were ringing as I tried to rise, but a heavy weight had lodged against my back. I lifted and turned my head. The weight belonged to James. Nearly half of his six foot four frame lay against me, his legs stretched out on the street. He'd been my human body shield. I lifted my scraped and bleeding palm and touched his shoulder.

"You okay? Talk to me." Wouldn't blame him if he didn't. I was the source of most of his troubles.

His head rose slowly. He blinked, stretching to look behind him, then back to me. "It's never a stroll in the park with you, is it? More like a stroll in the dark. With no flashlight in sight." He got to his knees and into a sitting position. His knuckles were bleeding.

I blew a sigh of relief and joined him, brushing away the dirt and pebbles from his shirt. "Can't argue with you on that one."

He nodded. "You okay?"

I stood and gave him a hand. "Yep."

James was up and surveying the scene. The cars around his SUV were virtually unscathed. A small crowd assembled by the charred remains of his engine. Debris scattered around the car. The front portion was exposed and smashed, the hood had blown off.

"How did you know?" I asked.

"Know what?"

"That someone tampered with your car."

He blew out a sigh. "I placed invisible tape on the hood gap, gas cap and trunk. The tape on the hood was broken when we got back."

"Clever. I'll have to remember that." I pitched my chin in the direction of the building across the street. "I saw him there. Must've used a remote detonator."

"He's all over the place, isn't he? Could be ex-military or ex-law enforcement."

"He's made numerous attempts on my life. And missed each one, although this one came closest."

"Either he's dopey when it comes to getting a job done," James said. "Or he's trying not to kill you. Or, we got lucky."

"He's working with Shaw." That thought jumped into my mind that very second.

"The previously living Shaw or the dead one?"

"We could've been killed," I said. The reality hit me hard, as did a wave of nausea.

"We could've."

We faced each other.

"I just wanted to say..." I started.

"You should know..."

We spoke at the same time. I broke into a small smile. "If anything had happened to you because of me, I'd never—"

He took my hand and squeezed it. "We can't keep—"

"You guys a'right?" A stocky guy had left the group and joined us.

"Uh, sure," I said. "Just a few cuts and scratches."

James gave a quick nod, which the man returned.

"We called 9-1-1," he told us and jogged back to the vehicle.

James hobbled forward.

"You sure you're okay?" I asked him.

He let loose a smile that would've melted a snowman in deepest Antarctica. "Nothing like a molar-rattling explosion to jump-start a dull day." He pulled out his phone.

"Ask for Sorkel," I told him and crossed the street.

"Where do you think you're going?" James asked. "The guy's not waiting around for you."

"Just a quick once-over before the cops arrive."

I scurried to the single story warehouse. Wrought iron bars shielded the windows; a matching gate protected the front entry. Edging my way to the spot where I'd seen the guy hiding, I slowed and peeked around a corner. The compact parking lot sat empty. A privacy fence separated it from an adjacent lot crammed with vehicles, parked tandem style. I was about to leave when I spied a small piece of paper fluttering against the stucco, stuck with a strip of duct tape. I grabbed the note and read it:

Next time will be certain death.

CHAPTER 47

Change in Plans Again

"It's hard to take him seriously," I said. "He's been threatening me all along. And he hasn't made good." Yet.

James and I sat in the back of an unmarked Crown Victoria, Officer Ramirez at the helm. We'd been checked out by medics, provided statements to the cops, got a long lecture from Sorkel about getting in the way (that was meant for me), and were now being escorted home.

"How does Deepak Nangia know where to find you?" James stared out the front window.

"He's been following me." I craned my neck behind me.

James redirected his stare to me. My cheeks warmed from the heat of his gaze.

"What?" I faced him. "No comment?"

Officer Ramirez exited the 405 freeway and got onto Rosecrans Boulevard.

James faced forward. "How long have you known?"

"First, I thought he'd placed a tracker on my car. But I searched and couldn't find any trace. Then I had Michael inspect my phone. It's clean. I'd been checking for trackers since and only found one. Placed there by the federal agent. I wasn't in my car today, yet he knew where I'd be. He must be tailing me, all the time. The brute."

James lowered his voice and dropped his mouth to my ear. "What have you got that he wants?"

"It's not what I've got. It's what he thinks I have." I wasn't sure if it was the warmth of his breath, but the chill scattered. "He expects me to lead him to what he wants."

"And once you do that..." James started.

"Which I won't," I said. "Even if I did know what he wanted."

"Any guesses on what he's expecting?" he asked.

"Something to do with Shaw's science project," I said. If anyone would know, it'd be Lacy. Why wasn't he after her?

"We figure out what he wants and what his business is, and we unlock an important key," James said.

"I'd love to lure him in," I whispered. "And nab him. We could engage in a little mild torture to find out what's up."

"By 'we' do you mean us?"

"Care to join me?" I asked.

"You're the bait?"

"I'm his favorite worm."

"What kind of torture did you have in mind?" James asked.

Ramirez made a sharp left. He lifted his chin and frowned into the rear view mirror. "You two okay back there?"

"Fine and dandy." I glanced behind me.

"I could use a cold beer," James said.

"So could I, but I gotta wait until after my shift," Ramirez said. "But you don't." He grinned. "On tap or bottle?"

"A long neck." James grinned back.

I turned away and grabbed my phone. I texted Michael: *What's new? James' SUV exploded...a little. But we're okay.*

Ramirez' brown eyes watched me through the mirror. "Good thing you're out of harm's way."

"Thanks to you, Officer." I leaned forward. "But you'll let me know if you learn anything, right?"

"Sure," he said. "If it's something we can share with non-departmental folks." His eyes flicked back and forth between the rear view mirror and the road behind us. He pulled into the right lane and turned the corner through a red light. His eyes shot to mine again. "Don't worry. I checked the intersection first."

"Good work." I leaned into James and whispered, "Farm animals make great torture weapons. Especially hens."

"Isn't that cruel?"

"Oh, I'd never let any harm come to the hen."

James grinned. "Since when do you know anything about a chicken outside of the freezer section of the supermarket?"

"Since my fifth grade field trip to Farmer Macgregor's in Costa Mesa. I learned a lot about hens that day," I said. "They love to peck at shiny objects, and they can be fierce when they need to be." The skin behind my neck prickled.

Ramirez executed a quick left.

"They taught you chicken torture?" James asked.

"I figured that part out myself." My gaze skimmed the cars behind us and I faced forward.

"How are we going to capture the target?" James' face was close to mine.

I pulled back. "I know where to find the perfect hen—"

"I mean Deepak."

I clenched my teeth. "He's tailing us." I leaned forward and spoke louder, "We're being followed, aren't we?"

"Well..." Ramirez' baby browns in the rear view mirror shot to mine and out the back window. "...for a minute there, I thought we—"

"It's a silver pick-up truck," I said. I first saw it when we got into the Crown Vic. It hung back a good distance, and vanished for a while. He reappeared just as we got off the freeway.

"I'm not sure..."

James turned and looked behind him. There was still enough daylight to make out the cars behind us.

Ramirez used the next few minutes to execute a number of sharp turns. I came close to throwing up my late lunch. Ramirez pulled into a driveway that curved behind a building, and parked.

"See any good movies lately?" he asked.

Appreciating his calm under pressure, I rattled off a list of my favorite old films starting with *Key Largo* and ending with *Charade.* Ramirez rolled back into traffic.

"I'll be sure and look some of those up," Ramirez said. "We're fine now. I took a class on escaping from unwanted tails." He made a right into a side street and aimed for Coast Highway.

Ramirez sailed through a small intersection just as an engine rumbled nearby. I looked out my window in time to catch the silver pick-up charging straight for us from a side street. I braced my legs against the floor.

"Step on it..." The clang of metal against metal swallowed my last words and sent the Crown Vic crashing into a telephone pole. My seatbelt yanked and tightened against my chest, knocking the breath out of me. I turned to James. The side of his forehead rested against the window, eyes closed, mouth slightly open. Blood dripped from the side of his face.

"James!" I shook his shoulder. I unbuckled and leaned forward. I gripped Ramirez' shoulder. "Officer!"

Ramirez slumped over, his face pushed against the white airbag that had burst over the steering wheel. A snapping noise stopped me. My neck slowly cranked toward my window. The door was caved in the middle, like a giant fist had landed a punch. My gaze inched upward. Deepak Nangia wrestled with the handle, but it kept snapping back.

"No!" My voice sounded low and hoarse. A gargle replaced my scream and flapped in my ears after I closed my mouth. I dug my hand into my purse, fumbling for my phone. I dialed 9-1-1 with my thumb, eyes fixed on the guy in the fedora. His hair was a wild tangle; there was a small cut above his expressionless dark eyes. He held a slim piece of metal, about two feet long and punched it hard against the lock.

"This is 9-1-1," the dispatcher answered.

"Officer down! Aviation and Fourteenth, Redondo."

James' hand reached out and gripped my shoulder just as

Lida Sideris

the door burst open.

CHAPTER 48

In For Trouble

I grabbed my pistol, aiming for Deepak's shoulder, but he gripped the nozzle, trying to twist it away. We struggled and I slammed my fist beneath his chin just as he knocked the gun from my hand. I kicked out, slamming his kneecap. He fell back onto the pavement. I hurled forward to punch his chin again, but I tripped onto the asphalt, landing on my knees. A stream of curse words blew out my mouth, and I stumbled toward the gun. Deepak grabbed my arm and dragged me, kicking and punching to his silver pick-up. He pinned his gun snugly against my back, just as James staggered out of the Crown Vic.

James snatched up my pistol and barreled forward on wobbly legs. I ducked to give him clear aim, but the guy encircled my waist with his arm and positioned me as his body shield. He yanked open the door and shoved me into the backseat of the truck. I glimpsed the weapon in his hand as he slammed the door.

"Moron," I mumbled.

He'd wielded a small Phillips head screwdriver, and had shoved the butt of the plastic handle against my back. I messed up a prime chance to nab him. Pumping the door handle proved no good against the childproof locks. I lunged headfirst for the passenger seat while he scurried around the front of the truck.

Screaming sirens howled louder. I flipped the door handle and it swung open.

"Help!" I screamed and nosedived for the pavement.

He grabbed my hair. Before my hands made contact, he'd yanked me back inside and flipped me around. My feet kicked out, over and over.

"You freaking..." I shouted.

He slapped my cheek so hard that I blinked away stars. He tried to stuff me in the back, but I gripped the armrest. Lifting my face, I spotted two cops racing for the truck. My grip slipped when Deepak shoved me into the rear seat. I managed to grab his ear and pull hard as I flew into the back. He punched my hand and I let go. He sped away.

"Where are we going?" I yelled. My hand throbbed like it was sitting under a hot iron.

"Shut-up."

The truck screeched around a corner. Stringy, dark strands hung around his angular face. His beard looked scragglier than ever. He breathed through pursed lips, blue aviators in place.

"You made a big mistake," I said.

He floored it through a yellow light, headed for the freeway.

"I'm your bargaining chip, aren't I?" I wanted to plant the idea in his head, in case he had more of a nefarious plan. My left arm throbbed like hundreds of needles pricked my skin. I flexed my feet and massaged my hands. My cheek burned, but most of my body parts seemed in decent working order. I moaned and bent forward. Better he think I was injured. A street lamp lit up the car and I peered through my hair at a map of Los Angeles on the seat beside me, highlighting a route from Redondo Beach to Venice. Why store the map in the rear?

Groaning, I slowly straightened. I flipped my hair back and unclenched my teeth. "Shaw Kota's your boss, isn't he?" If I struck his ego hard enough, he might talk. Or get rid of me.

He snarled, "He is nobody's boss."

Present tense! I stopped breathing. Shaw was alive.

Dark eyes shot to the rearview mirror, catching my gaze before re-focusing out the front window. Deepak maneuvered around vehicles at top speed. If he didn't kill me with a weapon or his bare hands, a car crash could do the trick.

"You can't outrun the police." I scanned the cars behind us. Not a cop in sight.

Moments later, he hung a sharp right into a residential street crammed with small homes. Porch lights were off, but the street lamps lit up weedy flowerbeds and dead lawns. We were only a mile or two from the 405 freeway. My guess was he was going to jump onto the 405 to a hideout in Venice, if the map meant anything.

Deepak parked in front of a house with a ratty sofa squatting on a sagging porch. He stuffed the fedora onto the floor by his feet. Reaching into the glove compartment, he grabbed a Dodgers' baseball cap and shoved it onto his head. He switched the aviator shades for horn-rimmed glasses, and hustled over to my side. He opened the door and gripped my arm, hauling me onto the sidewalk. The bony fingers of his other hand wrapped around a small revolver.

I tripped to slow him down and dragged my feet, but he tugged even harder. I stumbled along. A car rolled by without slowing.

"The map," I whispered. He didn't need it. He'd left it for the police to find, a false lead. My heart pounded against my chest.

He lugged me over to a gray Jeep parked a few cars away. Like the pick-up, the Jeep lacked a license plate. I was done for, unless I convinced him of my usefulness.

"I know these roads well. I can drive," I told him. "You concentrate on finding Shaw."

He cocked his head my way and rolled it around, until he cracked his neck. His gaze stuck on mine, unblinking, like a snake about to strike. "You're full of it."

"What? I need to close this case, so I can concentrate on

my real job. I'm a lawyer."

A nostril flared. "I hate lawyers."

"I'm not the kind of lawyer you hate. I negotiate and make deals with difficult, wealthy and powerful people. You've never met a lawyer like me before." I gulped and lifted my chest and chin. "I can be very useful."

"You negotiate?"

"All the livelong day," I said.

"Move it." He pulled open the passenger door and pushed me inside. He duct-taped my hands in front of me, winding enough tape to hide bare skin. Reaching across, he buckled me in while I eyed the door handle. He slammed the door and rushed to the driver's side. Could I open my door with bound hands? I rubbed my knuckles against it, pressing up against the tip of the handle. No luck. I slammed my hands against the seat. I had to do something.

Seconds later, he'd hopped into the driver's seat, tucking the gun between his legs.

"Smart move," I told him. "Changing cars, I mean. They'll never follow you." Or me. A sharp, heavy weight filled my stomach, like I'd swallowed an anchor.

You'll sink if you get discouraged. Dad's voice came in loud and clear. *Keep your chin up. Use your head.*

I tossed a glance at my chauffeur. He could have duct-taped my mouth and tossed me in the backseat, but he didn't. Why not? He expected me to talk. My gaze dropped to the gun. "You've been following me," I said. "Why?"

He motored back onto Aviation Boulevard. "Why did you take a special interest in Shaw?" He hung a right on a side street.

"He was hired by the studio to play a part in a movie. It was my job to enforce his contract." That was a good one.

"You lie."

My heart pounded more fiercely against my ribcage.

"I watched you, watching Shaw, the day he disappeared," he said. "You were present when there was nothing to enforce."

My sweat glands opened like Hoover Dam had sprung a

leak. No amount of deodorant could help me now. "There were complaints about Shaw before he...disappeared. He didn't show up on time, forgot his lines and breached his contract in other ways, that needed enforcement...what do I call you?"

"Deep," he said.

"Deep?" I studied his high forehead, thickly lashed eyes, copper colored skin and curvy lips. I searched my memory. "During the filming of that last bicycle scene. You stood behind me, near the corner."

"I watched when you tried to get into the brick building. And when you went to your office. And when you drove home. And when you *got* home. I was always watching."

"Why plant the dummy and hack my home security?" I asked. "And the hat in my engine?"

"Even a professional killer needs...how do you say... comic relief?" He laughed. His hollow cheeks quivered with each evil chuckle.

An icy stream trickled down my spine. "None of that was remotely funny."

"The dummy was symbolic, to show I knew Shaw was alive."

I didn't get that at all. "How did you know?"

"I saw him running like a scared dog, before he vanished."

"What about Calvin?" I asked. "You attacked him."

"He should have taken me to Shaw."

Both Shaw and Calvin were still alive. It was all an elaborate ruse.

"And Debbylynn?"

"She should have helped me like she helped Shaw."

"She knew Shaw was alive?" Of course she did. She'd played along with the fake murder. She was the one who discovered him. "You haven't been a professional killer very long, have you?"

He shot me a look.

I was right. Because he couldn't seem to do anything right. "You're not much older than me. Your job was to convince

Shaw to turn his project over to an investor."

"The government hid Shaw in India. I was hired to find the hiding place. I did. Before I could transport him to my boss, he escaped."

While I digested that nugget, Deep ambled around the block and back onto Aviation. He pulled a cell phone out of his pocket and held it out to me. "Call the lady."

"What lady?" I asked.

"The crazy movie actress."

"I'm not calling her," I said.

"You will."

"First off, my fingers aren't exactly free to call. And second, all she feeds me is false information. Plus, she's as mean as heck." And I needed to buy some time.

He sped up. "If she doesn't help, you'll be dead."

My throat constricted. I managed to say, "Let's go to the studio. I know where she is. We'll make her talk."

He darted in and out of the traffic and slowed as he turned into another side street. He wasn't going anywhere. We were driving in circles.

He finally pulled into a gas station, parked, and picked up his phone. He punched a button and scrolled up with his finger. I leaned closer and craned my neck. He was tracking someone on Overland and Washington, at Ameripictures. He tossed the phone in the pocket of the driver's side door.

"How long have you worked at the movie studio?" he asked.

"About five or six...years." More like barely six months. And I'd been on the main lot only one of those months. Before that, I'd worked for the production arm in Orange County. "I know the lot like the back of my hand." If that hand were frozen in front of my face, that is.

"I'm going to give you an opportunity," he told me. "To prove yourself worth keeping alive."

Now we're talking. Once I was out of the car...a chill slid down my spine as I caught his arctic stare.

"If you don't find what I'm looking for, you'll be dead tonight."

"What are you looking for?" I asked.

"The plan."

CHAPTER 49

The Destination

"I'll need details if I'm going to find anything," I told Deep, as he maneuvered between traffic on the 405 freeway. We'd passed the LAX exit. Culver City was coming up on our right. If only Lacy'd given me something more about the plan. I stifled a sigh. It didn't matter. I'd gone on less in the past. My sweat glands had dried up, and a welcome calm settled over me despite the kidnapping and death threat.

Deep didn't utter a word until after we pulled into the Overland gate. The glowing Ameripictures' sign loomed overhead. He knew I had territorial advantage, yet he'd brought me to home territory. Whatever he needed was on the lot.

Cradling the gun in his left hand, he reached into the backseat and threw a sweatshirt onto my lap, over my hands. Leaning the gun's grip against the door, he pointed the muzzle my way. He rolled down the window a few inches, dark gaze superglued on me. The security guard appeared by his side. Deep shoved his badge through the opening; the guard took a look and raised the gate. I couldn't see the badge, but how hard could a forgery be? He'd managed passports. A studio pass must've been a breeze.

Deep motored inside the lot and made a right, gun resting on his lap. I couldn't wait to see how he planned to transport me to our destination. Wherever that was.

"When will you tell me where we're headed?" I asked.

"You're going to tell me." He dove his hand into the side pocket of his door and pulled out a long, rolled paper. Angling into the parking structure, he pulled the Jeep into an open slot in the dimmest corner of the first level. I scanned the deserted surroundings. No one stuck around this time of night except a handful of execs and creative teams with odd hours. And if they did, they'd nab a spot closer to the buildings. Parking spaces were plentiful.

Deep deposited the gun in the side pocket and spread the paper between us. A small flashlight lit up a detailed map displaying a portion of the studio.

"What are you trying to find?" I asked

"Shaw."

He believed the missing Shaw and his plan were stashed at the studio. That would explain Shaw's paranoia in the day before his so-called murder. He must have known Deep was after him and found a place to lie low. "What's your relationship to Shaw?"

"If you ask another question, I'll stab you enough times for you to remain conscious to feel the pain and watch yourself bleed." He'd pulled out a jackknife. "I ask. You answer. Understand?"

I gave a nod. Anger seeped through my veins. I sat up straighter. I was done being manipulated. Deep lowered the knife and focused on the map while I eyed the gun sticking out of the side pocket. I slowly lifted my left elbow and tensed my legs.

"The structures are outlined in detail here…" he tapped a broken and dirty fingernail on the map. "Except for two buildings."

The commissary and the Otis buildings were highlighted on the map.

"These were ignored during the extensive remodeling five years ago," he said. "Why?"

My elbow was nearly horizontal. "They have historical significance." I had no idea if that was true, but it sounded legit.

He jerked his chin up.

My elbow froze. "Shaw never left the lot," I said. "He's still here. Is that who you're tracking on your phone?"

Deep grabbed the knife and skimmed it across my forearm in two quick strokes, leaving slits where blood gathered and oozed out. He shoved the map onto my lap and shined the flashlight. "I require details about these two buildings."

Blood dripped off my arm, and onto the seat. I focused on the two spots highlighted on the map and spoke through clenched teeth. "One's the commissary. It has a large dining area and private rooms. Too many people come and go to make it a worthwhile hiding spot. Kitchen and cleaning staffs, the tired and angry. I mean, hungry. It's never empty." The sliding glass door in Lacy's private dining room had led to a compact patio enclosed by a high brick wall. Chances were slim the private spaces had their own exits. "No exterior doors in the private areas. There's a basement, but that's for the bakery. I wouldn't hide-out in the commissary." I swallowed the burning lump in my throat. Deep couldn't get rid of me. I was a wealth of information.

"What about the other one?" he asked.

I studied the H-shaped Otis building. My guess was the Otis hosted plenty of hiding spots. Not only was it the oldest structure on the lot, but rumor had it the former chairman's office had at least one side entrance where talent would sneak up for a private chat...or more. All the top execs were once housed in the Otis, which meant secrets galore.

"I roamed around the Otis the other day, but you already know that." Deep had been watching me, I was sure. "Security is extra tight. Cameras everywhere." I'd seen one outside the main entrance and two in the lobby. Only one on the second floor pointed to a fire escape. Security seemed loose in the Otis. "The guards are former black ops." I stifled a giggle at my creativity. "There are motion sensors after hours. No way could Shaw get in and out without being seen." Now I knew where he was hiding.

Deep switched the knife for his gun, and pointed it at my chest. "You're not being helpful."

Come on, get careless. All I needed was one chance to rip his heart out. "What's your problem? The building is fully secure. Want me to lie to you?"

"You've outlived your usefulness."

I had to admit, this little corner of the parking structure would be prime to commit a murder. There were security cameras, but none pointing near us. Deep had a sharp eye for detail.

I leaned closer to him; the muzzle nearly touched my chest. "Fire away. But, I do have one last question. The brick building wasn't remodeled either. Why isn't it highlighted on your map? It's the perfect hideaway. Tons of unused space, and people are scarce. No one would look for Shaw in there. It's where he was fake-killed, after all." We locked stares. The gun barrel lowered ever so slightly.

"He's not in there," Deep said.

My mind raced. Did he conduct a search? Or did someone else do it? Did Lacy double-cross him? That would explain her lurking in the brick building. But one person lurked in the building more than anyone. "Vanderpat. You work together, don't you? Or is it..." I tensed my arms. Before he could blink, I slammed him with my hands as hard as I could beneath the chin. His head flipped back. His crown pounded against the window. The gun fell hard against my foot as I whacked him on the side of his head with the back of my hands. He groaned and yanked my hair so hard it felt like my brain was being pulled through my pores. Anger turned to rage, and I smacked him harder, across the face. And again. His head snapped back and lolled to one side. I pointed and pressed my elbow against the unlock button above the Jeep's radio. I pushed my back against the unconscious Deep, aiming the toe of my shoe beneath the door handle. I snapped my foot backward. The door clicked and unlocked, and I kicked it open. Less than a minute later, I was outside and running.

CHAPTER 50

Up the Wall

I hightailed it to the nearest security guard. Kimika was handling the night shift. She was walking back to the Overland Gate with a cup of coffee in her hand, which she promptly tossed when I told her about my kidnapping. She cut off the duct tape binding my hands and gave me her phone to call Sorkel, while another guard spread the word via a walkie-talkie.

Sorkel's call was brief. He was on his way. I tried Michael next. No answer. I called James. He picked up on the first ring. I fast-talked my update.

"You okay?" he asked.

"Sure am." I massaged my aching hands.

"As much as I'd like to, I can't come in person right now," he said.

"You know you're always welcome to my crime parties."

"I would've already been there, but I'm waiting to be treated in ER. Something about a concussion and a sprain."

I'd forgotten he was hurt. "If I hadn't asked for your help..."

"Life would be a lot less...exciting," he said.

"Officer Ramirez?"

"He'll be fine. He's got a fractured rib, besides his concussion."

I blew out a deep sigh of relief.

"Just for once, remember...dangerous situations are never predictable. Wait for the cops...oh, never mind." He disconnected.

I handed the phone back to Kimika and pointed behind me. "Direct the police to the Otis building. That's where I'm headed."

"I'll let the guard in Otis know," she said.

"Thanks." I took off at an unsteady gait with my left thigh and sliced arm throbbing. A dull ache riddled my hands from clobbering Deep. No amount of pain or wobbly legs would stop me now.

* * *

Minutes later, I rapped on the double glass doors of the Otis building. I was surprised the guard wasn't waiting for me. Hopefully, Kimika had reached him. My studio badge was MIA, as was any other form of ID. I rapped again, harder and stopped at the sight of a bulky figure edging to the side of the elevators. As he closed in, his eyes stuck on mine. It was Vanderpat. I stepped back. I knew why he was in the Otis.

He lifted a hand to unlock the door; his other arm curved around his back. That's when I saw it. A tattoo on the inside of his wrist, the small dark circle Veera had seen. As he stomped closer, the circle turned into an evil eye, matching the one on Deep's wrist. I turned and sprinted, ignoring the pain in my legs. I glanced over my shoulder and dove behind a large shrub. Where was he? Vanderpat hadn't come after me. Why? Because he had a more important task.

I stayed away from the front doors and street lamps, and hustled to the west part of the building. There was a side entry leading to the second floor. I stopped short of the entrance when I remembered the interior camera. I jogged around to the back.

A narrow, Z-shaped cement staircase would lead me to the doors on the second and third floors. I glanced around and climbed with the barest of lighting from the building behind me. The stairs served as a fire escape and were locked, that much I knew.

I'd nearly reached the top of the second floor when I realized two things: I had no means to pick the lock, and I wasn't alone. I spied the back of a figure in a black coat bending over the doorknob.

"Veera," I whispered.

She shot up, a can of pepper spray in her hand. "Corrie? You didn't answer my texts."

"My hands were tied. What are you doing?"

"Lacy and Michael went in through the front of this place about twenty minutes ago. I've been trying to get inside, but no amount of friendly persuasion would convince that Vanderpat."

We had to work fast. "Are you picking the lock?" I peered around her. I was definitely a bad influence.

"I've been trying to. I watched a video on the Internet, but I can't get the jiggle down." Veera held up two paper clips, bent straight at the ends.

I eyed the building. "There's a surveillance camera that'll catch us as soon as we enter from this door. We'll need to find another way in. Got any lip gloss?"

Veera dug into the pocket of her black slacks and pulled out a tube. "You know I do. Since when can you use gloss to break-in?"

"This is for afterward." I stuffed the tube down the front of my dress, beneath my bra strap.

"Need anything else?" Veera patted her pockets. "I've packed just about everything."

"Keep the pepper spray handy," I said.

"You know I will." She dug a hand in and pulled it out. "What's next?"

"We're going straight to the top." I stared upward. "And

onto that patio." I pitched my chin up. "To Otis' private dining area. I'll get in and open the door to the third level."

Veera swiveled toward the walled dining area above us. A short glass partition ran around the patio. She wheeled around to me again. "You plan on climbing the walls? 'Cause last time I checked you haven't got suction cups on your hands and feet or Spiderman's skill set. You can't scale that wall."

"Watch me," I said. "That tree's going to be my ladder." I pointed to a tall magnolia with limbs bending and stretching in different directions. They practically welcomed me aboard.

"What if you fall?" she asked.

"I won't."

My kitten-heeled, suede pumps could double as climbing shoes, thanks to the rubber sole and pointy toes. Perfect to catch jutting edges in the bark. It wasn't like I was scaling Mount Everest. I darted down the stairs.

"Corrie...wait." Veera chased after me. "That tree must be thirty feet high. You seriously climbing that thing, in a dress?"

"That's the idea."

"Least I can do is break your fall if you should go south."

I surveyed the branches above.

"You ever climb a tree before?" she asked.

"Sure. It's been a while, but it's like riding a bike."

My father believed the more risks his little girl took, the better she'd be trained to take care of herself. We spent many weekends tree and rope climbing, when we weren't target shooting or throwing shuriken, that is.

"Hands are for grabbing and gliding," I said. "Feet are for pushing and climbing."

Veera stared at her hands. "Not these hands."

I gazed up at the legion of glossy, rubbery leaves and took in the sweet lemony scent. Thank goodness for old trees. Every time a branch had been removed, a foothold formed by a large knot jutting out from the trunk. I stretched out my arms and jumped to grab a branch. My hands slipped before I could cop a grip. Hardly a promising start. I rubbed my hands together and tried again. I gripped the branch, lifted my legs and slipped my shoe into a deep V between the trunk and another branch. I hoisted myself up. I continued the slow climb and only slipped once, legs dangling, but managed to grab the nearest branch and muscle my way back up, panting.

Veera gasped below me, holding out her arms. "Hope I don't get a coronary watching you."

I gazed down at her shuffling around, hovering beneath me, arms outstretched, head tilted back.

"Don't worry so much. Keep an eye out for anyone approaching."

"We're expecting the police, right?"

"Any moment." I wiggled up the trunk until I faced the glass wall of the patio. I extended my shoe, landing a foothold on a slim pane sticking out above a tall window.

"Steady now," Veera said.

I blew the hair out of my face, leaned forward and stretched an arm. My fingertips touched the ledge beneath the patio wall. I pulled myself closer, grasping the two-inch ledge below the glass wall. I plunged forward, reaching out my other hand, aiming for the same ledge. I barely grabbed hold. Veera muttered below.

"Dear Mother of God. Please don't let her end up flat out."

I tightened my grip, using every bit of aching muscle, and pulled myself up, pointy toes lodged on the narrow ridge of the windowpane below. My dress flapped in a frisky breeze. In a few more moves, I'd heaved myself up and over the patio wall, landing with a smack on my rear. A dim glow of light from a streetlamp illuminated silhouettes of metal tables and chairs scattered around the tile floor. Heat lamps sat dormant. A short pile of tablecloths filled a cubbyhole near the entrance. I knelt, and peeked over the glass wall. Down below, Veera made a bee-line back to the fire escape stairs. I was about to stand when the shadows shifted and parted behind her. A beam from a passing car lit up the wide trunk of a tall tree. A man crouched next to the trunk, head turned in Veera's direction.

CHAPTER 51

The Invasion

T he shaft of a beam from an exterior lamp lit up a man with a dark beard and bucket hat. It was the agent that had talked to Mom and I. While I debated the next move, a siren wailed and the guy took off.

"Corrie?" Veera called out softly from the top of the stairs.

"Give me a minute." I dashed to the dining room entrance. A glass door and a row of windows stood between the interior section and me. I tried the doorknob. Locked. I peered through the windows into the darkened area.

I grabbed a tablecloth and wrapped it around my shoulders, laying another on the floor beneath a window. I picked up a stool near a bar in the corner of the patio. Pulling the cloth over my head, I raised the stool and hurled it crashing against a window. The impact shattered the glass and scattered the silence. I yanked off the cloth and glass shards rained down around me. Draping it over the window, I climbed inside and shook off any glass remnants. I dragged the cloth along while I glided toward the corridor.

A small dome stuck to the ceiling, waiting to capture my every move. Sliding a chair beneath it, I climbed up with the cloth wrapped around me with only one eye exposed. I pulled out Veera's lip-gloss. The sweet scent of coconut filled the stale air as I rubbed the goopy stuff against the dome.

Minutes later, Veera was inside.

"Sure smells good in here," she said.

"We have to be careful. Vanderpat could be anywhere." I gave her a quick run-down.

"I knew that man was dirty. Fortunately for us, it's gonna be hard for him to get to this floor."

"Still, we'd better hurry, in case," I said.

I made a dash down the hallway, Veera at my heels. "We've got to find a way to Lacy's office without being seen. Hold it." I froze and backtracked. I stopped near a pair of tall double doors. I pressed my ear against it.

"Did you hear something?" Veera asked.

"Talking."

"You think that's where Lacy and Michael are?"

"Hard to say." I waited a few beats. "I don't hear it anymore." I looked up at Veera. "Wait. Listen."

"Sounds like it's coming from over there." She pointed back toward the dining area.

I'd barely taken a step when I was interrupted by a loud thud.

I quick-stepped toward the noise, Veera trotted behind me, pepper spray raised in firing mode. I skidded to a stop just before reaching the entry to the dining area. I stood beside a tall potted palm. A narrow door was pressed into the wall.

"I didn't notice this before."

"I did," Veera said. "I'd have to duck and turn sideways to fit through there."

The slender doorway rose only a few inches higher than me. A sign read, *Roof Access.* I sucked in my breath. "I can't believe it. It was here all the time."

"What was?" Veera asked.

I told her about the notes Lacy received. "RA is roof access. Sit-O is Otis spelled backward with a dash. The dash could have something to do with Indian accents."

"I still don't get what it means."

"The answer is through this door." I turned the knob, but it was locked. "Do you have any credit cards on you?" I asked Veera.

She stuck her hand into a pocket. "How about this?" She handed me her driver's license.

"That'll work."

Two minutes later, I'd pulled the door open. I handed Veera her license. "Stay put," I told her. "Wait for the police, while I take a look on the rooftop."

"And if Vanderpat shows up?" She held up the pepper spray.

"Spray and yell, Veera, and I'll be right down." The door closed behind me.

I'd nearly made it up the first flight when Veera yelled.

"Don't you touch me," she said.

I froze.

"You should've stayed out," Vanderpat's reply boomed through the door.

"I need to see some ID," Veera said. "I'm wearing my badge. Where's yours?"

I crept down the stairs.

"I'm off-duty," Vanderpat said.

"Then you've got no business telling me to leave. Hey..."

I grabbed the doorknob, turning it slowly.

"Step away from the door," he told her.

"Since when do security guards carry guns?" Veera said. "Don't you—"

The door rattled and thumped. A crash sounded. I yanked it open. My gaze dropped. A large figure lay sprawled, a nasty cut on the forehead.

"You okay?" I asked Veera.

"Damn straight. Good thing I had this ready." Veera held up the pepper spray. She stared down at Vanderpat. "He knocked that fat head of his against the pot after I sprayed and slugged him one. Look what he did to that poor pot."

Clay fragments lay on the floor beside him.

I stooped and picked up his gun. "I don't suppose you have any rope in your pockets?" I asked Veera. "We should tie him up."

"Got something better." She reached into a pocket and pulled out a travel size, flat version of duct tape.

"Would you mind?" I asked.

"My pleasure. I'll shut his mouth first, in case he comes to."

"I suggest hands and feet first."

Vanderpat groaned. Veera raised her pepper spray and I raised the gun, pointing it at his chest. He opened his eyes and lifted his head.

"Freeze," I said. "Deepak Nangia is in custody. If you co-operate, the Justice Department will be more likely to cut you some slack." I've always wanted to say something like that. "We know you work together."

He shook his head. "He messed it all up. Shaw was about to lead me to the plan when Deep banged up that girl."

"Why would he lead you to it?" I asked.

"So I'd go away quietly. I'd spotted him hiding on the roof. I'd gotten Shaw to trust me."

Like I believed that. "Deepak was sent when you didn't get the goods fast enough," I said.

"He's a distant relative of the boss. That's the only reason. Deep kept messing things up."

"You two thugs worked for the same outfit?" Veera asked him. "I knew you couldn't be a security guard."

Vanderpat shot up, but this time, he wasn't fast enough. Veera sprayed him and I knocked him in the head a few times with the butt of the gun. He yelled and crumpled.

"Please tie him up, Veera."

"Gladly."

I turned back to the door leading to the roof.

Veera knelt. "Be careful." She raised her head. "What's that?"

Voices drifted our way again. I dove closer to a window

near the dining hall entry. A group of men in black stood around Sorkel, necks pitched back, staring up. One officer shined a mini spotlight skyward, past the patio to the rooftop. I edged closer and pressed my face against the glass. A man stood on the edge of the roof, gazing down at the small crowd, like he was ready to jump. His face showed clearly in the beam of light.

"What is it?" Veera asked.

"Not what. Who," I replied. "It's Shaw Kota."

CHAPTER 52

Loose Ends

I raced up the two flights to a door leading to the roof. I turned the brass knob, cracking it open. Cold air grazed against my face. A car alarm howled in the distance, tires screeched on the street and horns honked. Nothing unusual, except for the man on the ledge with his back to me. I pushed open the door enough to squeeze through and onto the small cement rooftop.

"I'm finished," Shaw said with a moan.

Lacy and Michael sat behind him on a small, raised wooden deck. Both of their hands were tied, ankles bound and mouths taped shut. The thudding we'd heard came from Lacy pounding her heels on the floor. Michael was struggling to get free of the rope binding his hands. His brows shot up when he saw me, eyes widening, his gaze darting between Shaw and me.

"Mr. Kota," Sorkel's voice sounded loud and muffled. "You understand we can't help you until you surrender yourself to our custody. After which, we'll do a full search to retrieve the plan you lost. But you will be liable for the consequences of your actions if you hurt the citizens you're holding hostage."

"They are not my hostages," Shaw spoke. "I have bound them for their own safety. This way, if they attempt to keep me from jumping, they will not be hurt. As for the plan, you won't find it." His voice dropped. "I've looked everywhere."

He continued the back and forth with Sorkel while I crouched and tiptoed to Michael. I pulled out his knife and cut through the rope on his hands and feet. I yanked the duct tape from his mouth.

Michael squeezed and stretched his lips. He whispered in my ear. "That hurt like heck."

"Nutshell please," I said.

"You know most of it already. Shaw and his uncle didn't con anyone. They managed to get a prototype to Wetzel that worked, but it needed an alteration. Shaw had a new plan with proper adjustments. He wanted to bring it to Wetzel in person. He didn't trust anyone else."

Lacy nodded her head.

"After Shaw discovered he'd been followed, he and Calvin staged his death with a little help from officials that Wetzel brought in. No one's admitting who these officials were. That's Shaw's version."

Lacy nodded and mumbled through the tape.

"That's right," Michael said. "Debbylynn was in on it, too. Shaw hadn't told Lacy much, for her protection. Last Thursday, Shaw was attacked, but escaped. That's what prompted the fake death. He hid the blueprint of the plan by cutting it in half, sending one portion down the mail chute in the brick building, which he retrieved, and the other half in the mail chute here. No one uses the chutes anymore, so it was the perfect plan. But the half in this building vanished, and Shaw freaked."

"Didn't he keep a virtual copy?" I asked.

Lacy mumbled again.

"No, he was hacked constantly. He kept the blueprints on his person until he divided them up."

"Why didn't he give them to Wetzel when he arrived?"

"Wetzel has been out of the country. He returns tomorrow."

"Did Lacy know Shaw was alive?" I asked. Shaw was still focused on the guys below.

"Not until today. She got a note to meet him on the roof. That's why she invited me. When we arrived, we finally figured out what the notes meant. RA was roof access, can you believe it? Shaw'd been hiding here, right under our noses. You'd think with all of our snooping around—"

Lacy mumbled louder. I ripped off her tape. She bared her teeth and wrinkled her nose like a rabid wolf. "Do that again and I'll—"

"We could have avoided this if you'd confided in me," I said.

She cut me a killer look and whispered, "I couldn't violate Shaw's confidence. I knew you'd figure it out, even if it was a little later than I'd hoped. Unlike me, the boy's a straight shooter. If Shaw says he dropped it in the mail chute, he did." Her gaze shot past me. I rose and turned.

Shaw and I stood face-to-face.

"Why tie these two up?" I pointed to Michael and Lacy. Michael was cutting away at Lacy's tape.

"I wanted to jump. They tried to prevent me," he said. "I've embarrassed and disappointed many. Uncle said not to be involved with the investor. I didn't listen. There've been death threats to Uncle and his family because of me."

"People have short memories, kiddo," Lacy told him. She tottered to her feet, as Shaw backed away. "I can help you get through this."

"No, you can't," he said. "Debbylynn was almost killed because of me."

Sorkel and two officers burst through the door.

"No one move." Sorkel sped up to Shaw and grabbed his arm. Another officer frisked Shaw and took him into custody.

"What happened to Deepak?" I asked Sorkel.

"We've got him."

"What about Calvin?" Lacy asked. "Is he alright?"

"We understand he's in some kind of protective custody," Sorkel replied. "He's the one that tied up your housekeeper. Shaw used Calvin to send messages, which everyone seems to have deciphered tonight."

"Excuse me for interrupting," Veera stooped inside the doorway. "Corrie, I got this message for you."

"From who?" I asked.

"Some older white guy with a beard and a hat that belongs in a bait shop," Veera said. "Know him?"

I raced forward and snatched the note.

Check chute, second floor.

Sorkel escorted Shaw toward the exit. I blocked the path and showed Sorkel the note.

"Here's your chance to help the Feds," I said.

"What are you talking about?" Sorkel asked me.

"Follow me." I headed down the stairs, with everyone else behind me.

Minutes later, we'd crowded around the center of the second floor eyeing a glass chute that disappeared into the floor and ceiling.

"This hasn't been used in decades," Lacy said.

"Nothing's in there," Shaw said. "I looked already."

"Did you drop it from the third floor?" I asked him.

He nodded.

"He made a copy of my Otis keys without telling me," Lacy said. "If it was anyone else, there'd be hell to pay." She placed a hand on Shaw's shoulder and spoke quietly, "Why didn't you tell me you were working with the feds?"

"I could not," Shaw said. "Your safety would have been jeopardized."

I pressed my cheek against the glass of the chute. I focused up, then down.

"Did you fold up the plans and drop them in?" Lacy asked him.

"Triple folded both halves, so they'd fit properly," Shaw said.

"I'd have done the same thing," Michael said.

"Did you consider they might unfold along the way?" Lacy asked Shaw. "Gravity shifts things around in a fall. For an

Einstein, that wasn't smart. Then again, Einstein nearly choked eating a raw olive."

I tilted my head and squinted upward. "Can someone check the third floor chute?"

Sorkel sent an officer upstairs. A minute later, Sorkel got a call. "He says there's nothing up there that he can see."

"He dropped it from the third floor, and it unfolded and got stuck somewhere in between," I said. "Anyone have a heavy object the size and shape of a letter?"

Mumbling ensued and Michael removed his knife.

"This should fit," he said.

I took it and handed it to an officer. She was instructed to go upstairs and drop it down.

We didn't wait long for the downpour. First the knife, then a package, followed by letters lodged for who knew how long, and finally the blueprint. We raced down to the first level and retrieved the missing half.

While the cops sorted through the mail, the feds arrived, in time for Shaw to put the two halves together. And in time to take over custody of the two thugs. It gave me a warm, fuzzy feeling to view the damage I'd done to Deepak. Black eye, swollen cheek, cut lips and missing teeth.

Sorkel exchanged words and back pats with the feds before the agents escorted Shaw away.

"Excuse me." I stopped one of the agents. "Who played the victim?"

"Mr. Kota's cousin, Calvin Singh," the agent replied. "Mr. Singh was taken into protective custody after the staged stabbing, but..." the agent shook his head. "...managed to escape for a short time, before he turned himself in. Mr. Kota also failed to cooperate. Both men are lucky to be alive."

"One more question," I said. "Where's the guy in the beard who wears a bucket hat?"

"You mean Archie?" the agent said. "He called this job in and left for another."

"He works for the Department?"

"Special agent," he said and continued to follow the escorting crew.

"How did Archie know about the clogged mail?" I asked.

"Same way you did," Michael said. "Deductive reasoning. Maybe he was called away before he could try it out."

After statements were collected, Sorkel turned to me.

"You're a chip off the old PI block," he mumbled, with the shadow of a grin.

It was the best he could do.

"You mean the guy who passed me the message was a special agent?" Veera wanted to know.

"Special agent, bullcrap. I told you your dad would help you solve this," Lacy told me.

"That's not—" I started.

"I know I'm not the easiest to work with," Lacy said. "But I'm going to make it up to you. I'm going to recommend a promotion out of kiddie flicks to be my personal, in-house lawyer."

"We'd like that." Veera broke into a wide grin.

"Who's she?" Lacy asked me.

"My right hand," I replied.

Lacy rolled her eyes over Veera. "Nice aura. Welcome aboard." She turned to me. "Michael was helpful in talking Shaw out of jumping before he stuck the tape on our mouths. The two of them really are kindred spirits." Lacy gave Michael a fist bump. "By the way, you're fired," she told him.

"That's a step for the good of mankind," Michael said. "My acting skills rusted over the years."

"It's not about your acting, although I was going to talk to you about that. I'm shelving the movie to film a documentary on the radiation suit and Shaw. I'll direct this one myself. It'll be full of intrigue. But first..." She dropped her chin.

"You alright, Miss Halloway?" Veera asked.

"She's having a vision." I turned my head for some privacy while I did a few eye rolls.

"A what?" Veera wanted to know.

Lacy's chin jerked up. She aimed her spidery lashes at me.

"You're going to enjoy working for me, but it won't be right away. There's trouble brewing."

"You mean like another murder investigation?" Michael asked. "'Cause that's no trouble for her."

"That's not what I mean." Lacy's eyes remained fixed on me. "You'll find yourself in shark-infested waters."

"That would be terrible." Michael sidestepped over and stretched his arm around my shoulders. "She's not good in water."

He referred to my Achilles' heel. I didn't do well in or around bodies of water, large or small. A giraffe could swim better than I could.

"Should she sharpen her swimming skills? Maybe take some classes at the Y?"

"I'm not talking literally! Jeez, it's like you've got a swarm of bees buzzing between your ears," Lacy said and refocused on me. "You'll be okay in the end, kiddo. Look forward to working with you again. And watch out for the monkey." Lacy strutted away, chin up, arms swinging at her sides.

"What mon—" Michael started.

"Don't bother," I said. "Her visions are all over the place."

"I'm looking forward to calling her boss," Veera said.

"Brace yourself, Veera," I said. "She might change her mind tomorrow."

"It won't matter," Veera said. "I know something wonderful's brewing on the horizon for us. We don't need Lacy for that."

"You've got an admirable attitude," Michael told her.

We breezed out into the cool evening. As we landed on the sidewalk, a hairy creature knuckle-walked in front of us into the back lot.

"Holy macaroni...isn't that a..." Veera's hand shot to her mouth.

"Technically, it's not a monkey," Michael said. "Chimpanzees are apes."

"See what I mean? Lacy's visions are never accurate," I said.

The End

ACKNOWLEDGEMENTS

Tons of thanks to:

The marvelous, dynamic duo of Verena Rose and Shawn Reilly Simmons of Level Best Books, and to sharp-eyed readers Barb Goffman and Kim Pendleton for providing valuable comments.

More gratitude to many wonderful friends for their support of my writing life, in particular: Marilyn Metzner and the Honorable Thomas Anderle, Alyce Scerbo and Jeanette Hudgens.

Big thanks also to retired police sergeant Mike Hadley who stepped up to the plate when I needed help authenticating my fictional police work.

And major gratitude to the three incredible men in my life. Where would I be without you?

ABOUT THE AUTHOR

Lida Sideris' first stint after law school was a newbie lawyer's dream: working as an entertainment attorney for a film studio...kind of like heroine, Corrie Locke. Unlike Corrie, Lida has never been blackmailed, never investigated a suspicious death, an alien encounter, a catnapping, a missing corpse or been involved in a low-speed car chase. Lida lives in the northern tip of Southern California with her family, her rescue dogs and a flock of uppity chickens. Lida was one of two national winners of the Helen McCloy/Mystery Writers of America scholarship award for her first book.

Made in the USA
San Bernardino, CA
03 January 2020